DEVOTION IN THE MIND

DOCTOR WISE BOOK 5

ARJAY LEWIS

MIND
BENDER
PRESS

Devotion In The Mind: Doctor Wise Book 5

Copyright ©2018 Robert J. Lewis; Updated January 2026

Cover Design: Marianne Nowicki, PremadeEbookCoverShop.com
Editing: Brandi Aquino, editingdonewrite.com

ISBN-13: 978-1732659308
ISBN-10: 1732659303

Published by:
Mindbender Press
474 South Main Street
Phillipsburg NJ 08865
www.mindbenderpress.com

DEDICATION

To the other authors who inspire
and help my work, and especially
Michelle Garren Flye who writes great
romances with truly magical characters.

Prologue --1

1. Faithful Practice --5

2. Familial Fidelity ---22

3. Sanctified Thievery --32

4. Dedicated Detective---51

5. Steadfast Burglar---71

6. Devout Courtship---86

7. Venerated Tale---100

8. Committed Location--114

9. Crime Scene Constancy ------------------------------------131

10. Ancestral Allegiance ------------------------------------140

11. Tracked with Zeal--160

12. Bygone Blessings --174

13. Dutiful Search ---185

14. Consecrated Grind ---------------------------------------199

15. Hallowed Renewal ---------------------------------------216

16. Applied Accomplice--------------------------------------229

17. Coveted Cult ---243

18. Reverent Raid ---258

19. Earnest Excuses--268

20. Solicitous Survivors ------------------------------------279

Epilogue--293

Asylum In The Mind --301

Author's Note --306

About the Author--307

Books by Arjay Lewis---308

"To succeed in your mission, you must have single-minded devotion to your goal."

—A.P.J. Abdul Kalam

"What is enthusiasm but a passionate belief in what seems to be a high and holy unselfish devotion to some noble cause — a consecration of heart and mind and soul to the attainment of a great object?"

— Orison Swett Marden

PROLOGUE

The lights flickered and shimmered ominously, casting distorted shadows that danced across the cold stone beneath her.

She loved the lights — the way they played tricks on her mind — until she realized that a chilling darkness beyond her punctuated the vibrant glow.

Was it the drugs coursing through her? A giggle escaped her lips, tremulous and hollow. She tried to remember where she was and why terrible music filled her ears. It was a low, echoing chant — Gregorian, or something equally sinister. Somehow, it was dimming her high, turning pleasure into a creeping sense of dread.

As a sudden chill slithered down her spine, another giggle bubbled up, unbidden and mocking. She lay sprawled on a surface that was both familiar and utterly wrong — cold, smooth, like the granite countertops in her mother's kitchen but vastly more foreboding.

She pushed herself up slightly, her body rebelling as if weighed down by an anchor.

What was happening?

There was something here — some sensation tangling with her thoughts. Her heart raced as panic cracked through her haze.

Yes, she had partied with those strange guys, delightful in their at-first innocent strangeness. But the tablet she had swallowed had promised ecstasy, not…this.

She squeezed her eyes shut and opened them again, desperately clawing for clarity.

She glanced around — a flickering multitude of candles lit the room, their flames dancing madly in the shadows, casting figures against the walls. They flickered atop twisted black iron rods, creating a ghostly sort of beauty that felt wrong.

She looked down, breath hitching — the fabric of her black velvet dress was gone. She was naked, exposed on what could only be a dark altar, rising ominously above the ground like a beckoning grave.

Something shifted beyond the circle of light as the chanting intensified, low and rhythmic, a sinister background to her terror.

Figures cloaked in deep shadows lingered just out of reach, their hoods shaping their faces into terrifying, formless voids. They were the ones chanting — she could sense it now.

Her stomach twisted violently; the thrill of the party had decayed into desperation.

Where was Erica? Her friend had promised to keep her safe, to watch her back.

And then she remembered: Erica had refused any drugs, standing as a sentinel against their reckless abandon. Where was she now?

Summoning every ounce of willpower, she pushed herself up on trembling arms, forcing her gaze beyond the candlelight. Only darkness pooled outside the flickering lights, and just as eerily, there appeared a hooded face above her — a specter emerging from the abyss.

The figure pulled back his hood, revealing a thin, drawn face framed by wild, shoulder-length hair. Recognition shattered the surface of her haze — the man from the party.

What was his name? Carl? Cameron? She couldn't remember. The softness in his smile twisted into something grotesque, a sickly façade.

"Y-you better let me go," she stammered, the words falling from her lips like frail leaves in autumn, scarcely holding her strength. His gaunt smile widened unnaturally, revealing too many teeth.

"Don't worry," he murmured, his voice like satin wrapped around a blade. "I will let you go."

He raised his right arm, and the sleeve slipped back, an ominous glint catching her eye. A dagger slipped into view, the blade reflecting the candlelight with a sinister brilliance, its wavy edge glimmering with a terrible promise.

Her breath caught in her throat, a gasp woven from fear and realization.

He moved around the altar, the dagger gliding toward her abdomen, and she felt paralyzed, her screams lost in the crescendo of chants rising like a storm around her.

"They will come looking for me." The words escaped her lips, feeble and desperate, a hollow threat.

"I'm counting on it," he hissed, a darkness flooding his eyes as he raised the blade high, and the world faded beneath the weight of her terror.

1. FAITHFUL PRACTICE

I had forgotten what winters in New Jersey truly felt like. After several years in California, a chilly day was simply one that required a jacket.

But over the past few months, I'd faced snow and biting cold — even a December trip to Maine, no less. Now, in the third week of March, just after St. Patrick's Day, winter was finally loosening its grip. Nights still dropped below freezing, but daytime temperatures climbed into the sixties, and the trees budded anew.

A sudden fall onto the mat shattered my pleasant reverie about the weather, pain radiating through me as I grunted.

"Your mind wanders, Leonard," Ashwan chided softly as I blinked up at the bright lights overhead.

I'd gotten up early on this cold Thursday morning and driven out to Bloomdale for a private lesson at my dojo. With my bad leg, I needed his help to rise.

"Forgive me, Sensei," I said, trying to steady myself. "I hoped your teaching would focus my mind."

"That's your first mistake," the small, older man replied with a knowing smile as we bowed. "You must focus your mind first, then take lessons. Show me your kamae."

I took the defensive stance I'd been practicing for two months since meeting Ashwan. It was called *Tachi Waza* — 'standing technique' — with my good left leg forward, slightly bent, and my frozen right leg behind. My left arm extended slightly, bent at the elbow. This was the proper form, even though I was right-handed.

Losing my right knee almost eight years ago in a car accident that also claimed my fiancée had left me with lasting challenges — physical and emotional alike.

"Your mind drifts again," Ashwan scoffed as he moved fluidly into position to be my *Uke*, my opponent.

I'd only started Aikido lessons in January after my Maine trip, where a couple of hoods had roughed me up. My girlfriend — odd to still call her that at thirty — insisted that if I was going to keep getting into trouble, I should learn to defend myself.

Aikido made sense: a defensive discipline rooted in understanding your opponent's perspective, matching my own beliefs.

Clad in my *Gi* and *hakama* pants, my bright orange beginner's belt tied around my waist, I began the familiar circular *Tai Sabaki* motions.

Ashwan lunged. I moved quickly, redirecting his fist away, then spun to harness his momentum — throwing him into the empty space he had just occupied. He landed on the mat, rolled, and rose with a gracious smile.

"Much better," he praised, advancing toward me again.

Dating Jyanette Emery these past five months had been a whirlwind of passion and thrilling nights. We both knew the heady rush would fade over time, but for now, we soaked in it fully.

People's eyebrows raised when we announced our relationship in January. Jyanette was an Assistant District Attorney, and I volunteered as an unpaid civilian consultant to the Mountainview Police Department.

The DA had even privately questioned Jyanette, ensuring no conflicts would arise from our connection. The last thing anyone wanted was for her to cross-examine her boyfriend in court.

Luckily, my work with Lieutenant Bill McGee kept me in the background — a position I preferred. No one wanted word leaking that the police were consulting a psychic to crack cases.

Even if it were true.

I found myself back on the mat as Ashwan lunged again, lights glaring overhead.

"You must focus," his voice was firm but kind, his white hair glowing in the glare above us. "I didn't ask for this lesson — you did."

He helped me up a second time.

"Forgive me, Sensei. Perhaps we should call it a day."

Ashwan glanced at his wristwatch. "Your hour's almost up. But next time, meditate before you come. You perform better that way."

I bowed. "You are wise, sensei."

His grin deepened. "And flattering me won't protect you from throws if you lose focus. Is something troubling you?"

I ran a hand through my short brown hair, frowning.

"Maybe it's the inactivity."

His smile softened. "As a teacher, I thought you were always busy with your students."

He meant my real job — as a professor of parapsychology at Garden State University.

"Or maybe your other work with your police friend?" he probed.

"It's been a while since Bill McGee needed me," I sighed.

"But you've spent your time coming to classes three days a week. You've been a devoted student."

I shook my head. "I'm just tired of getting beaten up."

He nodded knowingly. "Still. Meditate. Clear the clouds. Soon enough, you'll be busy."

"How do you know?" I asked.

He shrugged. "Yin and yang. You've rested — the yin — so action — the yang — must come."

Puzzled by his prediction, I headed for the locker room to change.

The drive back to Mountainview was quiet, as I watched the sun rise. Daylight savings time was still throwing everyone off their rhythm. Spring was officially returning on Sunday — Jyanette's birthday.

Driving west on a Thursday morning felt like a minor victory, watching the eastbound commuters crawl toward Manhattan while I had the open road. My silver minivan, specially equipped for my needs, with controls on the steering column that allowed me to speed up and brake the vehicle entirely with my hands.

Lieutenant Bill McGee, my friend and police contact, was meeting me at Mindy's Diner.

My mind had been elsewhere all morning, likely because of an email I'd received the week prior. A clinical paper I'd written for the American Board of Parapsychology had somehow caught the eye of a literary agent. He liked my prose but wanted me to adapt the academic text into a book for a general audience.

It was an "on spec" project — no guaranteed payday until a manuscript sold — but if it landed, it might help to stabilize my precarious finances.

I forced myself to stop counting unhatched chickens as I pulled into Mindy's crowded lot. Cars zipped in and out of the stalls, creating a frantic energy I wasn't ready to join yet.

I looked at my laptop sitting on the backseat, tempted to dive into my notes while I waited for McGee, but I knew better. I needed to follow my sensei's advice and center myself.

Meditation would help.

When my mental abilities first manifested eight years ago, they nearly broke me. Precognitive flashes and the ability to slip into the minds of others sound like a gift, but the reality was a nightmare of unbidden thoughts and intimate secrets screaming for attention.

I thought I was losing my mind.

To survive the psychic noise, I turned to alcohol. At first, it was a shield; eventually, it became a cage. I didn't just use it to cope — I loved it, right until I became a full-blown alcoholic.

Doctor Fritz Kohl saved me. He became my mentor, teaching me how to build mental barriers and harness my talents to help others rather than drown in them.

Meditation and controlling my mind were part of that process.

I killed the engine, set my phone alarm for twenty minutes, and closed my eyes.

In... out. In... out.

I slipped easily into an alpha state, detaching from the physical world. Outside, the highway hummed with the rattle of heavy trucks and the impatient honking of commuters, but within the cabin of the cooling van, I found a pocket of total peace. I was aware of the temperature dropping and the distant mechanical grind, but they couldn't touch me.

When the alarm finally chimed, I returned to the present feeling sharp and refreshed. Ashwan was right: I'm always better after I meditate.

The interior of the van had grown cold, but my winter coat and gloves kept the bite away. I reached back to grab my shoulder bag, then gripped my cobra-head cane. I could limp without it if necessary, but it was essential for balance and on stairs.

More importantly, the wooden sheath hid a twenty-four-inch blade — a tool that had proven its worth as more than just a walking aid frequently.

Cane in hand, I stepped out into the cold and made my way toward the diner.

Although the owner of Mindy's — Carl Sokolov — put in a rather impressive ramp to comply with the Americans with Disabilities Act, I took the stairs slowly, one at a time, as I preferred them.

As I went through the door, there was a line at the cash register, where Carl stood taking cash and running credit cards. The diner was a flurry of activity with people getting coffee, pastries, and breakfast sandwiches to go.

Carl wore a light-blue shirt that bore several food stains, undoubtedly from his most recent forays into the kitchen to assist the chef. In a small diner, the owner must wear many hats.

He waved and pointed to the back room — the 'party room' — where I knew coffee would be waiting.

McGee and I had started the habit of meeting on Mondays, though in January it had been more social than work. After the holidays, the caseload for Mountainview's newest lieutenant had shifted. Instead of pursuing cases, he was now following up on the people under him as they sought answers.

He enjoyed his new role as manager over other officers, but at other times he itched to get out and work cases.

The conflicted joy of being promoted.

It was odd for McGee to meet with me on a Thursday, and even odder that it would be here at Mindy's instead of at the Mountainview Police Department.

I was still a half-hour early, but as I had brought my bag, I took out my laptop and opened the word processing program that had the notes for my story.

I based the book on an actual event that involved a jeweler who was also an insurance scam artist named Phillip Mishan. He came to a terrible end when his partner-in-crime incinerated him. He and several other people died, including a young woman I was dating at the time named Wendy.

Well, that's not quite true. We'd had a total of two dates. But we'd become intimate, which led to her jealous psycho ex-boyfriend killing her right in front of me.

I had changed the names and the locations, though still based the tale in New Jersey. Writing it as a novel, I hoped to avoid any lawsuits if anyone didn't care for how I depicted them — even though I gave all the characters different names.

I was about ten thousand words in, and had to admit I enjoyed the process. Though still unsure of my competence as a storyteller, I felt I could correct any major mistakes in rewrites.

As I tapped away at my keyboard, Bill McGee came in carrying his battered briefcase. I shut down the computer as he poured himself a cup of coffee.

"How's the writing?" he asked as he sipped from the mug.

"Slow. I still haven't found my pace with it yet."

He pulled out the chair across from me and put the cup in his place.

"Are you ordering what you usually get?" he asked. "'Cause I need to order if we're eating. Captain scheduled a meeting today."

"Oh, uh, sure. I have a class later myself. So, I would get—"

"Yeah, I know, vegetable omelet, no potatoes, no toast. Really, Len, you could use some weight on you. You should hit the carbs a bit more."

"Thank you, I already have a mother. Do you want me to give Emily our order?"

"No, I will. I'm more fleet of foot than you," he said as he walked to the door to speak to our regular waitress.

I wasn't sure that I needed more pounds on me. At six feet-four and one hundred and eighty-five pounds, I carried myself pretty well, and with all the Aikido I was doing, I was gaining muscle, as well as strength and endurance. This was in contrast to the soreness I felt, because Ashwan had so little trouble throwing me.

McGee is my height, but stronger, wider. He'd been with the FBI. On one assignment, he met Laura, the daughter of a very rich man. Despite their differences in social status and the disapproval of her family, they married, and her family disowned her. Now, they had two sons.

A couple of years back, Bill was in a raid that went bad and almost cost him his life. Laura informed him that either he changed professions or she would leave. Bill left the bureau and got a job as a detective in the sleepy college town of Mountainview. He quickly rose through the ranks and became a lieutenant just last November.

He returned to the table, poured a cup of coffee for me without even asking, and sat down to open his briefcase.

A pile of manila files swelled the sides of the case, but Bill only pulled out one folder, which he placed on the table as I put two of the little creamers in the dark liquid in my mug.

"When are you going to switch to black coffee?" Bill asked, taking a sip from his own cup.

I glanced at him. "I thought you wanted me to have more calories," I said, nodding toward the briefcase on the table. "So, anything good in there?"

He looked up. "Hmm? That? Burglaries, a carjacking, a couple of missing persons—"

Missing...

A small but persistent buzz ignited inside me — a flicker of precognition, my personal code word for those subtle flashes. Sometimes they were faint nudges to pay attention; other times, they roared like a lion, impossible to ignore.

"I know it's not why you brought me here," I said, "but can I see the missing persons files?"

Bill frowned, fishing three files from the middle of his briefcase, and positioned them in front of me. "Sorry to bring so much," he said, "I've got cases for all the detectives now, not just my own."

I flipped open the first folder, scanning the details. "How's Laura?" I asked.

"Good. Busy." He sighed. "We actually got a sitter for Valentine's Day, and I took the night off."

"You are the LT," I said, using the verbal shorthand for lieutenant. "You can do that now."

He shrugged. "Old habits die hard — I still put in long hours. But Laura's patient. Speaking of patient souls, how's Jyanette?"

I couldn't help but grin. "Gorgeous."

"Now, now, calm down. I guess everything has been pretty steady with you not running around with me."

"Things are wonderful, but we're still adjusting. She's got trust issues from her ex-husband—"

"Oh yeah, that's right. You told me he did drugs."

I nodded. "And I have issues about women I date getting killed."

"So far, nothing's happened to her—"

"If you discount what went down with that crazy psychiatrist last September."

"True, but you weren't even involved then. Didn't even know her."

I grinned. "I wanted to."

He pointed at the ignored folder he first pulled out. "Let me know when you're ready. I really want to get to this."

I turned to the folders in front of me. "Sure, just following up on a buzz."

McGee sighed, quite familiar with my terminology. "Of course you are."

I turned to the first folder. A forty-year-old woman who disappeared about two weeks ago. "Anything about this one I should know?"

"You're the psychic, not me," Bill shrugged. "But she had a terrible marriage and an abusive husband. I'm inclined to think she just ran off."

I picked up another folder. "This one's outside your jurisdiction, right?"

"The two girls from Staten Island? Yeah, but the NYPD sent the bulletin to every tristate precinct since one's underage."

I read the names aloud. "Constance Newhouse and Erica Marconi?"

Missing...

The buzz grew stronger.

"Something about the name?" Bill asked.

"I told you about the gangster in Maine, right? The one who had a detective killed?"

"Yeah. Was his name Marconi?"

I nodded. "Anthony Marconi. He owns an island."

Bill smirked. "Who says crime doesn't pay."

"I'm getting a strong buzz on this one."

"Well, as you pointed out, that investigation is outside my sphere of influence. Unless, of course, they were being held here in Mountainview. Otherwise, you gotta go with the NYPD."

"Who might not appreciate a psychic getting involved."

"What can I tell you, Len? Most cops don't have an open mind like me. But, if it looks like you might have something, we could contact Stan Frazier."

"From the FBI New Jersey Task Force?"

"Exactly. Your help impressed him when we had the case of that gang targeting underage girls."

"We were lucky to have stopped them when we did."

"And we prevented Anna Sokolov from becoming another human trafficking statistic."

I pulled the flyer from the folder. "Can I keep this?"

Bill nodded. "Sure, I'll print up another copy at MPD."

"Great," I said as I returned the other two folders to Bill. "Now, you asked me here about this one?"

"You got it," Bill said, and slid the folder on the table over to me. "But I'm always interested in what you select on your own."

I opened the folder, and there was a picture of a silver knife with a wavy blade. It was bright silver and appeared old and unique. It had a handle made of what appeared to be gold, and next to the blade was a sheath, also silver with a green stone inlaid in the metal.

"What do you make of that?" he asked, his eyes hopeful.

"It's called a Kris or a Kĕris blade," I stated matter-of-factly, my eyes on the photo. "People produce them in many places, but primarily in the South Pacific, from the Philippines to Indonesia. It's used for rituals, as well as a weapon. This is like the Wiccan athame, which is a ritual knife used in rites."

"Rites?" McGee asked. "Like human sacrifice?"

"Not in any of the covens I'm familiar with. The point — if you'll excuse the pun—"

"I might not—"

"Its primary function is to focus the mind, like most ceremonial and ritual objects. The knife becomes a focal point for the mental energy of the user." I indicated the photograph. "This one is quite superb."

"All silver, and that handle—" McGee pointed with his finger.

"Is it really gold?" I said as I leaned closer to the photo. "Usually a Kris has a wooden handle. And this sheath, is that jade inlaid on it?"

"I wouldn't know."

"Who had this?" I insisted.

"A collector over on Upper Mountainview Road," Bill said. "You should've seen his place. He has a room filled with knives from all over the world, all different."

"But the only one stolen was this one?"

"You've got it."

"Hmm. Well, the blade is silver, probably no iron in it at all, which points to ritual use. Also, each curve is called a luk, and as you can see, there are multiple bends. In ritual use, the number must always be an odd number — never even."

"So why the wavy blade?"

I exhaled heavily. "Using it as a stabbing weapon, the edge of the blade 'dances' into a wound and shreds the flesh as it goes."

"Sounds efficient," he replied grimly.

I shook my head. "Very few people could survive a strike from such a blade."

I closed the folder just as Emily came into the room with our plates of food. Bill moved the pair of folders.

"How you two doing?" Emily said, her thin face showing deep circles under her eyes.

"We're good," I said. "But you look tired, Em."

"Yeah, Larry's on a cross-country, and Tyler was sick last night." Emily sighed, speaking about her husband and son. "I better have an energy drink to get through this day."

She placed plates of food in front of us, and I made a sympathetic noise. Emily's husband was a long-haul truck driver, and she sometimes felt like a single mom.

"Is Tyler with your mom today?" Bill asked.

"Yeah, thank God for her," Emily affirmed, and a hand went to primp her curly hair, and then adjust her uniform. "You boys need anything?"

"We're fine, Em," I assured.

"No problem. And, doc, if you can get those lottery numbers —"

I smiled. "Your boss asks for them every time I drop by."

"Well, you are his 'Wonder Man,'" Emily teased as she walked out.

"Is that your superhero persona?" Bill quipped. "I believe someone already took on 'Wonder Man'."

"Let me know if I can get invulnerability," I grunted. "I keep getting my butt handed to me."

Bill and I enjoyed our breakfast and some more coffee. Although I could keep the flyer on the missing girls, he needed to email me the stolen blade information.

I put a mouthful of omelet into my mouth. "I'd like to talk to the owner of the knife, see the place where he kept it, if that's possible."

"I don't see that will be a problem. I'll call him and make sure. Doug is still processing the evidence, but we don't have a lot to go on."

Doug Millbank is the county forensic chief, very thorough if a tad world-weary. I knew we could count on him and his team to find as much as possible from any crime scene.

"If the forensic evidence is sparse, could it have been the team from the 'Mister Burglaries?'"

"I believe we rounded up everyone in that group," Bill insisted as he scooped a forkful of eggs. "I'm sorry I have nothing more interesting for you."

"It's really not a problem. I am actually enjoying not being in the middle of bad people doing terrible things."

Bill put a forkful of eggs in his mouth and chewed thoughtfully. "Hopefully, this will be a calmer year."

We finished our meal and left cash on the table for Emily. Because Bill and I helped save Carl's daughter, he lets us use the back room, but we always leave enough to pay for our meals, as well as tip Emily.

Bill and I parted, he with his briefcase, and me with the computer bag and the one file folder.

I got in my car and decided I would head home and work at my home office when my phone rang.

My van was still fairly new with all the bells and whistles, and I answered the phone with the built-in hands-free Bluetooth equipment. "Leonard Wise."

"Len, it's Trisha."

Trisha Heywood was my boss's assistant, but she was the one who kept GSU running like a well-built watch.

"Good morning. What's up?"

"I know your class isn't until this afternoon, doctor," Trisha said, sounding very formal. "There is someone here asking for you. He insists he won't leave until he sees you. Can you come by?"

"I suppose. Who is it?"

"His name is Anthony Marconi."

2. FAMILIAL FIDELITY

Since I wasn't far from GSU, I was able to get there in less than ten minutes. Instead of pulling into my reserved space behind Williams Hall, I drove to one of the blue-signed spaces reserved for people with disabilities directly in front of College Hall.

I thought about leaving my laptop case in the car, but in the end, I grabbed the bag and threw it over my shoulder.

My concern was that the last time I crossed paths with Mister Marconi, he'd sent a couple of unsavory gents to rough me up and damage my possessions in a hotel room in Maine. Then he had a cop on his payroll murdered right in front of me.

I certainly didn't bear any warm, fuzzy feelings toward the man.

I wasn't sure if he'd brought his bodyguards with him, and I was unsure of why he was in New Jersey. Could the reason be the missing girl whose name I read about in the flyer from the NYPD?

I walked into College Hall. The building used to be a spectacular mansion, and this entrance showed the splendor of the original design.

This path took me through a large, impressive oak door and into a finely made marble hall, which led to the administration offices.

On the opposite side of the building, about five years ago, the university removed the traditional stone facade and replaced it with a glass foyer. On the one hand, at night you could see directly into the building to observe a pair of magnificent twin marble staircases, but it was like a greenhouse and rendered the inside broiling in the summer. In the daylight, it reflected anything that approached like a mirror.

I headed directly for Jon Baines' office. He was my oldest friend and the Associate Dean, which made him the reason I could head up the only college-level parapsychology department on the East Coast.

Of course, the department only consisted of me.

I gave the door a gentle knock and went through without awaiting a reply. Trisha rose from her desk as I entered.

"Where is he?" I asked, more sternly than I'd intended.

"I put him in Conference Room B," she replied. I turned toward the door, but Trisha approached, put her hand on my shoulder, and gently turned me to face her. "Is there something I should know about this man, Len? He was most insistent."

"Was he alone?" I attempted to sound less severe.

"Completely. But he seemed to be used to getting his own way."

"That's the truth. If there's a problem, make sure you have Campus Security on speed dial."

She gave me a concerned look.

"I'm kidding. But he actually is a criminal."

Her eyes grew wide. "Really?"

"The real deal. If he came without bodyguards, then I'm probably safe. Thanks, Trisha."

I exited the office and used my cane to push me in the direction of the conference room, grateful that if I needed a weapon, it was right there in my hand.

I pulled the door open, and there sat Anthony Marconi in one of the overstuffed leather chairs near the conference table. He wore a nice suit and tie. Nice? Hell, it probably cost twice what I made in a week. He looked good, tanned and relaxed since I'd seen him in Maine. His salt and pepper hair had a high and impressive pompadour as if blow-dried.

I stayed by the door and hung my coat on the hanger behind it. There was a cashmere coat already on one hook; I assumed it was Marconi's. I glanced carefully around the room.

"No one here but me, doc," Marconi reassured in his gritty tone, the strong 'New Yawk' accent in his voice.

He didn't get up.

"Louie and Pete still in Maine?" I questioned. I closed the door because I probably did not need to escape in a hurry.

He shrugged and tried to make it look casual. "I'm not at liberty to say. Come in, sit down, I won't bite."

He gestured to the chair across from him, and I limped over and sat, but kept my cane in hand. It was another large leather chair with those odd wings that always seemed to block one's peripheral vision.

"I appreciate you makin' time to see me on such short notice."

I sat stone-faced. "Our last meeting didn't go so well."

He shrugged. "Don't know what you're talking about, doc. Seems to me, we both got what you asked for."

"I wanted to bring your son's killer to justice, not watch them get shot down in the middle of the street."

He leaned forward and pointed at me angrily. "My Bobby ended up dead, and justice was served," he spat. He immediately composed himself and reclined back in the chair. "But that ain't why I'm here today."

I shook my head. "I've seen the newspaper articles. Things are pretty hot for you in Portland."

This didn't fluster him in the least. "In time, it'll pass. I'm here concerning a personal matter."

This piqued my curiosity. "A… personal matter?"

He nodded. "It affects my family directly." He looked up at the ceiling as if seeking answers there. "It concerns my niece."

I didn't need to be a psychic to get the obvious flash of insight. "Erica Marconi?"

His head snapped down to stare at me.

"How did you—?" he muttered.

I pulled the police report out of my shoulder bag and handed it to him. "There was an alert sent to the police in the Tristate area. I recognized the name."

He looked at the flyer, which included photos of Erica and her friend. "That was quick."

I pointed at the photos and said, "This is the girl she was with, Constance Newhouse?"

Marconi nodded sadly, his eyes fixed on the paper in his hand. "Her best friend since they started high school."

"I don't see how I can help."

His gaze shifted to me. "I want you to do that thing you can do."

I sighed. "Mister Marconi, it doesn't work that way."

"Really, doc?" he griped. "Just how does it work? You came to my house with a list of boats that had shipments — my shipments — that you just conjured out of thin air."

"Look, even if I could do anything, I don't have any official standing in Staten Island. I barely have an official standing here in New Jersey. You'd be better off hiring a private detective."

"I did," he said and extracted a business card from his pocket, which he held out to me. "This guy's an old family friend."

I leaned over and took the card. It read:

DARREN WARD
PRIVATE INVESTIGATOR

The card listed his phone number and the fact that he was 'licensed and bonded in New York and New Jersey.'

"Seems like you already have someone on the case." I offered to return the card.

He pushed my hand away. "Keep it. I need you, doc."

"Mister Marconi, I have commitments as a professor and I—"

"I know what you've been doing with the Mountainview Police." Marconi leaned forward in his seat. "After we last met, I had some people find out everything I could about you. That whole thing with the fires, and that cop who tried to blow up the police station? You figured those out — saved people both times. I also know what you did with me." His index finger tapped his forehead. "You got into my head."

"Mister Marconi—"

"I know you're the real deal. Look, if it's a matter of money—"

"I am not for hire," I stated firmly.

"Yeah, but you helped that old couple, the Stollers? You found out who murdered their son. You can help me, help my family."

I shook my head, frustrated with this entire turn of events.

Marconi went on. "Doc, my niece is innocent. She's got nothin' to do with my business. I'm asking — not for me, but for my wife. It's my brother's kid, and she was always Barbara's favorite. Y'know like the daughter she couldn't have. I mean, she's a teenager, rebellious and stupid, but she's family. After losing Bobby…well, to be honest…it's been rough on my wife."

I looked at him, knowing how hard it was for him to ask this of anyone. Usually, he told people what he wanted, and they did it without question.

He went on. "You don't believe me? Then do that thing. Go ahead, I give you permission." He stared at me.

I frowned, met his eyes, and slipped into his mind. Of course, it was easy. He'd given me permission and opened himself up.

At once, I experienced pain over the loss of his son. If he'd been any other man, it would have crushed him. And I also saw him as he held his crying wife, as she dealt with their loss and the fear that their niece was missing.

I instantly pulled back and broke eye contact, finding my eyes were wet.

The experience had touched me deeply. After a moment, I spoke. "I believe you are sincere."

Marconi shook his head as if awakening from a dream. "You can help. I know you can."

"I wish I was so certain. There appears to be very little to go on."

"The PI will take care of anything you need. I want you to give him an edge."

"You have to know, I can't promise anything."

"Can you tell me one thing?"

"What?"

"Are they still alive?"

I met his eyes again. "You have very high expectations about my abilities."

He held out the flyer with the photos. "Just try."

I took the paper.

"Please," he murmured.

I glanced at each photo, small squares on a police bulletin. The quality suggested that they were high school yearbook pictures. Focusing on Constance's photo, I gazed into the printed eyes.

Nothing came.

I shook my head. "I get nothing from Constance, good or bad," I reported.

"Try Erica," he stated flatly.

I moved my eyes to her photo, staring directly into her eyes as if she sat across from me.

Scared…

The fear flashed into my mind, hot and hard.

Tired…

Alone…

I shut my eyes and imagined white walls to block me from the momentary contact. If I had tapped into her consciousness, she was very much in an agitated state.

Marconi wore a weary smile. "You got something, didn't you?"

"Perhaps, but nothing conclusive." I put the flyer back into my bag.

"See! I want your help. You can find her."

I exhaled heavily. "If I agree — and I haven't yet — you must understand I cannot promise anything. I know you researched me, but I've got to tell you I've had my share of failures. And people ended up dead."

"Like that Wendy Wallace girl. Or your fiancée?"

I raised my head and gritted my teeth. He'd researched me thoroughly. I really didn't appreciate a man like Marconi knowing that much about me. "If I get involved, I don't want to be blamed if I can't find her."

He rose from the chair at this point. "I understand."

He reached into his pocket and pulled out a small phone. It was an older model of flip-style phone, which, in the age of mobile devices that do everything but your laundry, was rather a surprise.

"This phone's got one number on it. If you have news for me or need me to clear a problem out of your way, you call it."

I took the phone and looked at it. It was probably what people in the trade referred to as a 'burner' — a prepaid device bought at a big-box store with a limited amount of time on it. Drug dealers and criminals favored them to communicate under the radar. It reminded me of just what kind of man I was dealing with.

"Just so you know, this doesn't mean—"

"Relax, doc. I know you don't work for me. But I also know from our past encounter that you're a guy who'll be straight with me."

He headed for the door and grabbed his winter coat from the back of it. He pulled a scarf from the sleeve and wrapped it around his neck.

"Not to pressure you, doc," he explained, "but you need to understand that if someone grabbed her, we probably have a limited time to find her."

"I've been involved with kidnapping cases in the past," I said. "I promise I will call your detective."

He nodded. "I won't forget this."

He went out the door. I sat in the chair with my shoulder bag and the flip-phone in my hands.

Why the hell did I agree to this?

3. SANCTIFIED THIEVERY

I put the flip-phone in my pocket, pulled out my smartphone and the business card, and quickly input the number for Darren Ward.

The man answered after one ring. "This is Ward."

"Good morning, Mister Ward," I said and glanced at my watch to see it was almost eleven. "My name is Doctor Leonard Wise—"

"I was told you might call," he said, his tone matter-of-fact.

"Yes, well, Mister Marconi is quite persuasive," I pointed out. "At least this time it was just him, instead of several of his large associates."

"Yeah. Look, Wise, can I be honest with you—"

"Please do."

"I'm not sure what Tony thinks you can do that I am not already doing."

I could hear the annoyance in his voice. "I understand. I'm not trying to step on toes. But, can you tell me any of the events that led up to Erica and Constance's disappearance?"

"I suppose," he grumbled. "They caught a bus Tuesday, early evening, saying some cock-and-bull story about their school having a dance to celebrate Saint Patrick's Day."

"Which was yesterday," I affirmed.

"You got it. Turns out that was a tall tale, 'cause their school, Staten Island Regional, didn't have a dance Tuesday."

"That's when they vanished? Tuesday?"

"Yes. I've been looking into it, and there were no dances at any high school on Staten Island. There were a couple of parties at schools in Manhattan and Jersey. I've been in touch with the schools and spoke to a couple of chaperones, to see if either girl was at these events."

"Did you check about any cars or if they could drive?"

"Of course I did. Constance is eighteen, has her license. But like I told you, the girls took the bus, which doesn't suggest they left the island, unless they took the ferry to Manhattan. The police talked to the bus company, and I got the name of the driver."

"I see. Mister Ward, it appears you've been very thorough."

"Yeah, this is what I do. I'm going to go talk to the bus driver in an hour."

"That might help. But I think I can help even more."

"Do tell?"

"I have friends."

That made him give a curt laugh. "Yeah, well, some Jersey cop wouldn't be much help here."

"I was speaking of the FBI. I know people with the New Jersey Task Force, and they might give us access to their databases."

He considered this. "If I agree, what do you want?"

"Is it possible that you could get your hands on a personal item of both girls?"

"Personal?"

"Yes, a favorite charm, a piece of jewelry, maybe a childhood toy. Anything will do."

"I'm in touch with the parents. I'll put a call out and see. How do you suggest I explain what I need it for?"

"DNA testing?"

"That'll do. You are a doctor, right? Are you, like, an actual doctor?"

"In full disclosure, I graduated medical school and studied for two years in a psychiatry fellowship. But my doctorate is in parapsychology."

"Great," he grumbled. "If you want, you can swing by after two. You got my address?"

I looked at the card and read aloud the Staten Island address printed on it.

"Yeah, that's right. There's a lot. Park your car next to the building."

"Okay, I'll do that. See you at two."

I ended the call and pushed myself up with my cane. I grabbed my coat from the door and headed for my office, which is more of a glorified closet.

As I stepped into the hall, I got a momentary flash.

Danger…

I glanced up and down the hall. It was empty except for our custodial engineer, Jim Stevens, emptying a wall-mounted wastebasket into a large container of trash.

I raised my hand in greeting.

"Hey, doc," Jim said, and approached me. He was a lanky African-American gentleman who was a fixture at GSU and had come to my very first lecture the night I met McGee.

His hair was curly and gray, though his face was unlined, despite his years.

"Hey, Jim." I glanced around the hall to see if my buzz was for something more threatening. "How's your missus?"

"Ronnie? She's off at her sister's. Her niece just had a new baby and ran into some complications, so Ronnie's been there a few months to help."

"Oh, that must make it lonely for you."

"No, we've stayed together for over forty years. Sometimes, time away is the best thing."

I smiled. "You would know better than I, Jim."

Jim drew close, and his expression became serious. "So, who was the fancy dude in the conference room with you?"

"Just someone who needed help," I said, a bit surprised Jim had noticed Marconi. Then again, there was probably a lot he noticed of which I was unaware.

Jim shook his head. "Well, I don't want to tell you your business, doc, but he looked like a man you might not want to be mixed up with."

My smile grew. "You're probably right, Jim."

"I know I am, doc. Don't look now, but your boss is comin' over."

Jim backed away as Associate Dean Jon Baines approached us. Jon was almost as tall as I was, wider, but not solid like McGee. He was more like a really large, friendly dog.

He's my boss, but also my oldest friend.

He gave Jim a wave as he approached, then moved close to me.

"Len," he murmured with concern. "Trisha told me you were meeting with a gangster of some sort?"

We turned away from Jim and started down the hall, as he matched my pace. "Yes, but he came to ask a favor."

"Was it like…a favor you could not refuse," he said as his voice lowered and took on the sound of Marlon Brando's Godfather persona.

"Nothing like that. His niece is missing."

"Missing? If you get involved, could this be something that reflects badly on the university?"

I stopped, and Jon did too. I smiled at my friend. He was always thinking like a dean. He wanted to make GSU look good at all times and avoid any kind of controversy.

After all, controversy could affect fundraising, which was his number one job.

"It happened on Staten Island, so I think we're far enough removed, Jon."

"Still, criminals coming to the university—"

"It's okay, Jon. I'll make it my mission to protect GSU from scandal."

We walked on in silence for a moment.

"So, how is the 'family planning' going?" I asked. Jon and his wife — short, petite Jenny — were attempting to have a baby. They had given me no updates, so I was curious.

Jon beamed. "Don't want to jinx it, but Jenny's period was due two days ago. I think we might have hit it."

I smiled. "You guys'll make great parents."

"Yeah, it's weird. I think about it, and sometimes I feel like I'm walking on air, and other times I'm scared to death that I won't be up to the task."

"You sound like someone who will do the right thing. And I'm afraid the only way to really learn parenting is to have a child."

We reached my office, and he said, "Thanks, Len. I'll let you know."

I nodded and stepped into my office. Behind my desk, in front of my desktop computer, sat my teaching assistant, Teddy Santos. He glanced up at me through the thick lenses of his glasses, and his jaw fell open. "Doc? What're you doing here? Your class isn't until one p.m."

I smiled. "Some work on a case. If I can have my desk, that is."

Teddy looked about; his shoulder-length, straight black hair waved as he nodded.

"Oh…uh, sure. Sorry to take over, doc. It's just that you usually go directly to your class without stopping here."

My smile broadened as he assembled the items scattered on my desk and put them in his bag.

"Teddy, relax. Mi casa es su casa. You're my TA; you have as much right to come here as I do. That's why I gave you a key."

He nodded and picked up his backpack to shove his laptop into it. "It's okay, doc. I can just set up in the computer room. More light anyway." He threw the backpack over his shoulder and headed for the door.

"That's because the computer room has a window." I gestured at my windowless domain.

He looked back over his shoulder. "At least you got an office on the first floor." He shrugged and went out the door.

I walked around and sat at my desk. My desk was far larger than I needed. The extra space in the kneehole allowed me to fit my unbending right leg under it comfortably. I leaned my cane against the side so I could grab it easily.

I moved to the keyboard of my desktop and switched users, which made all of my personal settings come up instead of Teddy's, and opened my email.

McGee had sent the information with all the attachments. I had the police report and photos of the crime scene and the Kris knife.

McGee had been right about the collector. Glass cases lined the walls of the room where the robbery occurred. Each case contained impressive knives, swords, or other blades. I made the photo larger so I could examine it carefully.

McGee had also written the name of the owner, Brett Morgan, on the email, and left a phone number with the instructions, all clear to call him.

I checked my watch and decided I could fit him in before I went to Staten Island, if he was available. I called the number.

"This is Brett Morgan," came a cultured voice on the other end of the phone.

"Mister Morgan, my name is Doctor Leonard Wise. I'm a consultant with the Mountainview Police Department. Have I caught you at a bad time?"

"No, I'm working from home today, in case any of you people can find my dagger."

"I understand. I know you've had forensics in and out of your house today, but I'd like to stop by and have a look."

"What are you, a profiler or something?"

"Something like that. I offer the police insights, and sometimes it helps."

"When do you want to come?"

"Would a half-hour be convenient?"

"He will win who knows when to fight and when not to fight."

This caught me by surprise. "I'm sorry?"

"That was a quote from Sun Tzu and The Art of War. Yes, a half-hour will be fine."

He ended the call.

I shrugged and pocketed my phone. So much for niceties.

I turned on the printer behind me that sat on a small bookcase and loaded it with photo paper so I could print hard copies of the photo of the knife.

I just needed to take care of one detail.

I went to the computer room, happy that Teddy had moved there after being displaced from my office. He was in the corner of the large multi-user workstations that held several large monitors where teachers and teacher assistants could log into the academic accounts.

I knocked on the doorframe, and Teddy turned.

"Can you cover my class today?" I asked. "It looks like I have to go see a crime scene."

Teddy considered it for a moment. "I think so. I need to review the lesson plan."

"It's pretty easy this week. The class is presenting oral reports on Helena Blavatsky, the nineteenth-century medium."

Teddy pulled up the online lesson plan and looked at it; the monitor reflecting in his overlarge glasses.

"Yeah, I can handle it and record it for you to review. What do I tell them you're doing?"

"Something important. Make sure the camera is on and that you video their presentations. I can review it later to grade them."

He nodded. "That'll work."

"Thanks, Teddy," I said as I walked out. Because it would only take me ten minutes to reach the address on Upper

Mountainview Road, I used the time to ensure my lesson plans were up-to-date. If I had to run off to work on the Marconi case, I wanted Teddy to be prepared. It was funny — I now saw the inquiry as the Marconi case instead of a missing persons investigation.

After I posted my changes to the cloud-based lesson plan, I shut down my computer, grabbed the crime scene photos, and headed out.

After a brief drive through the more affluent area of town, I arrived at Mr. Morgan's residence. The house was an impressive Victorian structure, its large white-brick facade adorned with copper domes that had weathered to a soft green under the New Jersey sky. Facing the street, there appeared to be a hundred windows, spanning three stories, all set on a generous plot of roughly an acre. Mountainview, with its proximity to Manhattan, boasts some of the most expensive real estate in New Jersey.

I parked my van so it wouldn't block the circular turnabout near the front door. From the back, I extracted a pair of latex gloves from the box I carry for crime scene work. I shoved them into my pocket, used my cane to help me up the steps, and rang the bell.

A man of average height with the body of a power lifter opened the door. He wore jogging pants and a black T-shirt, which fit tightly against his six-pack abs and well-developed arms.

"Mister Morgan?" I said. I was much taller than the man, and a part of me wondered if his well-defined physique was in reaction to his stature.

"Hey, yeah, Doctor…what was it again?" he asked.

"Leonard Wise. You can just call me Len, if you prefer."

"Then call me Brett. You're the Mountainview Police profiler guy," he chatted away. "I just finished my workout. C'mon, I'll take you to the armory."

"The armory?" I repeated in wonder.

He stepped in the door, and I followed. "Sounds better than 'the weapons room' or 'my collection'."

He took me through his nicely decorated home and up a grand stairway to a second-floor hall, which was also well-appointed. Down the hall, we came to a door, and he reached for a small numbered panel on the wall and pushed in a code without hesitation.

The keypad made a beeping sound, and there was a click. He pulled open the door, and lights flickered on in the room as we entered.

The photos had not done it justice. Glass cases rose up the walls and displayed weapons from many bygone eras.

He'd filled one case with Japanese katanas, the traditional weapon of the samurai. Another case contained swords of European design — British, I would guess — with shining blades and simple hilts. Implements of death from many cultures filled each case. I found the number of items and the extent of this man's obsession overwhelming.

He'd label each item in the cases so you could see what it was as well as the time it came from.

"Wow!" I murmured under my breath.

"Yeah, it's something, isn't it?" Morgan boasted.

"It certainly is!" I replied. "All this, and they only took the one item?"

"Yeah, weird, huh? I was really afraid they would've taken this," he said and pointed to a large cutlass that hung inside a case marked 'Pirates'.

"Why that one?" I said.

"That's my prize. I have verification that it was one cutlass used by Bluebeard."

I looked back at the weapon in awe. "Really?"

"I have the paperwork in a fireproof safe in a separate room, along with photos of each item."

As I stared at the sword, I asked, "When did you first notice the Kris was missing?"

I heard Brett chuckle. "At least you know what it is called. The detective who came here just called it a 'wavy knife.'"

I smiled. "Hopefully, you understand why the police requested I become involved."

"Yes, I can see that," he agreed, and I noticed he focused his eyes on my hand. I looked down to see that he was staring at my cane. "Is that…what I think it is?"

"I'm sorry?" I questioned, still unsure of where he was going or what he was asking.

"It is!" he announced and crouched low and put out his hand to touch the wood of my walking stick. "That's a serpent cane, isn't it? Can I look at it? I mean, you won't fall over or something, will you?"

I shifted my weight to my left leg and handed him my cane. "No, please do. Perhaps you know something of its history."

With an expression like a child on Christmas, he took the cane and held it lovingly. He turned the stick one way and another, then carefully hit the hidden switch, as if he'd known it was there, and slid the head away from the wood, the concealed weapon sliding slowly into view.

As the sword glided out inch by inch, he became more and more excited until it separated from its wooden encasement. He handed me the empty shaft and, with wide eyes, ran his thumb carefully along the cutting edge to feel the sharpness of the blade.

He whistled in admiration and held the hilt at eye level as he judged the straightness of the weapon.

"A serpent cane with a twenty-four-inch blade," he gushed. "I've never seen one any longer than sixteen-and-a-half. Where on earth did you find it?"

"It was a gift from my mentor," I explained. "It comes in pretty handy sometimes."

"You work with the police and they let you carry this thing around? New Jersey law classifies this as a concealed weapon."

I merely smiled, as no matter what I said, it would lead to more questions, and I was there to examine a crime scene, not debate statutes.

"How much do you want for it?" he offered, as he held the blade aloft by the cobra-head hilt.

"It's not for sale," I responded. "It has sentimental value."

"Are you kidding? This has a history," he stated as he looked at the edge again. "That sheath is newer, added recently. But this sword is older, at least a hundred years old."

"Really?" I realized I had never thought about it very much.

"Oh yes, and this catch," he said as he pointed at the small spring-loaded button that linked it to the cane. "A model of engineering. You have a collector's item here, Len. This is valuable."

"I repeat, it's not for sale."

"Not even for five grand?" He suggested, not looking away from the sword.

"I'm afraid not."

"I couldn't go any higher than ten," he proposed. "I would have to track down its history, and that would take time. Look, I'm taking a risk offering that. It probably isn't worth it—"

For a moment, I considered it. Ten thousand dollars would certainly take a lot of financial pressure off me. I could get Jyanette that string of pearls I had seen at the jewelry store in town — with plenty left over. Her birthday was Sunday, and I had gotten her a small gift, but something more would be nice, especially with her parents in town.

"Afraid not," I stated as I shoved the thought of fiscal security out of my mind.

"Pity," he said and turned it over in his hand.

"I would be grateful if you could find out any of its history."

He nodded, turned the blade in his hand, and offered me the hilt. I took it.

"Hold on one minute, then," he said and stepped out of the room. He returned in mere moments with a state-of-the-art camera with a large lens. "Can you put that on the floor?"

I bent carefully and placed the two parts on the floor as requested, then limped back. Brett placed a yardstick between the blade and the shaft, then snapped photos. He focused on certain parts, snapped some more, then turned both pieces over and took a few more shots.

I glanced at my watch and realized I would have to head for Staten Island within the hour.

"Mister Morgan, if we can focus on the task at hand. The robbery?"

"Yeah, sorry," he said, the camera still in front of his eye. He hung the strap around his neck and let the device lie on his chest. Picking up the two parts of the weapon, he reinserted the blade before handing it back to me.

He quickly put the yardstick behind one bookcase where it probably lived.

"That is quite a piece, I'll tell you. I have a research guy whom I'll contact. It might take a few weeks. How can I get in touch with you?"

I extracted one of my university business cards from my wallet, and he glanced at it. "Parapsychologist? I thought you were a police profiler."

"I work for the police voluntarily. And since the stolen Kris has ritual overtones—"

"And since you actually know what it is," Brett grinned.

"Exactly."

He led me over to a case, which was filled with knives that were mostly from the South Pacific and the Polynesian Islands. There was another Kris, but the blade was plainer, far less grand than the stolen one. Plus, there was a thirty-four-inch blade, which lay diagonally across most of an entire shelf. The label read: **Philippine Island Sword dated 1900.**

I could easily see through the glass shelves to one beneath it, which had several knives; the first one an evil-looking short sword with a handle carved to resemble the head of a dead man. The label read: **Malay Dyak Mandau Headhunter Sword.** Next to it was a twenty-inch dagger marked: **Philippine Insurrection Horn Grip Dagger.**

In the middle of the shelf was a blank space, where I assumed the stolen item had lain. There was residue from fingerprint powder on the glass. It had a label which stated:

Silver Ceremonial Kris blade.

Origin Unknown

Discovered among the Korowai clans.

"The Korowai?" I was puzzled. "Is that significant to the history of the knife?"

Brett peered over my shoulder. "It's very significant. The Korowai are an indigenous people in New Guinea. No one even discovered them until the 1970s. The knife was a ritual tool used to conjure the ancestor gods."

He took a step back and looked into one of his other cases as he went on. "The strange part is that they really didn't have the smelting ability to create such an objet d'art. When I bought it, I couldn't tell that it was silver or that the handle was genuine gold. It was dirty and covered with…who knows what. Now, you add to it the fact that the sheath was a replacement, and it was still ancient. Then there is the fact that the Korowai have no access to the amount of jade on the sheath. It all begs the question, where did they get it?"

"Very unusual," I marveled. "How old do you think it is?"

He stepped back to me to peer at the empty spot on the glass shelf. "My researcher thinks it might be a thousand years old."

"Really?" I blurted.

"It was also strange that they would part with it. The person I bought it from said that the Korowai traded it to be rid of it. He said the Korowai believed it to be filled with evil.

I looked at the empty shelf with trepidation.

He went on. "Can you beat that? He got a good deal, but when he learned the materials used to make it, he made me pay an excessive price. I didn't mind. It is a one-of-a-kind artifact. That's why I want it back."

I nodded as I pulled the latex gloves from my pocket and put them on. "Is the cabinet unlocked?"

"Yes, I knew you were coming."

"Could I ask you to leave me alone for a minute or two?" I said.

He frowned. "Why?"

"I need to eliminate all distractions," I said as an excuse. I didn't want to tell him I was about to attempt an energy reading to see if I could receive a vision. Most people don't react well to that concept.

He watched me, then shrugged. "Is it okay if I wait outside?"

"Fine. I should only be a few minutes. I might observe something the forensics team missed."

"Okay." He headed for the door.

"By the way," I said, which stopped him. "Was the lock on the cabinet damaged?"

"Not even a scratch."

"Thank you."

As he stepped out, I closed my eyes, took a deep breath, relaxed my body, and opened my mind. I focused on my breath and felt myself sink into an alpha state. Once I perceived I had gone deep enough, I opened my eyes.

The room had undergone a change. Instead of the secluded room lit with fluorescents, with the colors of the different weapons in their glass cases, the room was now all in sepia tones, like a black and white movie, and dark.

The only thing lit was the cabinet before me, which was illuminated by what appeared to be the beam of a flashlight. I could see the silver knife on the shelf.

My hand went to the cabinet handle, and I opened the door, as the gloved hand in my vision did the same thing. I saw the hand grasp the knife, and I could sense ragged breathing.

I put my hand in the same place as the one in my vision...and the world fell away.

Images smashed into my mind, unbidden and unwanted. I saw flashes like a fast-paced montage. But it was all the same. That twisted knife, as it came down and pierced flesh. I saw faces — it seemed like dozens — as they screamed and howled in pain from the weapon as it sank into them and tore them apart.

I saw a room lit with candles and a chanting Middle-Eastern man who brought the knife down. Then it was an Asian man in a room with beautiful screens. Then, finally, a Filipino in a dark jungle. Each time there were cries and pain, and I staggered from the unyielding impressions as wave after wave of them battered me.

I fought to regain control, to clear my mind of this object's bloody history, and focus on the hand I saw. I tried to remove myself and remain an observer of the events.

Yet a part of me saw myself as the figure who wielded the blade, and I was the person who suffered from the killing stroke.

I calmed my mind, detached, focused my attention on this room and the person as he carefully lifted the dagger and slyly closed the door.

I was still in my sepia-toned vision but free from the impulses and energy of the knife's history. In the flashlight beam, the man lifted the weapon in his gloved hand, and for a moment I saw a reflection of a face in the cabinet's glass as the door closed.

I recognized that face immediately in the pseudo-mirror. Unshaven, fortyish, a thin Caucasian man with the smirk on his face I was familiar with.

It was Stephen Potts, a burglar I had run into on another case.

What was his connection to this knife?

4. DEDICATED DETECTIVE

A few minutes later, I was in my van after giving profound thanks to Brett Morgan. From his powerful frame, I assumed he went back to his workout.

Using the hands-free Bluetooth connection in my car, I immediately called McGee.

"McGee," came his big voice as he picked up.

"It's Len," I said. "I've just left Brett Morgan's house. Can you pick up Stephen Potts?"

"Potts? You think he stole the dagger?"

"Well, limited forensics and a picked cabinet lock. Sounds like him if he had help. There was a numeric panel with pretty high-end electronics, and he's not good with that. I thought he was in jail since last November?"

Around Thanksgiving the previous year, McGee had arrested Potts because of his connection to a series of mysterious home robberies referred to as the 'Mister burglaries', as the members of the gang only knew their leader as 'Mister'.

"He made a deal with the DA. He offered to give testimony once we showed him that Juan Espinoza had not returned from the dead. I was told he was under house arrest with an ankle bracelet."

"Well, he was at the Morgan house. I saw him reflected in the cabinet glass."

"Hmm. What excuse do I use to pick him up?"

"I don't know, but the job fits his skill set."

This got a chuckle from McGee. "I remember the last time he saw you, he covered his eyes so you couldn't peek into his mind. He fears you."

"So, tell him I read his mind."

"I'll get on it. You around?"

"I'm meeting a PI in Staten Island about the missing girls."

"So you are pursuing that case. You know I can't help with anything that isn't local to Mountainview. You definitely should call Stan Frazier."

"I will after I get done with you. I kind of suggested to the PI that I was friends with the FBI New Jersey Task Force."

"Did you? Well, Stan does like you. I think I'll call Potts' probation officer. Maybe I can get him to bring Stephen in."

"I'll let you know when I'm back in Mountainview."

"Good luck. Or don't you need that?"

"Every bit I can get," I countered, and McGee ended the call.

I headed for the New Jersey Turnpike, a stretch of toll road that travels diagonally from the top of New Jersey down to Delaware.

I hit the hands-free button on the console and gave a vocal command to call Stan, who picked up on the first ring.

"Frazier."

"Stan, it's Leonard Wise."

"Len Wise." Stan chuckled. "The Wonder Man!"

"Please, Stan, it's bad enough Carl Sokolov and his staff call me that."

"What's up, professor?"

"Someone asked me to take part in a case on Staten Island. The two missing girls that the FBI sent out a bulletin about."

"A bit out of your locale, isn't it?"

I proceeded onto the NJ Turnpike; my car's transponder paid the toll as I talked.

"A bit. I was wondering if you were involved."

"I saw the bulletin as it went out to law enforcement in the tristate area. But without an interstate crime, I would have to go through the NYPD."

"I thought kidnapping was always FBI."

"That's the problem, professor. It is uncertain if someone kidnapped the girls. We only know they're missing."

"Oh, right."

Stan was silent for a moment. "I could check with CARD."

"Oh yes, the Child Abduction Rapid Deployment team."

I pulled off Exit 12 for the Goethals Bridge, which I took toward Staten Island.

Stan kept going. "Right. Their regional headquarters are based in New York. If they can interface with my team, they could offer us as a help to the locals."

"That would be useful."

"Good. And I'll do what I can on my end. Do you think you'll be able to get anything?"

"Too soon to tell. I'm meeting with a PI—"

"You work with a private investigator?" he chuckled. "Since when?"

"Since this case. But I'll call you if I find something that gives us a direction to pursue."

"Do that." He hung up without further comment.

I had now reached the Staten Island Expressway, which is an oxymoron if there ever was one. It undoubtedly comes to a screeching halt for miles, no matter what time of day you travel it.

The GPS in the van directed me to Clove Street, which exited to an overpass over the expressway and down toward the north side of the island. I passed a sign that read "Vanderbilt College" as my GPS continued to lead me toward the Ferry Terminal.

Vanderbilt…

I received a buzz and considered this for a moment. Why would that one word stick in my mind?

I knew it was a small college on Staten Island. Cornelius Vanderbilt, the railroad magnate, grew up on Staten Island. Toward the end of his life, he moved into philanthropy and contributed to many charitable institutions from his sizable wealth. The more famous school was Vanderbilt University in Nashville, Tennessee, but he'd also built a smaller college in his native state.

I also recalled that a fellow student of my mentor, Fritz Kohl, was a teacher somewhere in New York, and I believe he was on Staten Island. He graduated the year I joined Dr. Kohl's program.

I put this information at the back of my mind. If there were a former student of Fritz's nearby, he might give me the lay of the land.

As I drove, I noticed the unusual landscape. Staten Island goes through areas that are squeezed with individual homes, all built in differing designs. Then it changes, and you are passing enormous brick monoliths filled with apartments.

I drove along Silver Lake Park, a large open space that allowed city dwellers a chance to interact with nature. Then, a side street led me past an urban renewal project that more resembled a prison than a place to live.

Finally, with just ten minutes to spare, I pulled off the street into a small parking lot next to the address given on the business card. A man in a heavy coat held up his hand to stop me at the entrance.

He approached my window. "Private lot, buddy."

"I'm here to see Darren Ward," I said, and pulled the business card from my pocket.

The man nodded and pointed at a space, which I pulled into.

As I got out and put on my shoulder bag, he drew near and said, "Leave your keys, in case I gotta move some cars."

I nodded and dutifully turned my keychain over. Not that the van used a key, but one of those electronic fobs that sends out a signal so the vehicle would function.

It was amazing how much low-level radio waves we had around us every day. Phones, keys, devices of all kinds, all bombarding our bodies and minds with frequencies that we are told are harmless.

Sometimes, I wondered if they were indeed benign.

The gentleman pointed out the main door, and I made my way to the entrance. It was a three-story stucco building painted white, looking as if it belonged on the West Coast rather than the East. It had an overhang on the top floor with curved red tiles instead of shingles, and painted trim around each window frame to match.

I found Ward's name on the directory and took the single elevator to the third floor, where I looked for Room 324.

It was fairly nice digs. The floors were clean, and the halls appeared freshly painted. It was not the office one imagines houses the hard-boiled fictional detective of old.

I knocked on the solid wood door, which bore a legend in gold letters:

Darren Ward
Investigations

A man about six feet tall, solid, with short blondish hair graying at the temples, pulled the door open. He wore a nice suit, sans tie, and gave the appearance of a stockbroker rather than a detective.

"You Wise?" he said gruffly.

"Yes. Mister Ward?"

"Come in." He stepped back to allow me into his office.

There was a small outer area with a couple of chairs and a glass partition where I could see a large, clean, organized desk in the next room.

He led me through a second door, which was open, and he sat behind the desk. This allowed him to face the window into the waiting room. I sat in the chair opposite him and looked around.

There were plaques on the wall, which I couldn't read because of the distance, but the awards granted an air of success and solemnity to the man.

"Were you able to talk to the bus driver?" I asked, recalling our discussion from the morning.

He leaned on the desk and looked at me. "I got back an hour ago. The driver remembers the girls and says he thinks they got off at the Ferry Terminal."

The Staten Island Ferry, which wasn't too far from Ward's office, runs twenty-four hours a day between Richmond Terrace on Staten Island and Battery Park in Manhattan, carrying thousands of people every day between the two boroughs. The problem was that once in Battery Park, the vast NYC subways were available to travel to any of the other boroughs, as well as offering connections to trains and buses out of town.

I exhaled. "Were they headed for Manhattan if they caught the ferry?"

"I don't even know if they went in the terminal. I have someone reviewing the video feed to see if they can spot them."

"Really?" I pondered. "I thought that would take a warrant."

"The police are very interested in solving this case. I'm former NYPD, so they will share what they can if it helps bring those girls home safely."

I frowned. "And how do you know Mister Marconi?"

"That's not important. Look, Wise, you're here to lend assistance, not interrogate me."

He rose and went to a shelf where sat a battered stuffed bear. The fake fur was gone in some spots, revealing brown terry cloth underneath.

He put it on the desk in front of me and eyed me suspiciously.

"Which girl owned that?" I asked.

"You tell me." Ward smirked as he returned to his seat. "Tony thinks there's something special about you. I'd like a demonstration."

I nodded and closed my eyes to focus on my breath. I felt myself slip down into an alpha state, and with both eyes still shut, I reached my hand out and took the bear.

Images flooded my brain. I saw the bear, new and undamaged, as tiny hands reached for it, and flashed through so many moments of looking at it in the same place in a small bed. Then the bed grew larger as I watched.

I heard a woman call, "Connie! Come for dinner. Now, please!"

Jumbled images went through my mind, and I passed through years at an alarming rate. I saw the bear cuddled, then on the bed, and finally moved to a shelf in a white bookcase that was filled with mementos.

Then I saw candles and a cold slab as a knife rose above me, ready to strike. As the arm came down to impale me, I yelled and found myself with my eyes wide open and breathing hard as if I'd run a marathon. My body was damp with sweat.

I put the bear down on the desk and pulled away from it.

"So?" Ward demanded, unfazed by my reaction.

I fought to calm my pounding heart. "The bear belongs to Constance."

"Good so far. Where is she?"

I met his eyes. "She's nowhere."

"What?"

"I think she's dead," I said, numb from the experience.

"And you know that, how?"

"I'm sure Mister Marconi told you about me. For a moment, I was there. I watched through her eyes as someone stabbed her."

"Come on, Wise," Ward jeered and leaned back in his chair. "You expect me to buy this crap?"

"It doesn't matter to me if you believe me or not, Mister Ward."

He shook his head in disgust. "Okay, maybe you'll do better with this."

He rose and took a woman's sweater off a different shelf and put it on the desk, replacing the teddy bear.

"I assume this is Erica's?"

"Wow, amazing!" he sassed. "You should have a TV show."

I ignored his comments and rolled my shoulders to loosen up. Being thrown out of a vision was always a jarring experience, and Ward's sarcasm didn't help.

I picked up the sweater as I focused on my breath. A faint perfume, something flowery, struck my nose. I tried to let myself drift, tried to push myself into the observer role, in case Erica Marconi experienced the same end as her friend.

Images passed through my mind. She bought the sweater at a mall and wore it in a school hallway as she jostled her way past other students. I tried to let my mind follow the girl and not the object. I didn't want images from inside a closet. I focused on Erica.

If she were still alive.

There was a fog all around me that made my way hazy. Deeper. I needed to go deeper, to follow the mental spoor where it took me.

I separated from the object in my hands and felt myself lock onto the person, and I tried to see her most recent impressions.

Abruptly, the clouds faded away, and I was traveling inside a New York bus, everyone preoccupied with themselves or their phones. Next to me was Constance, who looked like her photo, with a heavy coat and a smile. The image was brief, a snippet of memory that filtered to me.

I focused on Erica.

Then, instantly, there was loud music and strobe lights. I was at a party — one I assumed they had attended. I spoke, whether or not it mattered to Ward. It was the technique I had used successfully with McGee.

"A party — recent — flashing lights. She's there with Connie — that's what she calls Constance — both of them in coats, but they have dresses on under them. The ones they think make them look older."

I didn't know if Ward wrote anything down or even cared one iota, but from far away I heard his voice say, "Where's the party? Can you tell?"

I stayed focused on this moment and fought to try not to let the images pull me further. Everything seemed to slow down as I quickly surveyed the room.

"Nothing to identify it, but people appear well-dressed," I said as images came to me.

"How old are they?"

"Twenties mostly, I think." Then, the face of an African American man came into view. He dressed in a nice suit with a tie and seemed to greet the girls. "No wait, there's a black gentleman who has to be in his thirties. He seems to know the girls."

I got a very clear look at the man's face, thinning hair, mustache, but a look of success and prosperity. He stepped aside as a young, thin Caucasian man with a scrawny beard came forward. He took Erica's hand and kissed it.

I knew that face. It was the man who had held the knife in my last vision of Constance.

That brief flash of Connie's last moments.

I focused intently, which made the image slow to almost a still frame as I tried to take in every nuance of his face. I wanted to describe him perfectly so I could tell a sketch artist the details.

"A man, a thin white guy, is kissing Erica's hand."

"Any distinguishing marks?"

"His eyes bug out a bit, and he's got a beard, not much — one of those patch things men grow nowadays. Shoulder-length hair, very straight."

He offered the girls some champagne in glasses — or some kind of sparkly beverage. I sighed and wished that young people, especially young women, had more sense than to accept drinks from a stranger at a party.

I got the impression that everything was bright and colorful, even in the sepia tones I saw, but I couldn't hear any sound. I didn't know what they were saying or spoke about as I watched the girls take off their coats and sit at a table with the thin white guy. The tall black gentlemen took their coats away, then returned to linger nearby as the skinny guy's mouth moved and he told the ladies some grand story, which made them laugh.

I had to admit, from what I could sense, he was not trying to 'come on' to them, and I got the feeling he had met them before. He reached into a pocket and withdrew a solid silver cigarette case. When he opened it, instead of cigarettes, there were rows of capsules in it.

The flashing lights made it hard to see, but the capsules I could discern in full color, as if they contained a magic that allowed them to be perceived in their true state within my vision. Each capsule comprised two parts: a purple side and a bright green side.

I spoke. "He's got a cigarette case, but it has what looks like gelatin capsules in it — green and purple. I think some kind of custom drug."

With bodies slowly gyrating in the background, I saw Constance reach out and take a capsule, and without hesitation, put it in her mouth and chase it with the champagne.

The thin man offered the open case to Erica, but she just shook her head and declined. The man nodded happily and grabbed her almost empty glass. He lowered it behind the table to refill it, and I saw a move I knew all too well.

Since my point of view appeared to be through Erica's eyes, I knew she wasn't aware. But I plainly saw him pull a standard move magicians use called 'loading'.

My brother is a professional magician in Las Vegas, and we used to do shows together in our early teens. I had to master palming techniques, as well as hone the art of misdirection.

As 'thin guy' went to pour the drink, he lowered the glass out of sight as he let something drop into it. He pointed at Constance just as he did it, which distracted the observant Miss Marconi at just the right time.

"Constance took a capsule willingly, but he dumped something into Erica's drink."

"How did he do that?" came Ward's voice from a million miles away.

"He distracted her when he did it."

I saw Erica take the glass and take a sip, and then she put the glass down. She looked over at Constance, who smiled broadly and drunkenly back at her.

She rose and talked pointedly to Constance, who smiled and giggled. Erica grabbed her friend's arm as the skinny guy watched, with no attempt to stop them or help them.

Constance rose and sat back down and broke into a fit of giggles. Erica's hand went to her head, as whatever the man had put in her drink took effect.

The black gentleman drew near, as the skinny guy helped Erica to sit, and the room faded to darkness.

I inhaled deeply as I rose out of the altered state.

"Water," I groaned.

Ward stood and retrieved a bottle of water from a small refrigerator nearby. I downed it.

Anytime I have a deep or powerful psychic experience, it always seems to suck the moisture from my body. Doctor Kohl wants to do a study to understand the correlation.

"So, can you describe this guy you saw?" Ward asked, still doubtful that I did anything more than pull his leg.

"Easily," I said between swallows. "I work with a sketch artist at the Mountainview Police Department. I could call him and—"

Ward raised his hand, the palm facing me in a 'stop' position. He picked up the nearby phone receiver and hit a button I assumed was for speed dial.

"Hello, Tommy? Darren Ward... got a job, make it priority... my place... ten minutes? Sooner if you can... okay, see ya."

He hung up the phone and looked at me. "You say you've worked with police in Mountainview? What's your job title?"

"I'm a civilian consultant who offers insights voluntarily."

"That's a load of gobbledygook, if I ever heard one. You got police ID?"

I nodded. "Yes, but I didn't bring it."

That was a lie. My wallet and my ID badge were in my pocket, and the ID badge lets me in the main doors at MPD because it is magnetized. I didn't know if someone could clone or copy it. I also didn't like his attitude, and I just didn't want to show it.

What could he do? Fire me?

"Naturally. So, you want me to believe that you just saw Erica Marconi and Constance Newhouse in your head?"

I sighed patiently. "Once again, Mister Ward, it doesn't matter to me what you believe. My only interest is trying to help Erica."

"Do you know if she is alive?"

"I think so. I certainly didn't see the same end that Constance came to."

"But you could be wrong about any of this, right?"

"Sure. But if any of what I saw could help find them—"

"All right. I called my sketch guy, you heard me. You give him the descriptions, see what he comes up with."

We sat for a few minutes as Ward turned his back on me and made a few phone calls in hushed tones.

I still wasn't happy about my 'collaboration' with Darren Ward — or even getting involved in the entire matter. Marconi was a criminal, and to have a detective who was a former NYPD seemed to suggest some kind of illegal activity on his part as well.

Then again, when you're a private investigator, I guess you need to take the jobs that come along, as long as you're not doing anything illegal.

I thought of the knife as it came down to strike Constance and end her brief life. If I could stop that from happening to Erica, didn't I have a duty?

The knife…

The buzz was there and persistent. I had missed something. As Ward ignored me anyway, I closed my eyes and tried to get back to that momentary flash of the man with the knife. From the scene with Erica, I had a much better idea of his face.

I needed to watch but stay disconnected. I could not allow myself to fall into Constance's last moments of terror and pain.

I went lower in my consciousness, my mind focused on that man, that strange location with the candles, and the weapon he held aloft. I allowed myself to slip back, back and down into that image, as I fought to focus on every detail.

For a moment, I was there, and then it slipped away as I felt Constance's terror and desire to escape.

I pulled myself back and used my will to be aware of what she saw through her eyes in the last seconds she lived.

And there I was.

I felt cold stone under my body, and I looked up to see that slim man. He wore a robe, and he pulled it back as he lifted the knife.

I concentrated my attention on that blade and how it sparkled in the light. I could see it twist and turn and knew what it was: a silver and gold Kris dagger.

The stolen one that had been in Brett Morgan's collection.

I took a deep breath and brought myself back up from my trance, just as someone came through the door.

The guy was thin, average height, with a pair of glasses, and red hair with a bald spot in the center of his head.

Ward finished his call just as the man came in and turned to face him with a big smile.

"Tommy," he said gregariously. "Set up over there; the light's better." He pointed to a corner with a nearby chair.

Tommy didn't speak but sat down with practiced grace and pulled a set of pencils and a box of charcoals from his bag, and then, to my surprise, unfolded a small easel, which he began to twist and turn to extend it to its full size.

"Elaborate gear," I said to Ward.

"Tommy's a proper artist," Ward boasted. "He takes his work seriously."

Tommy continued to unfold the legs of the metal frame but gave a quick nod.

In a moment, it stood on all three legs, and he sat in the chair and looked at me.

"Go ahead, Wise," Ward insisted. "Tommy's ready."

I sighed, as the man hadn't even said "hello" and now stared at me expectantly. I began my description of Thin Guy, as I still called him in my head.

As I named each feature and conjured the image, Tommy nodded, and his hand moved behind the sketchbook. He still didn't talk, and I wondered if he was mute or merely antisocial. But he encouraged me with his gestures and looks. At some points, he stared at me so intently that I thought he might try to reach into my mind.

Then, like a magician revealing a rabbit, he stood, picked up his pad from the easel, and turned it to face me.

My mouth fell open in astonishment.

I glanced over at Ward, who smiled smugly. "Pretty good, huh."

I shook my head in disbelief.

The drawing was the face I'd seen in every detail, from the slight bulge of the eyes to the patch of beard on the chin.

"I'm, uh, very impressed," I stammered as I tried to find the right words. "I mean, I've worked with sketch artists before, but…that is amazing."

"Tommy's one of a kind," Ward chuckled as Tommy ripped the page from his sketch pad and handed it to Ward. "Thanks, Tommy. I'll get a check out tomorrow."

Tommy nodded with a half-smile as he broke down the contraption that was his easel. He put everything back into his bag, hefted it onto his shoulder, and still without a word walked out the door.

My eyes followed his exit, then I turned back to Ward. "He doesn't say very much."

Ward shrugged. "Spends all his time in his head. You should see his real art. He does these huge murals that take up entire walls."

"But you use him to find criminals."

"Not just criminals. Victims, missing people. He's even done reconstructions from found skulls. He helps me, and I send him enough work to pay his bills until a mural gig comes in."

"Could I take a photo of the sketch? It might help."

He put the paper on his desk and stepped back as I took out my smartphone and clicked a couple of shots.

"I have to tell you I saw something else—"

"Do tell?"

"The man who stabbed Constance used a very special knife. She was lying on a cold slab — I think an altar — and there were candles all around."

"So, you think this guy is into the occult?" he said and gestured at the drawing.

"It fits. I've studied many different rituals, but I was not aware of what he or his followers were doing."

"He had followers?"

"People in robes, chanting. I wish I could tell you more."

"I have to admit, you were pretty good, Wise. The detail you gave Tommy and all. I believe you when you say you've worked with sketch guys before."

"I told you I've worked cases before," I grumbled, once again not liking the assumptions Ward made about me.

"Look," he replied. "Everyone comes here with a story, and it might be true, it might not. I don't even know if this drawing is of a real guy or something you just imagined, but it gives me a place to start."

I relaxed. "I just hope we can find Erica while she's still alive."

"That we can agree on."

5. STEADFAST BURGLAR

L eaving any part of New York City after 3 p.m. on a weekday means you're in rush hour. The Staten Island Expressway moved at the pace of an inactive turtle or an incredibly underdeveloped snail. The half-hour ride back to Mountainview took an hour and a half.

Since I planned to stop by the Mountainview Police Department, I used my hands-free phone to send a quick text to Jyanette, informing her that our seven p.m. dinner would have to be at eight. She was grateful that I'd remembered to let her know.

I drove straight to MPD, and soon I passed the large, angular structure that sits on the corner of Bloomdale Avenue and Valley Road.

The building that houses our police and fire departments is a large, old-fashioned structure that possesses a curved tower, which houses the office of the chief of police on the first floor and the fire chief on the second. The grand office housed the mayor before the municipal offices moved to a separate building years ago.

When one walks in the front entrance, one sees the words 'Mountainview Municipal Building' carved into the stone above the door. To your left, a newer sign reads 'Mountainview Public Safety Building,' which was its current politically correct name.

Ever since I received my security ID, I had access to the back lot of the tan-brick building. The sturdy granite blocks that laid its foundation exuded a sense of permanence, grounding the structure in the bustling city around it.

As I navigated into the lot, my gaze lingered on the adjacent garage, where massive roll-up doors stood ready to unveil the city's fire engines. The sight of those gleaming red vehicles, always prepared for action, filled me with a sense of duty and community.

I grabbed the bag with my laptop and my cane, got out of the van, and made my way to the rear door, which was clearly marked 'Authorized Personnel Only'. I held my magnetic ID badge to the small plate and let myself in.

I moved down the hallway past the bunk rooms — small rooms with beds for officers to catch a few hours of sleep when necessary — and I passed the locker room entrance on my left.

I sauntered across the main corridor and entered the Administration Offices, where our head dispatcher, CeeCee Carter, swiveled in her chair to look at me.

"Leonard Wise!" she blurted. "Haven't seen you in a while!"

I shrugged. "Guess you've been catching the bad guys without me."

"Damn straight," she chuckled as she slipped her headset off her ears and down onto her neck, which released her shoulder-length, dyed-blonde hair. "So, when are you going to break down and take me out on the town for a good time?"

"Considering my finances, not soon," I shot back as I shifted my weight on the cane. CeeCee was a big flirt, but it was all harmless fun. "Besides, you know I'm dating Jyanette Emery."

"Huh," she grunted. "The DA's office gets all the perks."

"I'm sure you have no end of suitors," I said.

"Ha!" she blurted. "I intimidate the guys I meet because I'm a cop or annoy them because my schedule shifts around so much."

I considered it was probably CeeCee's powerful personality that intimidated them. She was of average height and not unattractive, though her face possessed features a bit too strong to be called pretty. She hit the gym constantly, and word was she could bench-press over two hundred pounds.

"Well, I'm sure you'll meet the right guy soon," I suggested and nodded my head toward the lieutenant's office. "Is McGee in?"

"He's probably in the detective's bullpen," she complained. "Honestly, I don't know why they bothered to give him a promotion and an office if all he does is stay there."

"Should I go look for him?"

"No, sit," she commanded with a gesture at a pair of chairs in the corner for guests. "I'll page him."

With a shrug, I carefully lowered myself into one chair, my right leg sprawled out straight in front of me. I hoped no one would come into the room in a hurry; I might trip them.

CeeCee put her headset back in place and hit a button on her console as she announced, "Paging Lieutenant McGee. Lieutenant McGee, you have a visitor in your office." Her voice boomed through the precinct, and I thought it might be a bit of overkill. Perhaps I should have merely called his cell.

I could hear McGee's shoes click in the hall outside, and he came into the room in his rumpled suit, to which he'd added a tie since the morning.

I stood, and Bill smiled. "Been so long," he joked, then turned to CeeCee. "Geez, CeeCee, did you blast that through the entire building?"

"If someone would remain in someone's office," she scolded, "then visitors wouldn't have to wait."

"All right, all right," McGee whined, his hands up defensively. "It's just hard to think in there. It's too quiet. I'm used to noise around me."

"Hmph!" was CeeCee's only reply as she turned away to face the monitor on her desk.

Bill shook his head and waved me into his office.

I grabbed my shoulder bag and dutifully followed him into the small room, which was taken up by a large horseshoe desk facing the window. Folders piled on the desk, similar to his old one, but he appeared to know the location of each needed file.

"I think this is the first time I've been in here," I said as I glanced about.

"Hm?" McGee said and followed my gaze. "Oh yeah, you barely knew Lt. Butler when he was alive, and I only moved in since the New Year."

"The only time I've seen you since then is our meetings at Mindy's."

"Yeah," he said, and looked at the large desk. "I hate the desk. It takes up the entire room."

"I couldn't help but notice."

McGee shrugged. "I guess Butler liked it."

"I guess," I countered.

"How did it go with the PI?" McGee said as he flopped into the big chair and turned to face me as I sat in one of the two chairs in the corner.

"Actually, pretty well," I said as I pulled out my phone and went through my photos. "He thinks I'm full of it—"

"As I told you, most investigators are not as open-minded as I am—"

"But he brought items owned by the girls, and then called a sketch artist." I pulled up the photo of the drawing on my phone, which I turned to face McGee.

"That's pretty good. You saw this guy with the girls?"

I nodded sadly. "I saw him kill Constance."

McGee inhaled sharply. "Really?"

"Yes, with Mister Morgan's stolen knife."

His eyebrows leapt up. "That is interesting. Do you believe Erica is still alive?"

"Yes. I could also be wrong about Constance."

"But you don't think so."

"No."

I saw McGee's jaw set as he handed me back my phone. "Email me the sketch, please."

"Right away," I said as I took the phone and tapped the touchscreen.

"I don't want to sidetrack you," McGee said. "But now you can bring Stan Frazier in with no conflicts."

"His resources would help," I considered as I sent the sketch to McGee's email account.

"We have a burglary in one state that has direct implications to a murder in another," Bill hypothesized as he opened the photo of the sketch on his desktop computer. "Plus, if you're sure this guy abducted the girls, then you have every reason to bring in Stan and the FBI and he might speed things up."

"My impression was that he killed Constance, and I am sure he's planning to kill Erica," I asserted.

McGee shook his head. "Then we have to presume we're on a tight timeline."

"Any luck with Potts?"

"I sent Galland to meet with his parole officer and pick him up," McGee confided, as he referred to his aide-de-camp, Ben Galland. He was a uniformed officer in the MPD and the resident computer wiz. "He should be here soon, provided Potts didn't skip."

"Should I stick around?" I offered and put my hand on my bag. "I have my laptop. I can hang in the break room."

Bill considered this. "It might not be a bad idea. You scare him." McGee looked at the mountain of folders on his desk and then turned back to me with a serious expression. "You go play with your computer. I'll give Stan a call and update him to see if we can get the federal gears turning."

"How will you explain the sketch?"

Bill smiled. "Come on, Len, I'm an old hand at this. I'll say that the description came from a reliable source."

I pushed myself to my feet with my cane. "I'll be in the break room, writing."

"Got it."

I walked out into the administration room and waved to CeeCee, but she was on a phone call and didn't look over. I assumed she spoke to someone who needed police aid as she tapped away at her keyboard.

Stepping into the main corridor, I walked the few dozen steps to the break room, laughingly called 'the Canteen'. It's a small room, but it has coffee, a microwave, a refrigerator, and several machines to buy food that's never as good as you hope.

In the center of the room is one small, round table. There, with a Styrofoam cup of coffee, sat Sergeant Joseph Tice.

I sighed inwardly and walked over to get a cup of coffee for myself. "Sergeant."

"Witch doctor," he smirked. "Shrunken any heads lately?"

"Only people with a big head," I replied.

"Present company excluded, of course," he said and leaned back in his chair. "I was wondering why things have been going so smoothly lately. I just realized it's because you haven't been around."

I shrugged as I grabbed a cup and poured myself some java. This was a constant situation with Tice and me. He thought little of me, despite my successes in previous cases, and considered me a fraud. He could get under my skin, and his constant barrage of insults only made me like him less.

Once he had gotten me so angry, I slipped into his mind to find some past recollection I could use against him. Instead, I saw the memory of a beautiful woman at the moment she left him, and I found the loss so staggering it embarrassed me I had glimpsed it.

With no other place to sit, I plopped down across from Tice and extracted my laptop from my bag.

"Word is that you're going to be an author."

"Trying to be," I said as I opened the lid.

"Well, I'd better not show up in any of your fabrications," Tice remarked as he rose. He took one final swig from the cup and gave it a toss into the nearby open trash can.

"Don't worry, Tice. If I wrote you true to life, no one would believe it."

He smiled at this. "That's the way I like it, doc. And now that McGee is on the opposite end of the building from us peons, make sure you stay on that side during your visits, all right?"

He rose and, without further comment, walked out of the room. I sighed with relief and took a sip of my coffee.

It was hideous.

I don't know what it is about cops and bad coffee. I decided if I finished the book and sold it, I vowed to buy MPD one of those coffee machines that brew individual cups with little plastic pods. It could only be an improvement.

Focusing on my screen, I opened the word processor to take up where I left off, quickly becoming engrossed in the story. Checking my notes — another file on the computer — I tried to keep track of the false names I had used for each player in the drama.

I didn't know how long I had been tapping away when I heard a knock at the door. I started as if woken from a dream and turned to see McGee in the doorway.

"Galland just brought Potts in through the holding vestibule. We'll put him in Interrogation Room B, as soon as he's processed."

"Do you want me in Observation or in the room with him?"

"Start in Observation and see what impressions you get. Then we'll move you in when we want to push him."

"Great. How did it go with Stan?"

McGee shrugged. "I sent him the sketch, and he's coordinating with the NYPD and the agency in NYC. He said he'd call you once he put people in place."

"It'll be weird not working with you," I told him as I shut down my program and stashed my laptop in the shoulder bag.

"I can't be everywhere, Len, and I'm just a local cop."

I walked down the hall and slipped into the squad room to enter the observation room from the side door. The squad room was busy as the officers were changing from the day to the evening shift.

Like most police precincts, officers move from shift to shift regularly. This makes personal life difficult, as they can move you from day shift to overnight from one week to another. Yet I have always found the officers to be professional and able to handle the strain.

I saw Tylissa Booker speaking to the new squad sergeant, Andrew Hastings. She was a short African-American officer and built like a fireplug, but I'd seen her in action. She could tackle a two-hundred-pound man, pin him, and cuff him without even breaking a sweat. I approached just as she turned to see me. She glanced away, but I spoke up. "Hi, Tylissa. I haven't seen you in months."

She didn't meet my eyes but looked at the floor. "I didn't think you'd want to see me because… y'know."

"Because you shot me?" I recalled in a low voice. "Tylissa, it wasn't you; it was Vanya. I'm just glad they reinstated you."

"Really?" She looked up at me, pleased. "I don't know if I'd be so forgiving. I mean, you were wearing a vest and all, but that still had to hurt like hell."

I gave her my best smile. "I'm just glad I didn't end up dead."

Her eyes grew damp. "Don't say that, doc. You know how bad I feel."

I opened my arms, and she moved in to give me a hug. "I'm glad you're back. What happened with Harrigan?"

"He's not up on charges, but he's still under investigation. He can't be a cop anymore."

"I'm sorry to hear he won't be back," I speculated. Several months earlier, I was on a case that involved a monster named Anika Vanya, who used a concoction of unusual drugs and hypnosis to control people, including Officers Tom Harrigan and Tylissa. Under her orders, Tom attempted to blow up the precinct, killed Lieutenant Butler, and the former squad Sergeant Tony Williams. I had testified on his and Tylissa's side for Internal Affairs shortly after Christmas.

"What're you doing here today?" Tylissa wondered.

"Missing persons and a burglary."

"So, the usual?" she smirked.

My mouth curved into a grin. "I guess so."

We parted as I went in the side door to the observation room. I got a cursory glance or two from the other officers as I went in and closed the door.

No sooner had I taken my seat facing the one-way glass than the light came on in Interrogation Room B. Officer Galland brought a handcuffed Stephen Potts through the door and sat him at the table. Potts looked the same as the last time I'd run into him: unshaven, with his longish hair going in wild directions and standing up in some places. His eyes were watery and red, and it looked as if Galland had picked him up at the end of a bender.

Galland undid the handcuffs behind Potts' back and fastened them to a metal loop in the middle of the table in front of him. As soon as he finished, and with only one quick look of derision at the burglar, Galland stepped out.

McGee walked in almost immediately with a file folder in his hand.

"Oh, Stephen, what are we going to do with you?"

"I din' do nothin'," Potts muttered. Even though he was only pushing forty, his drinking and hard lifestyle made him look like a man who was closer to sixty.

"Your parole officer let us search your room, Stephen. We found the signal generator. Nice piece of tech. It sends out a signal that matches your ankle bracelet. Which allows you to take it off and go somewhere else."

Potts just stared at his hands.

"Of course, the lock on the bracelet was child's play; you could undo that in your sleep. But you got that hi-tech generator…and a ride so you could do the job in Mountainview. I guess whoever sold you the tech gave you something to bypass the digital lock on the door?"

Potts shook his head. "I was in my room all night. I went shopping today, but I had permission for that—"

"Yes, and over four grand to shop with. Where did you get the money, Stephen?"

Potts continued to stare at his imprisoned hands. "I earned it."

"At that part-time job you got at the supermarket? It would take you ten years to set aside that much."

Potts didn't look up.

"Here's what I think happened. You got hired to break into the house of one Brett Morgan and steal a fancy knife for someone. How'm I doing so far?"

"I din' do it."

"I left out the best part, Stephen. That knife was used to commit a murder. So, if you don't tell me who hired you, we'll bring you up on charges as an accessory."

This made Potts lift his head to look at McGee. He immediately put it down again and muttered. "I wan' a lawyer."

"Okay, I'll get you a lawyer," McGee agreed. "Might take a few minutes. I'll have to have someone watch you while I'm gone."

He waved to the mirror, and I picked up my cue. I hurried out of Observation and opened the door to enter Interrogation.

Potts started in his chair. "Him? You're leaving me with him?"

"We're shorthanded around here, Stephen. Doctor Wise will monitor you while I get you a lawyer."

I looked at Bill. "I guarantee there won't be a mark on him."

Potts turned to McGee frantically. "You can't leave me with him." He gave me a sidelong glance. "He can get into your brain."

"Okay, then tell me who hired you to do the job!" McGee bellowed. "We have one dead girl, and we might have another if you don't talk."

"All right, all right," Potts spluttered and continued to avoid eye contact with me. "It was a black guy, tall, had a mustache—"

I recalled the man I'd seen in my vision. "Was he well-dressed with thinning hair?"

Potts looked at the table to answer. "Yeah, that was him."

"I need a name, Stephen," McGee demanded.

"That's not how it works," Potts muttered. "This guy approached me. He tol' me he had somethin' that would make it look like I was home. I just had to do a job. It was an easy five grand for a night's work. How did I know they were gonna off a girl? I thought he just wanted the frickin' knife."

"A name!" Bill demanded.

"I don't have one!" Potts shouted and glared at McGee.

"Here's what we're going to do," Bill announced. "My sketch artist will work with you, and I need you to tell me where and how you met this guy."

"Only if he ain't here," Potts grumbled with a nod of the head toward me.

"All right," Bill agreed. "I'll call my guy. You want coffee or anything?"

"A sandwich would be good," Potts muttered.

Bill and I stepped out into the hall. "You'll be able to check the sketch against what you saw?"

I nodded. "At least it's a place to start." I took a quick glance at my watch. It was seven-thirty. "Aw jeez, I gotta go."

"Meeting your lady friend?" Bill smirked.

"Yeah, she's cooking," I explained as I bolted for the door. "Once you get a sketch, please send a photo to my phone."

"You got it, Romeo."

6. DEVOUT COURTSHIP

I pushed the empty plate away as Jyanette smiled.

"Glad to see you like my cooking," she beamed across the small table in her tidy apartment.

"Very much." I rose to grab the dishes. "I can clean up."

"Okay, I won't fight you. But it seems unfair. When I come to your place, you cook and clean up."

"I cheat. Mrs. Higgins often cooks on the nights when it's my turn, and then I get pulled away on a project."

"I'm learning all your secrets. How goes the book?"

"Slow, but I get a few hundred words done each day. I might have to put it to the side. I got pulled into a case."

"Which you can or cannot discuss with your Assistant District Attorney girlfriend?"

"It's out of your jurisdiction, so I can tell you." I scraped the plates of any leftovers from our pasta dinner. I carefully inserted them into the stainless steel dishwasher Jyanette had built into her kitchen cabinets. It was a tiny thing, but for a single woman, it was enough. The larger pots, I would wash them in the sink.

"Then by all means, tell."

"Missing persons. That gangster from Maine asked me to look into it."

Jyanette frowned. "Marconi? Jeez, Len, maybe you shouldn't tell me anything after all."

"His niece was one girl abducted on Staten Island."

"His niece?"

I stood and paused for a moment as I thought it through. "I'm not sure why I agreed to help, but it seemed important that I do."

"Well, if it's in New York, you'll have to work the case without McGee."

I nodded. "It looks like I'll be working with Stan Frazier from the FBI and a PI in Staten Island."

"Would you mind if I had a glass of wine?" Jyanette rose from her small table. "I might need it if your explanation gets any more involved."

I smiled. Jyanette knew I was a recovering alcoholic. In consideration, that was a misnomer. I was simply an alcoholic, but I had chosen not to drink. Alcohol was the easy way to shut off the mental impressions that continuously bombarded my brain. This was before I learned the techniques to shield my mind.

Some nights, I could watch people drink without it mattering at all. Sometimes the desire for a drink could be so powerful it annoyed me to watch someone else drink it so freely. Jyanette was sensitive enough to always ask.

"No, I'm fine. Could you make me tea?"

"Sure, lover," she concurred and put a small teapot on the stove and turned a dial to start the heat. Then she pulled a wine glass and an earthenware mug out of a nearby cabinet. Since the kitchen is small, everything is nearby.

Jyanette chose her apartment complex because of its proximity to her office at the Essex County Courthouse, where she tries most of her cases. It was fairly inexpensive as she was a civil servant lawyer with college loans to pay off.

The kettle heated water, and Jyanette plopped in a bag for tea. Then, with a turn that even a ballerina would admire, she pulled open her refrigerator and extracted a large bottle of white wine, with the cork already pulled.

It always amazed me that most people could have an open bottle of wine and just dole out portions when desired. Once again, it must be the perception of an alcoholic. If I had any open wine, it needed to be finished.

I walked over as Jyanette returned the half-full bottle to the refrigerator. As she turned back, I pulled her into my arms.

"Now he gets romantic." She laughed as she held the wineglass carefully in my embrace. I pressed my lips to hers, and she made a little moan in the back of her throat.

Kissing Jyanette was always an experience. At six feet tall and built like an Amazon from her workouts in the gym, her frame was taut and her muscles strong. Yet, she possessed a delightful, full bosom and a rear end that made angels weep with joy. With my free hand, I patted that admirable rump lovingly.

She pulled back with a smile, and her bright-white teeth flashed. "Plenty of time for that, sir."

She took my hand, and I limped after her. I left my cane in the kitchen, which was fine. I mostly needed it for the stairs. The highest thing I would climb this night would be my lady.

We reached the sofa, whereupon she placed her glass on the coffee table a few feet away, and then pushed me. Without my cane, I fell right onto the sofa, at which point Jyanette hiked up her skirt and sat directly on top of me.

To say this instantly aroused me was an understatement, and she moved her pelvis against my crotch so that I gasped, which made her smile even more.

The kettle on the stove whistled, and she kissed me chastely. "Let me get your tea, and we can get to this."

I gulped. "I think I'm done."

This made her smile grow broader. "You're fun. You always react in ways that make a girl feel wanted."

She moved off me and went to the stove to pour the boiling water into my teacup. She brought it over to me, picked up her wineglass, and perched next to me. I adjusted my trousers and took a sip of tea as I tried to slow my racing pulse.

I looked at my girlfriend of almost six months. Her father was an African-American builder from Baltimore, and her mother, a dark lady who emigrated from Africa. Jyanette's sisters took their father's lighter skin coloring, but Jyanette's tone was as inky as her mother's. To me, it only enhanced her beauty, but she told me that growing up, she always felt odd being so much darker than her sisters.

Sipping my tea, it thrilled me again that I had been lucky enough to meet this extraordinary lady. Add to that, I got the sheer pleasure of making love to her. Our friends all knew we were a couple, and we were in that place where we were learning each other's habits — good and bad — and the physical side was still tremendously exciting.

Immediately, I noticed a good-sized box sitting on the floor next to the table.

The box…

The 'buzz' was strong, and my mind was now pulled to the cardboard container.

"What's that?" I asked as Jyanette followed my stare.

She sighed. "Things I want to send home. You know my parents are coming this weekend."

"For your birthday. I haven't forgotten." I knew it was a big deal because Jyanette had met my family the previous Thanksgiving, and now it was my turn to see if I could win familial approval. "What's in it?"

"Things for storage that I'm sending back with them. Mostly, stuff from my marriage. It's time I let them go."

Jyanette had gotten divorced a year before I met her. She had told me very little about it, except that her ex-husband had a substance abuse problem. Which at first made her nervous about dating an alcoholic.

"Can I take a peek?"

"I would prefer you didn't." She sighed and then met my eyes. "Oh no, I know that look."

"What?"

"You got one of those 'buzz' things of yours, didn't you?"

I smiled sheepishly. "Yes, but I'm also curious."

"Len, I'm trying to move past that part of my life. Can't we just finish our drinks, and then you ravish me enthusiastically?"

"I give you my all anytime I get the chance to ravish you. One quick peek?"

"Crap. You know how I feel about my privacy—"

"And you shouldn't be afraid to share things with me. I am aware you had a life before I showed up. I want to partake of that with you as well."

She shook her head. "Nicely played, but it's just your damn curiosity." She bent over and yanked the box open. "Go ahead, get it over with."

"Glad you don't say that when we make love," I joked as I bent to peer into the box.

"I was in a fine, sexy mood before you got nosey," she muttered as she leaned back and took a large swallow of wine.

I smiled sheepishly and turned to the box.

My smile fell away, and I froze.

There in the cardboard container was a framed photo. It was Jyanette, looking amazing as always, but a tall African-American man stood next to her and faced the camera.

Mustache, his hair not yet thinning, but I recognized the face instantly from my vision.

It was the man I'd seen helping Thin Guy.

"Len, what is it?" Jyanette fretted, as she could sense my changed mood.

I reached out my hand as if it moved through molasses, and I grabbed the silver picture frame.

I dragged it out, my mouth open.

"Okay, Len, you're freaking me out. What is it? What do you see?"

I turned the photo over to Jyanette. "Who is this?"

"That's my ex. That's Antoine."

"Antoine?"

Her mouth became a hard line. "Antoine Powell. He sells computer hardware. At least he did when I was married to him. What is it? What about Antoine?"

"Computer hardware?" I repeated.

"Yes, high-end stuff. He explained it to me, but I didn't follow. Law, I understand. Computers, not so much. Would you tell me what the big deal is?"

I exhaled heavily. "I saw him in a vision. He was working with a thin white guy to abduct the two girls I'm looking for."

She was shocked. "What?"

"High-end computers," I murmured. "He also may have given a burglar a device to break into a home."

"Len, that's impossible. Antoine has flaws — I mean, I should know — but kidnapping? Burglary? I can't believe that."

"Could I take a photo of that picture?"

"What? No! This is crazy!" Jyanette yanked the frame from my hands.

"Jyanette, I'm not playing around here," I insisted. "This could be pertinent."

She gazed at me, and then at the frame. "Len, do you really think — I mean — it makes no sense."

"At least let McGee check. If it's a mistake, no harm done."

"McGee can't. Antoine doesn't live in Mountainview."

"Do you know where he is?"

Her mouth was a tight line. "My last address is over a year old in Bloomdale. But that was during the divorce. Last I heard, he'd moved to Staten Island."

"The old address might help."

"Look, Len, I have issues with my ex-husband — faithfulness and drugs, to name a few. But I can't believe he has slipped into a life of crime."

"I'm working with a private eye in Staten Island. He could look into him and clear his name if he's not involved."

She sat next to me and handed me the photo. "Okay. But why does this crap have to happen the weekend my mom and dad are coming up from Virginia?"

I slid the frame out of her hand. "I don't know, it just happened. But I know one thing."

"What?" she muttered sullenly.

"That I am crazy in love with you, Ms. Emery. And that I want your parents to like me."

This got the smallest bit of a smile. "That'll be hard with my father. Any man who sleeps with his daughter is suspect."

"Well, then I'd better sleep with you now, before they get here."

"Great, after you've done everything one person might do to ruin the mood? Go through my things, bring up my ex-husband —"

I pulled her into my arms. "It wasn't intentional."

This didn't pacify her, and she looked at me with annoyance. "If you'd just kept your big nose out of my stuff…"

I leaned forward and pressed my lips to hers, with no response.

"My nose isn't all that big," I suggested.

She stared at the floor. "No, but you put it where it doesn't belong."

I brushed my lips to hers a second time, and she looked up. The third kiss got a reaction. She held on longer, and soon we kissed in earnest, and our tongues danced together.

She pulled away and sighed. "I guess you didn't completely kill the mood."

She finished her wine, stood, and held her hand out to mine. I took it and rose.

"Still mad?" I asked.

"Yes, but I will not let it ruin my night. I'll use my annoyance to have angry sex."

I lifted an eyebrow. "Really?"

"And you'd better make sure I'm satisfied."

"I might like this."

Cold, so very cold. I tried to move, but my body felt numb. I used the palms of my hands to press against the surface I lay on, to find out what was under me.

It was stone. A cold slab of smooth rock.

An altar.

Lifting my head, I saw a naked body, but it wasn't mine. Not unless I'd suddenly become hairless and grown breasts.

There was a circle of candles around me, and just beyond the firelight, a line of cloaked figures who chanted quietly. I fought to raise my head — or whoever's head this was — to get up on my elbows and try to identify the room or any detail that might give me a sense of the location.

One figure stepped beyond the ring of candles. I was certain it would be Thin Guy together with the silver Kris knife.

But as I focused my attention, I knew that the outline I saw was larger than the slim man from before.

It turned to face me, and my blood ran cold.

I recognized the face in an instant.

The tall frame and crimson features stood out from the hood. It pulled back the cowl to expose an enormous set of impressive horns on top of its head. The white, pointed teeth in the maw that was its mouth broke into a smile.

"You have to be careful what you conjure, boy!"

The booming voice made me fall back in terror. It was the creature, the monster that had appeared on that wet roadway years ago.

The night that Cathy died.

Cathy and I had gone to a party, a silly graduation event for medical school. I'd finished first in my class, with Cathy a close second. I had done it in three years instead of the traditional four.

At one point, we played with a Ouija board that would give amazing answers whenever I touched it. Without my hand atop it, the small shuttle hardly moved at all.

Someone at the party suggested we conjure a demon.

Most of the party is murky in my memory, but I could recall someone chanting in an odd tongue as the partygoers drew a pentagram in chalk on the floor. Then we all sat in a circle and joined hands.

I don't completely remember the attempt we made, but I know that something happened that night. All I can clearly remember is how beautiful Cathy looked with her long blonde hair hanging down. When I'd seen her in scrubs, whether in surgery or doing rounds, she always wore her hair up and usually under a hairnet.

It was on the way home, on the wet roadway over a mountain on the way to her parents' house in Mountainview, when it happened.

She had said something about our upcoming wedding, and I glanced over to the passenger side to give her a smile.

It was when I turned my eyes back to the road that I saw the huge scarlet monster directly in front of me. I jammed on the brakes and swerved as Cathy screamed. The car went into a spin, smashed through a protective guardrail, and careened down the side of a mountain, flipping over as it went.

As we came to rest, Cathy and I hung upside down from our seat belts. Cathy was unconscious, and I could see the blood dripping from a gash on her forehead. I assumed flying glass caused it, as the windows were smashed. I knew she was dying, but I couldn't do anything because of my pinned legs, which kept me in so much pain.

I tried to yell "Help," but all that came from my throat was a moan.

I looked out my window to see if there was anyone nearby who rushed to our aid.

All I saw was a pair of large, blood-red, cloven hooves.

And then he bent over so that his crimson face was in my line of vision. That was when he said those very words:

"You have to be careful what you conjure, boy!"

I leapt up from the slab and tried to fight, but a web or something held me down as I struggled to break free.

"Len!" came a voice as a light flashed on.

I panted from exertion, and all at once, I was in Jyanette's bed. The web that pinned me was nothing more than her bedsheets and blanket that I fought to throw off.

The clock on the nearby bureau read 3:00 in crimson letters.

Jyanette's hand went to my face, and I flinched.

My woman was totally naked from our lovemaking; her hair, usually so well-groomed, was a tangled mass.

She touched my face again. "You okay?"

I relaxed and tried to slow my breathing. "Yeah."

She shook her head as her own bosom heaved. "Sleeping with you is always a challenge."

"Sorry," I murmured, and took her hand and kissed it.

"You've been sleeping fine for weeks. The problem is once you start on a case…" She moved close and kissed my head.

"I'm sorry." I held her, our naked bodies against each other. "I guess my brain goes into overdrive, and stuff comes in I don't expect."

"Did you get any answers?" she asked and moved off me to lie on her side of the bed as my eyes worshipped her taut, firm body.

"Afraid not," I replied, and my hand reached down to caress her flank.

"Oh no," she chided with a slight smile. "No more of that tonight. You got yours."

"Tired of me so soon?" I slid across the bed and brought my lips to hers.

She kissed me back. "Len, you've jostled my insides enough for one night," Jyanette grumbled as she pushed my probing hands away.

"I thought you liked it."

"Quite a great deal. But I have to get up in a few hours, go to the office, and clear up paperwork. All this before my parents get here."

"Perhaps angry sex is too much for you."

"It was breathtaking, but I could use a few hours to recover." She gave my nose a platonic kiss. "Go to sleep."

I slid to my side of the queen bed and tried to clear my mind, but concerns kept popping in unbidden.

I saw myself in Constance's place, but why did I see the demon — my demon? Could there be a connection?

If so, what do Antoine Powell and Thin Guy have to do with it?

I argued possibilities in my mind as Jyanette's breathing became slow and steady. By that time, I finally relaxed and allowed sleep to pull me down.

7. VENERATED TALE

As sunlight streamed through the drapes, Jyanette smacked my bare bottom to wake me as she stood, fully dressed and apparently ready to walk out the door.

"Ow!" I objected. "Don't tell me you're still mad."

"No, I just wanted to slap your ass," Jyanette sassed. "You should get some sun, my dear. You are truly one of the whitest men I know."

"I'll buy a sunlamp. You taking off?"

"Yeah. Lock the door on your way out—"

"I know the drill." I turned my head to look at my love. "I've slept with you before."

"Well, work on the attitude or it might be the last time." She bent to kiss me on the cheek and gave my bare hindquarters a quick rub.

"I thought you weren't interested," I taunted.

"You've got a nice butt, even if it is pale. Don't forget dinner tonight, at seven. Not seven-oh-five or seven-fifteen. Seven."

"Got it. You're really nervous, aren't you?"

"It's my parents, for God's sake. What do I do if they don't like you?"

"See me but don't tell them?" I suggested.

Jyanette sighed. "Please don't joke, Len."

I rolled over and sat up in bed. "I'll dazzle them with my good manners, and if worst comes to worst, I'll get inside their heads and command them to like me."

Jyanette suddenly sat on the edge of the bed and gazed at me. "I feel like I'm in high school and I'm introducing my prom date."

I put my hand on her arm. "It'll be fine."

"I didn't introduce them to Antoine before I married him. Turns out dad never liked him, and look how that ended. Now, I feel like I've got to show him I learned from my mistake."

I kissed her hand. "It's important to me as well. I want them to approve."

"Sorry if I'm a little crazy about this."

"You met my family under unusual circumstances—"

"Unusual? You just got out of the hospital and couldn't drive yourself—"

"And they loved you. My mom thinks you're the best."

"For a shiksa," she said, using the Yiddish term for a non-Jewish woman.

"Well," I said as I gazed up at the ceiling thoughtfully. "She certainly would be pleased if you wanted to become Jewish."

I reached over, turned her face to mine, and pressed my lips to hers fully as she moaned.

She broke the kiss by standing up. "I-I have to get to the office —"

"Ten minutes," I said as I held onto her arm, my lack of clothing revealing the state of my excitement.

Jyanette sighed as she pulled off her jacket and untucked her blouse. "Sometimes, your timing sucks."

It ended up being twenty minutes. Everything differed from the wild time of the previous night. We were gentle and loving as I touched and tasted her, and after placing a condom, entered her tenderly. We moved together slowly until it built into a release for us both.

Then as I lay on the bed panting, she quickly threw on her clothes and headed straight for the door before I could rise.

"Seven!" was her last word as the door slammed.

I smiled. She was one hell of a woman, and she was with me. I wanted her parents to like me. I wanted them to adore me, if it would make her happy.

I took a few minutes to use my phone to take a picture of the framed photo of Antoine Powell, which I emailed to both Darren Ward and McGee with the explanation, "Possible suspect: Antoine Powell" under it.

Then, dressed in my previous evening's clothes, I left the apartment and headed home with a feeling of great contentment.

Jyanette and I were in a good place, and tonight we would take the next step in our relationship.

I knew her father was a builder and restorer of old buildings because Jyanette had worked on job sites with her father throughout high school, and even summers in college and law school.

Her two sisters had lost interest in construction work as soon as they left for college, but Jyanette liked it and also learned at her father's side the techniques used to bring historic structures back to usefulness.

I knew very little about her mother, who emigrated from Africa in the late 1970s. Jyanette told me she was a tall woman and very dark-skinned. I had seen pictures of Jyanette's older sisters, Natisha and Shanika, and they both had lighter skin tones — like coffee with cream, not the espresso of their younger sibling.

It was also a big step for me. The last woman whose parents I met was Cathy. My relationships since her death were fitful, to say the least. A few short ones, then I had lived with a woman, Susan Haring, who I'd recently seen again in Maine when I helped her with a haunted house. Then there were my two dates with Wendy Wallace — she had ended up dead.

With women who got close to me ending in failed relationships or getting killed, my time with Jyanette for these six months with nothing more than relationship issues any couple would go through was indeed a blessing.

I dropped it from my mind as I pulled into the circular driveway of my rented residence.

Mrs. Higgins, my landlady, had a great deal of money saved from thirty years as a cook to wealthy families. I had stumbled across the house and had even given her advice as to what to pay for it, and she bought it. In gratitude, she rented me a first-floor bedroom and sitting room with a separate entrance. The rent she requested was far less than market value for such a splendid space.

Add to that the benefits of someone who cooked for me — often without my asking — and watched over my well-being. It was an exceptional situation, and we had become fast friends.

Also, Mrs. Higgins has a remarkable ability to sense when I was on a case and push me in the right direction. I believe she is a far better psychic than myself, but she denies it. She claims any helpful suggestions are from, in her words, her 'wooman's intooition.'

I left my car in the driveway, and in the one parking space off the asphalt sat Mrs. Higgins' tiny car. It was a recent purchase and was one of those new 'smart' vehicles, which boasts huge economy on gas, but looks a bit to me like an oversized lunchbox.

But since most of her driving was local, it seemed a logical choice.

I got out of my van with my shoulder bag and limped to the front door. Since it was about eight-thirty, I decided she had been awake for hours, and I didn't have to go in my private entrance to be quiet.

As I took the front steps one at a time, the door opened, and there stood all five-feet-one inch of Mrs. Higgins. Her hair was gray with a touch of auburn and in a graceful pile on top of her head. She was in a simple floral dress with her trademark apron about her waist and a warm smile on her face.

"Good morning, doctor. Have you had your coffee yet?" she stated in her Irish brogue.

"Good morning, Mrs. Higgins. No, I'm afraid Jyanette had to run, so I waited until I got home."

"I have some made fresh. And mayhaps a scone or two?"

I came through the door and into the hall. "Please, Mrs. Higgins, easy on the pastries. I'll weigh three hundred pounds."

"Ooh, you're nothing but skin and bones. I talked to Jyanette and she agrees we need to fatten you oop."

As I always suspected, the women in my life were plotting against me.

"Maybe just one scone," I dutifully replied and followed Mrs. Higgins down the hall, past the large dining room, and into the kitchen.

The house was a marvel of construction. The outside was stone, probably built in the last century, but former owners had updated the inside with fine wood and beautiful built-in cabinets. There was a large kitchen, living room, dining room, as well as multiple bathrooms and closets, and three large bedrooms upstairs. Built as an addition were my bedroom, the bathroom I used, and the sitting room that worked as my home office.

I would consider it a mansion, except that in the town of Mountainview, the houses are of a large and impressive size. My mother would call them 'ungapotchka,' which is a Yiddish term for 'overdone.' In fact, this house was one of the smallest in the neighborhood, which was another reason Mrs. Higgins did well on the purchase.

We went through the large swinging door from the hall to the kitchen, and Mrs. Higgins led me to the small table where we ate most of our meals. The formal dining room was too large for her and me, so we only used it on special occasions.

As I put my computer bag on the floor and sat, she poured coffee, added cream, and put the cup on a saucer in front of me. A small plate with two scones and butter quickly followed.

I smiled. "I thought I asked for only one."

She smiled back. "Did ye now?"

I shook my head and sipped my coffee as Mrs. Higgins puttered about, cleaning as she went. I didn't see that any straightening up was necessary. As always, the kitchen was immaculate.

I buttered my pastry and took a bite.

I had to admit it was a little piece of heaven, and I sighed as I tasted it. I sipped my coffee and felt myself relax, glad to be home.

My phone played its classical music ringtone.

I pulled it from the breast pocket of my jacket and gazed at the screen, which bore the name 'DARREN WARD' in oversized letters.

"Wise," I said as I answered.

"The photo you emailed me, what am I looking at? Is this the guy you thought was the accomplice?"

"Yes. Did you see the message? His name is Antoine Powell. I don't know how he's involved, but he was with the man who drugged the girls and helped to get them out of the party."

"Great," Ward griped. "While you're at it, can you pull his address out of the air? Or a location for the girls?"

"I wish I could."

"All right. I'll run him down, see if anything pops. It's not much, but it's more than I had yesterday. If any of it's real."

"I'm available all day if you need me."

"Yeah, yeah. I'll let you know."

And he was gone. I replaced the phone in my pocket and focused on the flaky pastry on my plate.

"Are ye involved in a fresh case?" Mrs. Higgins questioned quietly.

"Hmm? Oh, yes, just happened yesterday. I forgot I didn't see you at all. Two missing girls. I believe that one of them is dead."

She frowned. "How terrible!"

"Yes, and if the case doesn't break soon, I have little hope for the other. Someone is performing human sacrifices with a stolen ritual knife."

"Why would anyone do that?"

"Don't know that either, Mrs. Higgins. I had a dream last night, which was linked to something I'd seen years ago, but I've gotten nowhere with it."

"Could be ye're tryin' too hard."

I shook my head. "Perhaps there's more to this case than I think. Something hidden."

"Weel, if you want to talk of something hidden…that reminds me of a story."

"Another one of your stories, Mrs. Higgins?"

"Hush now. Eat your scone and let me tell ye aboot it."

"I'm all ears," I said as I took another sip of coffee.

"Long ago, in Ireland—"

"Where else?"

"Dinna I say to hush? There lived at Loftus Hall a man named Charles Tottenham, a well-to-do man with the Irish Parliament. He had hisself two daughters, Elizabeth and Anne. Now Loftus Hall was an old rambling mansion with no pretense to beauty."

"For a mansion."

"There were passages that led nowhere, large, dreary rooms, small closets, various nooks and corners. The father t'were a cold, austere man, and the mother not much warmer. Elizabeth had gone off to marry, which left the younger girl, Anne, in this place with no friends to speak of and no contact with neighbors."

"Okay, a lonely girl. I've got it."

"One wild and stormy night—"

"Is there any other kind?"

"Don't ruin me story! So, as the family sat in the large drawing room, t'was a loud knocking at the outer gate, a most surprising and unusual occurrence."

"The plot thickens."

Mrs. Higgins put another scone in front of me. "Eat, so ye canna interrupt. So, the servant announced a young man, lost and with his horse knocked up, who was lookin' for shelter and lodging. They admitted the stranger, and he was a most agreeable gentleman… and young Anne was immediately smitten with him."

"An impress—nable young wo-fan," I said, my mouth full of scone.

"Aye. They invited this man to remain some days, and he made hisself quite at home. As they were now four in number, they played a game of cards called Whist."

"Whist?" I repeated.

"The stranger, with Anne as his partner, invariably won every point; the older couple never had success. One night, when Anne was in great delight at winning so constantly, she dropped her ring on the floor and dove under the table to recover it. In her haste, she discovered her agreeable partner had skipped off his shoes, exposin' a pair of cloven feet."

"Cloven?" I said, as she now had all my attention.

Mrs. Higgins nodded. "Her screams made him aware of her discovery, and at once he vanished in fire with the smell of brimstone. The poor girl never recovered from the shock, lapsed from one fit into another, and they carried her off to her bed chamber from which she never came forth alive."

"A sad tale indeed," I observed. "And I am sure you feel this has something to do with my current case."

"Whatever do you mean, doctor?"

"You always tell me these tales when I get on a case and get stuck," I pointed out. "So, what is the connection?"

"Well, ye said somethin' hidden. Sometimes the outside we see differs from what is inside a person. But if ye look deeply, ye ken usually find the truth."

I sighed as I finished my scone. "Well, sound advice, but it doesn't exactly open my mind to any amazing insights."

"Not yet." Mrs. Higgins shrugged as she removed her apron. "I'm off to the market."

"Mrs. Higgins, you're here all the time. Why do you go shopping on Friday, the busiest day of the week, as you did when you were a cook?"

She shrugged as she hung the cloth on a hook in a nearby wall unit. "Lifetime of habit, I suppose. Will ye be here for dinner?"

"No, Jyanette and I are meeting—"

"That's right! Her parents! Her birthday! That's this weekend!"

"Glad everyone knows my schedule," I muttered.

"Hush, now. Best to wear your blue suit, and I'd advoise a tie." She headed through the swinging door into the hall.

I followed.

"It's supposed to be casual," I explained, as she pulled on her coat and salvaged her large purse from the floor of the closet.

"D'ye think you'll impress her father'll more if ye wear a tie or not?" she stated bluntly.

"Probably if I wear one?"

"O' course! Sometimes, ye have no sense at all, doctor."

She grabbed an impressive set of keys from an ashtray — or was it a candy dish — on the small table by the door and headed out.

I turned and walked to my part of the house for a shower and a change of clothes.

Once clean and shaved, then in new clothes, I retrieved my computer bag from the kitchen and booted up the laptop.

I opened my email, and there was a quick note from Jyanette. It had Antoine Powell's address in Bloomdale and the address of the restaurant where we would eat that evening. In very large letters there also was:

7:00 PM

With a smile, I wrote a reply: Message received. I then copied and pasted Powell's address into separate emails for McGee, Ward, and Stan Frazier.

I opened my file of the book I'd been writing, and as I prepared myself, my phone went off.

It was McGee.

"Yes, Bill," I said.

"We showed the photo you sent to Potts, who we kept overnight in holding. He has identified Antoine Powell as the man who approached him about stealing the knife."

"And no doubt supplied him with the devices that mimicked his ankle bracelet and bypassed the security keypad at Morgan's house."

"No doubt."

"I just emailed you his address in Bloomdale. I don't know if it's current."

"How did you get a photo of him so quickly? And an address? I mean, even for you, that's pretty amazing."

"Not this time. Turns out Powell is Jyanette's ex. She had that photo boxed away to send home with her parents."

"Uh-oh, is that a problem?"

"Depends on what he's done. Arranging Potts to steal that knife and helping abduct the girls? That makes him an accomplice, from what I know of the law."

"That's why you need me."

"But there are other things. I got a glimpse of a large room with candles, an altar, and people chanting. There is something ritualistic about it all. Plus, I got a brief vision of the history of that stolen knife. The history of the knife includes human sacrifice for hundreds — maybe thousands — of years."

"Do you think it's like Juan Espinoza, some kind of cult thing? Maybe Santeria — or what was it—?"

"Santa Muerte." I considered this. "Could be similar, but the images I got from that knife suggest a tradition based on the Middle East or Asia."

"So you think Powell and his 'partner in crime' chose this specific knife because of its history?"

"They wanted that one. How they knew about it, I can only guess."

"Could one guy in this cult be like you? Maybe sees things in visions the way you do?"

"It's possible. But I don't know what the end game is. Whoever is behind this has called attention to himself by abducting the girls."

"So you think it is some kind of ritual thing?"

"That's where my mind goes."

"Then I might have more bad news for you."

"What?"

"Well, I'm not an expert in the occult like you, but I would say there is one fact that might be important—"

"Please spit it out, Bill!"

"Sunday night is a full moon."

I paused as the concept sank in. A full moon at midnight would be the perfect setting for a ritual sacrifice.

"And it's the Spring Equinox as well," I realized.

"Yes, and isn't that called something special, like the ecclesiastical full moon?"

"Yes, also known as the Paschal full moon," I informed him. The concept made me concerned. "I think you're onto something, Bill."

"If so," he stated bluntly, "we're running out of time."

8. COMMITTED LOCATION

Bill ended the call with assurances that he would have a fellow officer with the Bloomfield Police Department check on the address of Antoine Powell to see if he was in residence.

My head was still spinning from Bill's realization that the day after tomorrow was the Spring Equinox and a full moon. If Thin Guy was doing this because of a belief in the occult, the date made sense on several levels.

I went to my bedroom to the white built-in bookcases. The workmanship of these shelves was wonderful to behold. The shelves were made of strong boards that could support the weight of my copious books, and the clever support system allowed me to adjust the height of each shelf to fit my needs.

I quickly pulled some of my books on the occult I keep handy for research.

It didn't take long. In one of the older tomes, I found an 'occult calendar,' which listed important dates for pagan rituals. Under the listing for the Northern Vernal Equinox was this notation: 'Spring Equinox — Minor Sabbath but requires human sacrifice'.

I continued scanning the books. There were suggestions in several that an ancient order, the 'Illuminati', always performed a human sacrifice on March twenty-first.

The notion of a sacrificial murder taking place during a full moon and an astronomical event strongly suggested the selected day. But I still had no idea of the reasons behind it, or what Thin Guy was seeking.

Usually, with rituals, especially dark rituals, the person who presents it is seeking power — often from a deity or non-corporeal being.

But in my vision, I was aware of figures chanting around the altar, involved in the ritual. How did these people allow a young woman to be murdered right in front of their eyes?

With the Santa Muerte cult I'd dealt with just last November, they were seeking to bring someone back from the dead. I doubted they could have actually accomplished it, but they conjured great power from a collection of items imbued with mystical energies.

I returned the books to the shelf, and I pulled out a notebook and went through it. It was part of my collection of notes from when I studied with Doctor Kohl. He created the parapsychology department at the Southern California University of Health Sciences.

It was five years ago, and I was studying psychiatry in California and getting nowhere with the insights and flashes of other people's thoughts that inundated me daily. I went to a lecture where Fritz Kohl was speaking.

Doctor Kohl's theorem was that there were true psychics, and with training, they could focus their skills and help law enforcement, like a forensic pathologist.

I quit my psychiatric program the next day and signed up to study with Doctor Kohl.

It had been tough going, as I no longer had the financial support of my surgeon father. I worked odd jobs, even as a night guard, to keep myself in the class.

Unfortunately, I still used alcohol to deaden my abilities so I could sleep. But, as I learned techniques from Doctor Kohl, I found other ways to shut my mind away from the endless input.

He brought me on as his teaching assistant, which also helped, but I finally reached a time that my drinking became so bad I couldn't use my abilities at all. Fritz told me I would either stop drinking or he would remove me from the school.

I remember what he told me in his heavy German accent. "Leonard, you vill never master your gifts if you do not stop drinking. You are far enough along mitt the techniques that you do not need it. You must choose, or you can go no further."

A local chapter of Alcoholics Anonymous and my sponsor, Chuck Granger, got me free. It was scary the first week; getting my body used to it was a shock. Adding to that was the challenge of using Kohl's techniques to protect my mind from the constant chatter of thoughts and impressions.

But Kohl had been correct. It was a big breakthrough for me, and I could face my future sober and clear.

In the notebook, I found the section I sought: notes about human sacrifice. I quickly reviewed the pages.

Ritual sacrifice had been around since the dawn of time and in every culture. In ancient Japan, they would bury a maiden alive at the bottom of a building to protect against disasters. In Pharaoh's Egypt, priests would murder servants to be buried with their master. Even in the Americas, the Aztecs killed eighty thousand prisoners to consecrate the Great Pyramid of Tenochtitlan, and that event occurred only slightly less than six hundred years ago.

I moved through the grisly information and went to my notes about cults. I had noted that all sects followed certain parameters: First, they needed a charismatic leader. My vision had pointed to Thin Guy as the man in charge. He was the one who drugged the girls and wielded the knife.

Second, cults needed to use intimidation or psychological manipulation to keep members loyal. Being co-conspirators in a murder certainly was a powerful motivation to keep the group's secrets. Also, if Thin Guy had experience with designer drugs, this could give him a way to attract and control people through addiction.

I still wondered about the man's overall motivation. Then again, what was the motivation for Charles Manson or other ritual murderers? And yet dismissing him as a psychopath seemed too easy.

My phone rang, and I pulled it from my jacket pocket. "Wise," I said.

"It's Darren. I got the info from the NYPD. Those girls did not go into the ferry terminal. Officers are now scouring the area in the neighborhood near the ferry with photos of the girls, that sketch, and a copy of the photo you sent me of Powell."

"Well, that's something. Thanks for keeping me in the loop, Darren."

"Actually, what are you doing now?"

"Now? Reviewing some notes."

"I think...that is if you want...you might...I don't know, help or something."

I was stunned. "You mean, you want me there?"

"Yeah, well, what could it hurt? And if there is any of the occult stuff... you... uh... probably know more than I would. Or even the NYPD."

"Uh, sure. Give me an hour."

"Great, I'll text you an address near the terminal where you can park."

"Okay. See you soon."

I ended the call, surprised by this turn of events. I quickly put my laptop in my shoulder bag and decided I would have to be prepared to go directly from Staten Island to the restaurant for dinner with Jyanette's parents.

I packed my blue suit, white shirt, and tie in a garment bag. Experience had taught me that my clothing could easily get stained with mud, blood, or some other noxious substance if we located a scene. I could change in the back of my van if the need arose, and I consistently carried a supply of wipes to clean up.

Of course, I had no expectation of stumbling into or onto anything, but I also knew that to show up at dinner in a disheveled state would disappoint my lady.

I changed into jeans, black sneakers, and a less-than-nice shirt, with one of my cheaper tweed jackets. No point ruining a good Harris Tweed — not that I could afford more than the two I currently possessed.

I walked out of the house and quickly hung the bag filled with my clothing on a hook in the back, and then with my shoulder bag, I got into the driver's seat.

Ward had texted me an address, and I fed it into the GPS app on the dashboard. In a moment, it had my route planned, and I drove off.

I took advantage of the time in the car to call Stan Frazier on my hands-free car connection.

He answered on the first ring. "Professor, is that you?"

"Yes, Stan. I am just doing a follow-up to make sure you received the photos I sent you."

"Yeah, I got them. I've made headway with the team for CARD. I shared the photos with them, and they hooked me up with agents on Staten Island, and helped me interface with the NYPD."

"Good. I heard from the PI on my end. He said the NYPD checked the video at the ferry terminal."

"Actually, that was CARD. Yeah, the girls may have gotten off the bus near the terminal, but they didn't go in."

"I'm on my way to the neighborhood. If I get anything, you'll be my first call."

"Do that. My team is up and running."

I pushed the button to end the call and focused on driving.

Soon, the miles fell away as I tried to get my head around why Ward had asked me to become involved in this part of the investigation. Was he having second thoughts about my input? Or had Anthony Marconi called him and demanded I be part of his efforts, despite any misgivings?

I crossed over the Goethals Bridge and crawled across the Staten Island Expressway, as I thought about Jyanette's parents, dinner, and how to best impress them. I needed to relax. Any attempt to make myself into their desired image would merely make me come across as phony.

After fretting in traffic an additional quarter-hour more than planned, I pulled off on Clove Street and passed the sign that read "Vanderbilt College" again.

Vanderbilt…

There was that buzz again. I really needed to follow up and email Doctor Kohl to get the name of the man who studied with him and might teach there. For the life of me, I couldn't remember his name, but if I kept getting a buzz, it suggested I needed to take action.

I arrived at the location, which was a carport with the fanciful name of St. George Garage. It was a huge building, at least four stories of parking, directly across from a series of brownstone buildings that included an old hotel.

Even from the outside, the hotel looked seedy.

I found an open space, noted my floor, and went around the van to open the tailgate. I kept evidence bags and gloves for crime scenes. I put several pairs of gloves in one pocket of my jacket under my black winter coat, and the bags in the other. Then I took an elevator down to Central Avenue, texting Darren of my arrival. He replied, advising me to meet him at the corner of Central and Hyatt, and I was soon on my way.

My walk led me past the Staten Island Supreme Court, which seemed to have undergone renovation recently. It now boasted an impressive new facade and a small grass park in front with concrete sidewalks weaving through it.

Darren stood on the corner with an old-fashioned hat on his head and a trench coat, looking every bit the PI from a classic murder mystery, except he was holding a large paper bag.

"Hey, Darren," I said as I approached. He nodded in response.

"NYPD has been canvassing the neighborhood," he stated, looking about at the brick storefronts across the street.

"I'm sure that helps," I offered lamely to say something intelligent. "There is someone I've worked with on the FBI New Jersey Task Force. He told me CARD has helped him interface with NYPD."

"CARD? That's the Child Abduction Rapid Deployment Team, right?"

"That's right."

"Missing underage kids are a big deal," he noted, still focused on the building across from us. He then turned to face me. "So, how does this work?"

"I'm sorry?"

He lifted the bag toward me. "I brought the bear. Can you use that to get a scent on them or something?"

I smiled. "I'm a psychic, Darren, not a bloodhound."

He exhaled in exasperation. "You know what I mean. You said you saw the club they were at in that... vision or whatever you saw. Can being close to the location help?"

"It might," I stated. "Do you think we're close?"

"The girls didn't go into the ferry terminal, and there are a lot of clubs close by. Also, a couple of raves."

"A rave? Isn't that a place where the younger generation throws an unannounced party?"

"Yup. Usually with lots of electronic music..."

I felt old, even though I was just thirty. I glanced around the small park. There was a squat metal bench, which faced away from the courthouse, and I pointed at it. "Let's sit there."

We strolled over, and I sat with my cane against my extended right leg. Darren lifted the bag to me.

"No, please hold it. I have to get myself into a light trance."

"You should explain the rules first," he grumbled.

I closed my eyes. "Sorry, I thought I did."

I let the jibe fall away and didn't allow Ward's negativity to affect me. I focused on my breath, slowing it down and keeping my mind clear.

In… out. In… out.

I could feel myself slipping into an altered state, but I needed to do it carefully. Here on a busy city street, the random thoughts of the people nearby might invade and distract me. I focused on keeping some protections in place. I also had to maintain a certain amount of control to not let the toy flood my mind with countless images of Constance, as it did the last time.

Once I felt properly prepared, and without opening my eyes, I held out my hands and said, "Hand me the bear." There was a rustling of paper, and in a moment, I felt the worn, fuzzy plaything pressed into my hands.

I wanted to use the bear and its relationship to Constance, so I cautiously let down the barriers in my mind. I kneaded the furry stuffed companion with my hands, reaching out for a connection.

It took a few minutes, but I soon felt a pull, like a giant magnet, that literally drew me to my feet.

"Got something?" Ward insisted quietly.

"I think I do," I stated, and felt the tug that pulled me to my right. I walked up Hyatt Street, away from Central Avenue.

The pair of us reached St. Mark's Place and turned right. I was going a fairly good clip, my cane in my right hand and the battered bear in my left.

"So you think—?" Ward attempted.

"Shh!" I hissed, not wanting any distractions as I focused on that pull, the insistent demand I move forward toward an unknown goal.

With Ward following, I soon reached another street and made a left, still going strong. It was one block over at Montgomery Avenue that I paused for a moment, my eyes closed in deep concentration.

"You okay?" Ward asked, as a wave of scattered images pummeled my mind. I saw Erica next to me walking up this very street, but it was night. Then I was in the club, the lights dazzling my eyes, and the loud, pounding music distorted and twisted.

I focused on white walls to pull myself back from the mental pictures which echoed in my brain, fast and confusing.

I took a deep breath as my thoughts cleared, and I could see the sidewalk in front of me. Although it felt like it took minutes, the entire episode was only a few seconds.

"No, I'm fine," I said as I slowed down my breathing and came back into focus. "But I think we are close… to something."

I headed down Montgomery Avenue with Ward in tow. It was an interesting street, a collection of residential brownstones mixed with warehouses and the occasional restaurant or retail space.

The pull was strong again, and I had to control myself to keep from rushing forward. I heard a rustle and glanced back to see Darren extract a cigarette from a battered pack and pull out a cardboard holder of matches. He saw my look.

"What? I can't do this either?" he complained.

"No, it's fine. I just didn't know you smoked."

"I don't — I mean, I quit."

The buildings along the street caught my attention. "We're close."

"To what?"

"We'll know soon."

I walked up the block as Darren fought to strike a sad-looking match that appeared to have seen better days. I didn't need him to tell me he was a smoker who had quit. From the rumpled condition of the pack and the matches, he'd undoubtedly left them in the coat and only discovered them again today.

Why had he dressed in the trench coat and hat, anyway? If he wanted to blend into the crowd, he could have worn a clown suit and been less conspicuous.

It was halfway up the block when the feeling from the magnetic pull became a four-bell alarm.

I stopped in front of a large, flat, two-story building that appeared to take up several lots. There were two substantial, roll-up metal garage doors designed for trucks. Someone replaced the building's original doors at both ends with large metal ones. These new doors have a hole where the doorknob should be and a thick chain and padlock to seal them.

The five windowsills on the second floor had intricate wrought iron decorations on the outside sill, but a sheet of weathered plywood had replaced each window.

"Here," I told Darren as I stared up at the building.

"What? This place has been closed for years."

"Exactly," I reassured, as I slipped the bear under my right arm and pointed at the nearest door. "Check that one."

Darren took a drag on the cigarette he'd finally lit and blew out smoke in an annoyed blast. He tramped over to the door and leaned over to look at the lock.

He glared at it and turned his head, taking the hand with the cigarette and waving me over.

"It's not locked," he said as I drew near. "The lock is just put in place, but it's not fastened."

I reached into my pocket and extracted two pairs of gloves. "Here," I said as I held a pair out for him.

He looked at the blue nitrile gloves and chortled. "You come prepared."

"I was told it was a good habit to get into," I concurred. "Should we call the NYPD and my contact with the FBI?"

"Let's look first," Daren suggested. "I mean, to make sure this was... well, what do you think it was?"

"I think it's the location for the party where the girls went. I'll know once we're inside."

He flicked the still-burning butt to the gutter, took the gloves, and stretched them over his fingers. I followed suit, but it was a little more complicated as I had to juggle the bear and my cane while doing so.

He manipulated the lock, and the chain easily slid off the door, falling to the ground. Ward grabbed the metal door and yanked it open as rusted hinges groaned in protest.

I gazed into the complete darkness and pulled out my phone to activate the LED light, as Ward pulled a large, old-fashioned flashlight from the pocket of his trench coat. He flicked the switch, and a powerful beam cut through the blackness. Beer bottles, plastic trash bags, and other assorted garbage littered the floor.

As we stepped in, Ward inquired, "Look familiar?"

"Not yet," I answered, looking at the open space with parking for two trucks. I turned my light on a set of stairs near the door… and felt the pull again. "Up there."

We walked up the metal stairs, and although they appeared old and the paint was peeling, they were in good repair and quite solid. The building was still structurally sound. It was a pity it was no longer in use, except by party squatters. We climbed the steps.

Well, I climbed, and Ward ran up ahead of me.

When I reached the top, there was an open door that revealed a large room. There were pillars in various locations, supported by another set on the first floor — or else the pillars ran straight up both stories, with molding to make them look as if they were on separate floors.

The space contained abandoned furniture, old couches leaking stuffing, and tables and chairs scattered around in various states of repair.

In a flash, I saw the room crowded with people and Thin Guy on the ugly orange sofa just a few feet from me. The room pulsed with loud electronic music and sparkled with flashing lights. I closed my eyes to shut out the impressions.

"This is the place I saw," I told Ward, and opened my eyes to see him wander about with the light. "This is the party where they met the girls and drugged them."

Ward pulled out his phone, looked at the screen, and cursed under his breath.

"I gotta go outside to call," he said. "You okay here?"

I nodded and shone the light from my phone around the room. He took the steps at a clip I could never manage, and I heard the door creak as he stepped outside.

My phone lit up, and its musical tone went off, surprising me. The screen indicated the caller was "Unknown." I quickly shut off the light, hit the virtual button, and lifted it to my face.

"Wise."

I heard heavy breathing on the other end, but no one spoke. I wondered if it was a crank call.

"Hello?" I attempted, as if it were a malfunction of the phone or the nearby cell tower.

"I didn't think you'd find the club this soon," a male voice wheedled in my ear. "I was told you were quite talented, but I truly didn't expect a man with your physical limitations to work so quickly."

"Who is this?" I demanded, as an icy chill ran up my spine.

"I go by many names. I believe you are currently referring to me as 'Thin Guy.'"

My mouth fell open.

He went on. "On one level, I am honored, as I have always tried to stay in good shape. On the other hand, it does sound derogatory."

I tried to keep my wits about me. "Where is Erica Marconi?"

"Safe for now, but I am afraid her time is running out, just as it did for dear Constance," he said, and his voice sounded almost wistful. "She shall be missed."

"I know what you did to her."

"Yes, I was told you would. In fact, that was why she had to be dispatched so quickly. I wanted you to be aware I was here."

"Why?"

"You and I have different motivations. I seek to serve my master, who brings me others who serve me. You seek redemption."

"I don't know what you're talking about."

I heard him chuckle. "Of course you do. It was a pity about Constance. But as you know, sacrifices must be made."

Whoever it was, they ended the call while I stood in shock.

Sacrifices must be made.

Months ago, I experienced a vision when my life had been threatened, and I thought I was moments away from death. In the vision, I was back in the night of the car accident, when the sight of a giant demon in the road ahead of me forced me to spin the wheel and crash the car.

In the vision, I was in the moment when I regained consciousness enough to see Cathy as she hung upside down. She never regained consciousness, and I would soon black out after having a terrifying experience with the same demon who appeared at the broken window of the car.

But in that strange vision, an upside-down Jyanette suddenly replaced Cathy and it was her face covered in blood. Instead of the demon at my window telling me to be careful what I conjured, Jyanette stared at me with eyes that had no pupils, only sclera, as a strange voice came from her throat that clearly said:

"Sacrifices must be made."

9. CRIME SCENE CONSTANCY

It was a difficult afternoon. After my call from Thin Guy, the NYPD arrived. I phoned Stan Frazier, who assured me he also would soon be on his way to the scene.

In the meantime, I had to deal with a tall, gawky man in a uniform with sergeant stripes who led his team and proceeded to take charge. He and Ward obviously knew each other.

"So, who told you the girls were abducted here?" the sergeant asked Ward. He had big ears, as well as a large nose, which made him look even more ungainly.

"As I mentioned when I called you, an anonymous source," Ward retorted.

The tall man shook his head. "You know that Brass hates anonymous sources. They also don't like private investigators inserting themselves into ongoing cases."

"I know that better than most, Kelly," Ward responded.

The tall man, apparently Kelly, inclined his head in my direction and leaned closer to Ward. "Is this guy the source?"

"No, he's a doctor, my personal physician. In case I get a heart attack or something."

Kelly rose to his full height. "All right. Both of you get out of the room while the team goes over things. But stay close. I'm gonna wanna ask you questions."

"How about I bring you guys coffee, my treat?" Ward suggested.

"Bribin' an officer?" Kelly smirked. "That'd be nice. Now, get out."

We stood on the sidewalk, me still in shock holding my cane and that damn teddy bear. I could not for the life of me figure out how on earth Thin Guy got my phone number. Or knew I was at the location of the abduction. If he was a psychic, he had skills that outpaced my own. I couldn't just pluck phone numbers out of the ether.

If he was aware of me and had already researched me, how did he know that I was going to get involved? And how did he know that phrase 'sacrifices must be made'? Or was that merely a lucky coincidence for him? My mind went around and around in circles with questions piling on top of questions.

Meanwhile, Ward had taken it upon himself to get a coffee box filled with coffee and donuts from a nearby shop. The gesture was not lost on Kelly or his team. As men in gloves, face masks, and jackets emblazoned with NYPD ran in and out of the building, Kelly stood out front with Ward and sipped coffee. I retrieved the paper bag and freed myself of the stuffed bear.

Ward offered me a coffee, and still in a daze, I took it.

"You okay, doc?" Ward asked as he handed me the Styrofoam container.

"Yeah, just a little spacey," I replied.

"Well, don't know if we'll get any forensics that'll help us, but it does mean NYPD will increase the canvas of the neighborhood."

Just then, a large black van pulled up and into an illegal parking space. Several agents in full gear stepped out. They wore black turtlenecks and pants, with tactical vests marked FBI in reflective letters. The last person out of the vehicle was Stan Frazier.

His face opened in a smile. "Professor!"

I relaxed, feeling a little less spacey as I accepted Stan's firm handshake. "Stan, good to see you."

Kelly, who couldn't have missed the arrival of the team, approached. "I was told you guys might show up."

"Yeah," Stan said and held out his hand, which Kelly took. "Stan Frazier. I've been authorized to take the lead in this case." He added apologetically, "I don't wanna step on toes, but this is our crime scene now."

"I'm Sergeant Kelly, 120th," he replied, giving the number of his precinct, followed by a snort of derision. "Let me tell you, there's enough forensics here to keep both our teams busy for the next month."

"Any sign of CSI?" Stan wondered, getting right down to business.

"I was expecting them a half-hour ago. How about yours?"

"The Evidence Response Team Unit should be right behind us."

Kelly chortled. "Leave it to you Feds to make the name even more complicated."

This got a weary smile from Stan. "Can I trouble your men to secure the area?"

Kelly nodded. "That can be arranged. Are you going to need lights? We can get generators here and some high-powered portable trees."

Darren and I sipped our coffee as the men discussed plans and protocol. It was nice to see, as many times there was a competition between the FBI and local police. But Sergeant Kelly didn't seem to mind turning things over to Stan, and even offered things that would help.

As they spoke, another black van pulled up, and three men and two women quickly came out and pulled on gloves and face masks. They all wore khaki pants with multiple pockets and long-sleeved blue T-shirts emblazoned with 'FBI Evidence Response Team' in yellow letters.

Stan turned to me. "Anything they should look for, professor?"

The image of a locket came to me and filled my mind completely.

"Jewelry," I blurted.

"What?" Kelly pondered, gazing at me quizzically.

I cleared my throat. "I believe there's a locket up there."

"A locket?" Stan repeated.

I nodded. "Constance's locket."

The three men stared at me: Stan, Kelly, and Ward. I had to admit; I was acting odd, even for me. But the phone confrontation had left me in a strange place. I felt almost as if I was floating above my body and looking down. Having actually had out-of-body experiences, it was remarkably similar. Stan appeared to decide. He walked with Kelly toward the building and spoke in hushed tones. Kelly glanced back at me and shook his head, but after a moment, they both went inside.

Ward and I stood side by side sipping coffee.

"Frazier seems to be used to you, but Kelly's not really sure what to make of you. Then again, neither do I."

"Just trying to help," I stated flatly.

"Okay, but, doc, you've been acting funny since we found this place."

I blinked a few times and tried to suppress the running thoughts and floating feeling. "Sorry. This case is affecting me in ways I didn't expect."

"A couple of kids, maybe one dead?" he stated bitterly. "It would affect anyone."

Kelly came outside with a look on his face of a man who had been to the mountaintop and had seen the face of God, followed by Stan who wore a smirk. In Kelly's gloved hand was a small, clear plastic evidence bag, and within it sparkled a glittering gold chain.

"Holy crap," Ward muttered.

"How did you know this would be there?" Kelly boomed as he approached me and pointed his finger like a weapon. "I walked inside, and one of my men handed me this!"

Stan pulled him aside and lowered his voice to speak to him. I only heard a few muttered words, as Kelly gesticulated wildly and pointed at me repeatedly.

After a few minutes of this, I walked over with my cane. The pair of them stopped talking as I approached.

"Gentlemen," I observed, and peeked at my watch. "It's getting late, and I have a dinner date planned."

Kelly leaned toward me and put his long index finger to my chest. "How did you know that would be up there?"

"Easy, Kelly," Stan defended.

"I guessed," I sassed.

"Yeah, good guess, funny man," Kelly snapped.

Stan interrupted this confrontation. "Kelly, I've worked with the professor — Doctor Wise before. He brings information—"

"He knows more than he's telling," Kelly fumed. "I want to know how he knew we'd find that locket up there, or how he even found this place."

"I can vouch for him, sergeant," Stan clarified.

Moving slowly, I extracted my wallet from my jacket pocket and handed the sergeant a business card.

Kelly frowned as he gazed at the card, then cursed under his breath. "Parapsychologist? What the hell is that? You some kind of witch doctor?"

"Actually, I'm a college professor."

Kelly glared at Stan, who shrugged and added, "He is, really. That's why I call him professor."

He waved the card as his eyes went from Stan to me. "This explains nothing."

"I know." I retrieved a pen and extricated the card from his hand. I quickly jotted my cell number on the back. "But this is how you can get in touch with me, if you need me."

He stood with his hands on his hips as I finished scrawling and returned the card.

This didn't mollify him. "What if I said I'd like to take you into the 120th so you and I could have a little chat?"

It sounded like he wanted to bring me in for an interrogation.

"Is that necessary, Kelly?" Stan questioned.

"It's okay, Stan," I pointed out. "Sergeant, I will be glad to talk to you at any time, but I have to meet my girlfriend's parents tonight at dinner. I gave you my card to show you I am always available to you. I am sure that Mister Ward will vouch for me as well."

Kelly gave Ward the evil eye.

Darren opened his arms and spoke. "I asked him to be here. He's done work with the Mountainview Police."

"And the FBI," Stan said, standing up straighter. "He's assisted on several cases, including an abduction."

"I don't give a damn. I want to hear how he knew that locket would be there."

"Is there proof that it belonged to Constance?" I interjected.

"Yes," Kelly huffed. "Upon examination, I discovered the locket has two tiny photos. One is Constance. The other appears to be the other missing girl."

"Erica?" I asked. "She had a photo of Erica with one of herself?"

Kelly grimaced. "Yeah, and the locket has 'BFF' engraved on it."

"Best Friends Forever," Ward said with a nod and sipped his coffee.

"Need no more proof than that," Stan assured.

"But this doesn't explain how you knew it would be there," Kelly demanded. "So, tell me."

I exhaled. "I've had some success in reading energy at locations, for the police."

Kelly again looked at the surrounding men. "Reading energy? What the hell does that mean?"

"It means I can get impressions from objects and locations."

He held the evidence bag up in my face. "Does this look like an impression?"

"I'd explain it more accurately if I could," I responded. "My training enables me to interpret—"

Kelly's other big hand went up to my face in a gesture of 'stop,' cutting me off. The gesture was so succinct; he must have been a terrific traffic cop at one time.

"No more!" he bellowed with a scowl. "I don't want to hear it. Okay, doctor, you can go. But I'm going to check you out, and if

I don't like what I hear, you'll be in an interrogation room tomorrow morning."

"That will be fine, sergeant, as long as I can go to dinner tonight." I nodded to Ward and Stan, then limped away.

"Where'd you find that guy?" I heard Kelly mutter to Ward as I moved away.

"Someone recommended him to me." Ward replied.

"I don't think anyone was doin' you a favor," Kelly complained.

"The professor's unusual, but a unique asset," Stan told them. "Now about your men securing the site…"

I was soon out of earshot and on my way to the parking garage. You would think after the work I've done with McGee for the last nine months, I would have been aware that any time you are involved with a crime scene, you are on the hook for hours.

If I'd been thinking clearly, I would have just said no to Ward when he called. I could see it would be a rush to get out of New York and get to dinner on time.

As I walked, I wondered to myself why I was afraid to mention the strange phone call I'd received.

10. ANCESTRAL ALLEGIANCE

I pulled my van into the parking lot of the Hunan Dynasty at 6:55, with just five minutes to spare. I shoved the gear shift into park and took a moment to breathe a sigh of relief.

I adjusted my tie, thrilled that I'd actually pulled it off. It had required that I pull into a rest stop on the New Jersey Turnpike and change clothes in the back of my van. The drive had been two hours, instead of merely the half-hour it should have been, but I'd made it on time.

Perhaps my psychic senses had pushed me to leave when I did, for once helping me out of a sticky situation. Often, my abilities leave my personal life in shambles.

Realizing that the last thing I wanted was to be distracted while dining with my darling's parents, I quickly opened the van's glove box.

There, in a small zipper-lock plastic bag, sat a small resguardos bag. This was mixed for me by a powerful Palero, which is a high priest of an offshoot of the Latin American religion of Santeria known as Palo Mayombe.

When he gifted me with it, I thought the bag protected me from harm with its special oils, herbs, and crystals. What this charm did was block my abilities as long as I wore it on my person.

I was about to pull it from its plastic bag when a black sports car caught my eye. A mid-size four-door job, but it had an unusual red stripe down the front of its hood. I glanced around to see if there was anyone in the car or near it of whom I should be aware.

Seeing no one, I pulled the resguardos bag out and placed it into my jacket pocket, returning the zipper bag to the glove box. If it still held the same effect as before, it would help me not to be bothered by the mental chatter of such a public place.

As I sauntered to the door, it pleased me I was going to focus completely on her family and show my lady that I could be responsible, as well as sensitive — two traits a man tries to show when he wishes to win the heart of a fair damsel.

I walked through the red-painted door emblazoned with large gold Chinese letters, where a lovely young Asian lady wearing a traditional kimono stood behind a small lacquered wood podium.

"Good evening," I said. "I'm joining the Emery party."

She nodded and gave a quick glance at a paper seating chart on the podium. "Yes, they have arrived. Sheryl will show you the way."

Sheryl, an Irish redhead — also in a kimono, but not nearly as authentic — smiled at me, grabbed a menu, and led the way.

The restaurant was an open, enormous space with high ceilings and dim lighting. Asian food restaurants in New Jersey run the gamut of every type and price range. You can find excellent sushi places and every variation from Mongolian to traditional Japanese.

The Hunan Dynasty seemed to be a high-end, chic place devoted to people who wanted a grand dining experience. Following the woman's ginger hair and the tiny pillow of her outfit attached to her rump, she led me through the room.

In a moment, we arrived at the table, where Jyanette sat sipping a white wine. Across from her were her parents. All three of them rose as I drew near.

Her father was eye-level with me, which didn't surprise me. Jyanette is six feet tall, so I gathered her father would equal my six-foot-four-inch frame. I could tell he was a powerfully built man, even in his well-tailored suit. He had an expansive chest, and from the look of him, I guessed that one of his arms was the size of both of mine put together. His shaved head gleamed in the dim room.

What surprised me was Jyanette's mother. She was also tall, maybe even taller than Jyanette. An artist arranged her African features, including her full lips and wide nose, to convey a sense of royalty. Her skin tone was even darker than her daughter's, but appeared almost to glow in the dim light.

The man put out his hand to shake with a grip that had spent a lifetime moving lumber and masonry.

"George Emery," he said. "You must be Leonard."

"Yes, sir, nice to meet you," I replied, hoping he wouldn't crush my hand. He released me with a smile, and I turned to his wife.

"Mrs. Emery," I greeted her, and took her hand in a quick grasp that wasn't really a handshake, but we made contact.

"Deka, please," she said, not letting go of my hand and looking deeply into my eyes. She spoke with a slight accent, and her voice was almost musical in its delivery. She wore a very nice dress that exposed her shoulders. The garment had a subtle African print to it that was hard to discern but quite handsome. A frown appeared on her face. "Have you come from somewhere you found disturbing?"

"I-I-" came out of my mouth. Fortunately, my girlfriend covered for me.

She put her hand on top of ours and said simply, "Let him sit, mother. You can give him the third-degree over dinner."

This made her father snort with a loud belly laugh. "That's my girl, always talking like a lawyer."

We separated, and I sat on a chair between George and Jyanette with Deka facing me.

George went on, "So, you're the mystery man Jyanette has told us so little about."

I glanced over at Jyanette and could tell she was uncomfortable.

She piped up. "Really, daddy, I just wanted to... um... make sure that it was... uh... right."

I tried to save her. "Jyanette and I have both had unhappy relationships in the past, and we wanted to have time to get to know each other before we introduced family and friends."

"Exactly," Jyanette said, too brightly.

As we spoke, I noticed that Deka still watched me closely. If the resguardos bag in my pocket wasn't deadening my extra senses, I probably would have been able to feel her stare.

"Can I order you a drink, Leonard?" George asked.

George had a tumbler of amber liquid with ice in front of him, and I could smell the whiskey, even from my seat. It had a fragrance that called to me.

"Tea is fine," I said.

There was a pot in the center of the table with small earthenware cups at each place setting. George reached over, took the wicker handle of the pot, and poured steaming liquid into one for me. "I heard Jyannie met your family around Thanksgiving."

I looked at my lady with a grin. "Jyannie?"

Jyanette frowned. "Don't start. It's a nickname. Mom's is worse."

I met Deka's eyes with a smile. "What nickname do you call her?"

"It is only when I wish her full attention. Then I call her by her middle name: Ebele. It is Nigerian for compassion."

I smiled as Jyanette glared at her mother.

"I didn't even know she had a middle name," I chuckled, and took Jyanette's hand. "That's really beautiful."

"Well, you've embarrassed me enough for one night," Jyanette whined, and with her free hand picked up her glass to take a sip.

"Oh, it's all right, Jyannie. It's just family," George commented, as he took a sip from his own glass. "So, Jyanette tells us you're a college professor."

"Associate professor, so far. I have a new department, and we're working to get it fully established and accredited. Tenure and all that will be years down the line, provided I can keep the interest going and attract new students."

"And it's what? Jyannie told us, but I forgot."

"Parapsychology. We are trying to teach techniques where unusual phenomena are researched the way a forensic scientist treats trace evidence."

"You were the one at Scudder house," Deka suddenly snapped and pointed at me. "You are the one who found those treasures."

Jyanette looked from her mother to me. "Again? All I've heard about since I met this man is this Scudder House thing."

"It was well over a year ago," I explained. "It was a case I worked on in California with my mentor, Doctor Kohl, and a team from San Francisco University."

Deka was undaunted. "But you led them. You spoke for the spirits trapped in that house. I read about it in the National Inquisitor."

I raised my hands as if to ward off a blow. "That case got a lot of attention, but it isn't really what I do. I only investigate situations when I'm called in."

George's forehead creased, as if stunned that his wife went off on this tangent. He quickly picked up his menu and opened it. "Hey, maybe we should figure out what we want."

"Good idea, Daddy," Jyanette insisted and followed suit. Deka and I also flipped open our menus and looked over the selections.

The last thing I needed was to have Scudder House brought up at our first meeting. I had received a lot of publicity from helping locate a hidden trove of gold and money in a false wall of that abandoned home. The problem for me was that I had acted as a medium for entities there. I had left with the souls, spirits, or residual energy still trapped in that house, imprisoned there by forces beyond my understanding. I knew one day I would have to return to face them — and attempt to free them.

"I think I'll have the Kung Pao Chicken," George said as he perused the menu. A pair of horn-rimmed glasses had appeared on his face, though I wasn't sure when he'd put them on. "What do you want, Mamay?"

Jyanette touched my arm and leaned close to me. "Mamay means 'mother' in Kikongo, which is my mother's native language."

"Really?" I replied, delighted by this bit of information.

"The Moo Shoo vegetables will be fine," Deka said and lowered her menu. "I do like those little pancakes."

A waitress was suddenly at our table. It was another girl in a kimono, though my guess was she was of German descent. George and Deka repeated their requests. I asked for General Tso's bean curd, and Jyanette ordered Hunan chicken.

"How about we get vegetable dumplings and sweet and sour spareribs for the table?" George said to round out our order. The waitress nodded and headed off to deliver our order.

"So, tell us how you two met," George inquired.

Jyanette and I exchanged a quick glance, and she went poker-faced.

"I believe the first time we met, she was prosecuting me," I stated.

"What?" George blurted, unsure of what he'd just heard.

"All the charges were false, Daddy." Jyanette glared at me with a look that told me I shouldn't really have brought that up. "The next time we met, he — kind of — rescued me."

"Really?" George said.

"Yes," she sighed. "And he ended up in the hospital."

"But things have been much calmer since then," I reassured with a smile.

Jyanette took another sip of wine. "If you would stop ending up in the hospital," she muttered.

"I didn't know being a college professor was so dangerous." George snickered as he signaled the waitress for a refill of his drink.

"Some people go looking for trouble," Jyanette added.

I gazed over at my lady. Apparently, there was some resentment she had not been sharing with me. It is always interesting what happens when a loved one gets around family or friends. Suddenly, you realize things about your own relationship that you didn't know were a problem.

"But enough about me, George," I changed the subject. "I understand you're one of the top renovators of historic buildings in the country."

"Well, I don't want to brag…"

"You should, Daddy," Jyanette suggested with enthusiasm.

"He is quite good, I must say," Deka interjected. I looked over at her as she touched her husband's arm with affection. "But I will also want to hear about your work with the spirits, Leonard."

George reached out for his wife's hand. Their affection for each other was obvious. "Deka grew up in a village where her father was the Nganga, which is a spiritual healer."

Deka sat up straighter in her chair. "As was his father and his father before him. I had to leave because of the unrest in my country."

"So now it's my turn. How did you two meet?" I asked.

George beamed. "She came to America to continue her studies in accounting. We met at Georgetown University."

"Accounting?" I said, surprise in my voice. "Seems like an unusual choice for the daughter of a Nganga."

She smiled sweetly. "I like numbers; they speak to me. Much as the spirits speak to you."

"Mother, I don't think this is the place…" Jyanette said, just as the waitress returned to our table with a second glass of whiskey for George.

Deka was undaunted. "Yes, daughter. But there is something that your friend carries with him. It connects him to a terrible Bakisi."

"What's a Bakisi?" I asked.

"It is the term my father used for a spirit. You carry a minkisi, a symbol of this being with you," Deka insisted.

I looked at her, puzzled, then dragged the resguardos bag from my pocket and held it up. "The man who gave me this called it a resguardos and said it was to protect me from an Orisha, the gods of Santeria."

"Ah! Bakisi is a word that is much older, Leonard. It is the worship of gods and ancestors that began in Africa, long before the Europeans came. The Nganga's teachings form the basis of Voodoo and Santeria, yet they corrupted them. She pointed her finger at my resguardos bag. "You should cast that aside."

"But it helps. It shuts off my mind from any unwanted stimuli."

Jyanette looked at me. "I didn't know you had that."

I turned to her and lowered my voice. "I'm fine most of the time, but a big restaurant — so many minds all going so fast. It's tiring to shut it out."

"Wait a minute." George looked perplexed. "You have to shut out… what exactly?"

I looked at my girlfriend's parents. "I get… impressions from people and things around me constantly. I have learned techniques to control how I'm affected, but a room like this, so many people… it's a lot to shut out."

Deka nodded her head, her eyes bright. "You are like my father! You have the gift."

"It's not a gift; it's a curse. I lost the woman I was going to marry because of it," I said a bit loudly. I leaned back in my chair as the waitress brought our appetizers.

My outburst surprised Jyanette, and I felt sheepish. As they put the steaming dumplings and pungent ribs in front of us, she signaled the waitress for another glass of wine.

As the waitress walked away, I exhaled and spoke quietly. "I'm sorry. This isn't the time or place to talk about these things. All I wanted tonight was to meet you and tell you how much I adore your daughter."

I reached out my hand to Jyanette. After a momentary pause, she took it and regarded me with a smile. It appeared I said the right thing for the first time that night.

The meal seemed to go well after that, although I really focused on Deka and the stories she could recall of her father. At first, she was reluctant and confessed she hadn't spoken of such things in years, but I pressed on, and soon she regaled me with fascinating and often comical stories of the man.

"—and that was when he found the goat." She chuckled, ending a story about her father's search to find an escaped animal in the jungle using techniques of divination. After many comical escapades, he located the goat in his own backyard.

Everyone at the table laughed, George and Jyanette out of politeness, as they had probably heard the story before.

"It's a pity he could not escape the country when you did," I lamented.

"He loved Zaire, and at first he thought Mobutu would bring order. But like many, Mobutu sought power and money for himself at the expense of the people." Deka looked at her hands. And yet, the people of our village treated my father well, and soldiers with the government respected him. It was strange…" Her voice faded off with a glazed look in her eyes.

"What?" I hoped she would continue.

She looked up at me as if woken from a dream. "Forgive me," she apologized and smiled. "It has been so long."

"You appeared to have remembered something."

"Yes. My father did not fear for the unrest in the country, though it pained him to see the people mistreated. He sent me to America because of unusual occurrences. He believed mysterious men who were Nganga pursued him. But he felt that they used their abilities for a dark purpose."

She fell into silence as the staff cleared the plates from our meal.

George reached over and took his wife's hand under the table, which stirred her from her reverie.

I looked at Jyanette, who avoided my glance but sipped her wine instead. I then realized that her mother and I had been doing most of the talking.

It was then that several waiters and our waitress came through the room, carrying a small cake with several lit candles on it, and approached our table. They were singing the melody of "Happy

Birthday," but the lyrics were in Mandarin or Japanese; I wasn't sure which.

It was then I had a sinking feeling. Of course, it was Jyanette's birthday on Sunday. This was her birthday dinner, and I had left her card and her present on the desk in my sitting room at home! In my rush to go to Staten Island, I hadn't even thought to bring it.

I would have joined in with the singing if I had any idea what the words were. Instead, I just sat there with a silly grin plastered on my face as they placed the cake in front of Jyanette.

"Happy Birthday, sweetie," her father said as her mother retrieved her purse from the floor and pulled out an envelope, which she handed to her daughter.

"Yes, Happy Birthday," I repeated.

Since I had nothing to give, I leaned over and gave her cheek a quick peck. This got a smile, and Jyanette blew out the candles with the eagerness of an eight-year-old.

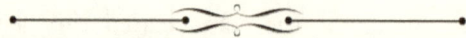

About an hour later, after dessert and polite goodbyes, I drove the short distance to Jyanette's apartment complex. It took a little while for me to find an open visitor's parking space, and it was a bit of a walk before I reached her place. The complex in which she lived was a series of two-story interconnected buildings. Jyanette lived on the first floor of her structure, and each apartment had its own separate entrance. I knocked on the door, and Jyanette let me in, a fresh glass of wine in her hand.

"You're… having another?" I asked.

Jyanette sighed. "It's my birthday, and I need it after that dinner."

I had been reading the cues correctly. Jyanette was unhappy with the way things had unfolded. "I'm sorry the conversation went into your mother's history and the whole spiritual thing—"

"You and my mother spent most of the meal talking about the different Orishas and Bakisi, as well as your philosophy of residual energy. The pair of you ignored Daddy and me."

"She's a fascinating woman," I confessed. "I mean, to find someone raised by an African healer, practiced in arts passed down for generations? I wanted to hear her take on the indigenous culture's concept of the paranormal—"

She held up her hand to stop me and spoke in an annoyed tone. "Enough for one night, please. You want tea?"

I felt a need to defend myself. "I assumed you'd be happy that I had a good relationship with your mother."

She waved her hand dismissively. "I am. It's just that, well, I hoped you and Daddy would bond more."

"Your father mentioned a football team he likes…"

"And you saying that you didn't follow sports shut that down," she mocked.

"Jyannie," I said playfully.

With fury in her eyes, she turned to me and pointed her index finger right in my face. "You don't call me that. Not ever!"

I could see she meant it. "Sorry." Her hand went to her hair to move a few strands out of her face. I ventured further. "I'm also sorry I forgot your present—"

"I don't need a damn present," she barked.

"And I'm sorry if I ignored you during dinner."

She shook her head. "You are one sorry guy, Len."

I exhaled to push down my annoyance. "You want to tell me what's going on?"

"Why don't you just read my mind?" she sniped and sat in a straight-back chair in the open living room area.

I walked behind her, leaned my cane against the chair, and touched her shoulders. "I don't have to be a psychic to see that you are on edge."

I massaged her shoulders, which were tense, the muscles taut. A sigh escaped her lips, and I felt the tension in her body release a bit.

"It's just — I had so many things I wanted this dinner to accomplish," she explained as I continued to rub.

"It surprised me to find out that you were upset about my getting injured," I consoled, yet I immediately felt her shoulders grow tight again. I pulled my hands away. "Do you want to talk about it?"

Jyanette exhaled deeply and rose with her glass, polishing off the half-full goblet in one slug. "I do want to talk about it. But it will only lead to a fight. I need more wine."

"Don't you think you've had enough?"

She turned to me, her face livid. "Says the alcoholic?"

I held my tongue, but that was a low blow, throwing it in my face like that. I felt my own temper rise. We had been dating for about six months, and it was only at that point when people begin to relax and truly express their feelings. I had been unaware that we had major issues seething under the surface. I followed Jyanette to the refrigerator, as she removed a large bottle and refilled her glass.

"Instead of lashing out at me," I attempted, weighing my words carefully, "perhaps we could discuss it. Or maybe it would be better if I just went home and we talk tomorrow."

She glared at me, and I was sure she was about to throw me out of her apartment, perhaps beating me with my cane for good measure. Instead, tears appeared in the corners of her eyes.

I immediately felt my irritation fall away as she blinked back the flow. "I'm sorry... I didn't mean to—"

"You almost died!" The words sprang from her throat in a wail of despair as the tears came. She put down the glass and grabbed me in an intense hug.

"I'm fine, shhh," I soothed. "I'm here, all in one piece."

"You don't know what it's like," she sniffled. "To see you lying in a hospital bed, all battered—"

"But I'm fine now."

"You could've died. And it's not just a one-time thing; it's every few months. Even when you went to goddamn Maine to help your old goddamn girlfriend. You got beaten up—"

"Sweetie—"

"I just don't know if I can handle it," she sobbed. "And then when the dinner didn't go the way I imagined it in my head, I got all bitchy and I wanted to take it out on you—"

I would have responded, but she raised her hands to my face and pulled my mouth to hers. She was all over me, her mouth on mine, which started a fire in my loins. Her hands moved up and down my body, stroking me. I pulled back to grab some air.

"Look," I grunted. "Maybe we should talk…"

She slid my jacket off my shoulders, as she used my tie to pull me to her mouth. Then her hand was on my belt, loosening it and undoing my pants.

"Are you sure you don't want to talk about this?" I gasped feebly as she reached down and pulled her dress over her head. In only a bra and panties, she grabbed my pants and pulled them down, so I stepped out of them.

She knelt there with a solemn look on her face as her hand gently stroked my right leg. This is the worst reminder of the accident that had killed my fiancée and crippled me — the series of scars and unnatural bumps and crevices in my flesh.

She looked up at me. "Can't you see what I am afraid of? All this suffering and pain you've already gone through."

I pulled her to her feet. "It only makes the joy I have more meaningful."

She took my hand and led us to her bedroom. Still sniffling, she unhooked her bra to expose her dark breasts and pulled my hands to them, moaning as I caressed her.

I quickly removed my shirt, and we fell into bed. I wanted to touch her, to arouse her slowly, the way she likes. But she would have none of it. She grabbed a condom from the nearby drawer and sheathed me in it before I could catch my breath. Then, overcome with desire, she pulled me on top of her and inside her in one fluid motion.

The admission of her fear and the expression of it was all the stimulus she had needed. She had put up walls to block me off, but they had fallen away and she wanted — no, demanded — physical contact to re-establish our bond.

She filled my senses: her scent in my nostrils, her warm ebony flesh against mine, the taste of her mouth on my tongue. Our intimate contact, overwhelming and overpowering both of us, as nerve endings flashed and exploded with sensation after sensation.

She needed this; we needed it: the contact, the loving, the connecting of our two bodies into one. I was on top, then she flipped us and she was uppermost and writhing over me. The pair of us moaning out words of love and desire, of want and need.

Passion this strong could not last, and in a few minutes, our bodies reached the pinnacle, and spasms racked us as her hips vibrated and I emptied myself into her, both of us crying out as we fell from the crest and lay conjoined, our breathing ragged.

"I'm sorry," she muttered once the tremors subsided.

"If this is the apology," I wheezed, "feel free to yell at me anytime."

We lay side by side, holding hands with our fingers intertwined.

"I guess I don't tell you how I feel about a lot of things," she finally murmured.

"I can read minds, but it's a lot easier if you just say what's bothering you. Not that I'm against drunken, weepy sex, but I want to know what you're feeling, what you're going through."

"I get scared, okay? Christ, back during Thanksgiving when I saw you in the hospital? That scared the crap out of me. And then you come back from Maine, looking like you'd taken up prize-fighting…"

"That's why I'm studying aikido. I need to handle myself."

"Until someone shows up with a gun? Then what do you do, Len?"

"Try not to get shot?" I attempted.

"Or that crazy cult leader with the knife. If you hadn't been wearing that thing your mother gave you—"

"The mezuzah—"

"You'd be dead. How can I have a relationship or plan a future with you, if you're constantly exposing yourself to this kind of danger?"

"My darling, you're a prosecutor. There are people out there who would kill you if they got the chance."

"It's not the same. I don't go looking for trouble."

We both lay there staring at the ceiling. I tried to think of words that I could say, things to reassure her. But the long day and the lovemaking had befuddled me. I felt the grip of her fingers relax and looked over to see Jyanette had fallen into a boozy slumber.

I sighed and let sleep take me.

11. TRACKED WITH ZEAL

The light poured in through the window past drapes we had forgotten to close in our passion. I was facing the mirrored door of Jyanette's closet, and I could see her supine form as she lay asleep beside me.

I rolled over to watch her as she dozed. Her facial features had really followed the strength of her father's with her Romanesque nose and strong eyebrows. But her lips were as full as her mother's, and her hair was a cloud laid out over the pillow in all its glory. I constantly marveled at how she twisted her hair into a tight bun when she was in court or her office.

Feeling a tad naughty, I lowered the sheet and blanket to gaze at her tight, firm physique. My eyes contemplated her strong arms and muscular legs, which contrasted wonderfully with the soft fullness of her breasts and hips.

I covered her up and slid out of the bed. Stark naked, I limped to the bathroom to relieve myself, then moved out to the kitchen to retrieve my cane and start her coffeemaker.

As the pot bubbled and steamed, I tried to get my head around some things her mother had told me the previous evening. Her father — Jyanette's grandfather — felt mysterious men with abilities pursued him. During dessert, as Jyanette opened the card containing a substantial check her parents gave her, her mother told me the circumstances of her father's death.

"I was in America and dating George. This was in nineteen eighty-one, and I received a letter from one of my cousins. There had been a raid on the village, and government troops took young men to become soldiers. My father stood up to them, but out of respect, they did not hurt him. It was later that men came, abducted my father, and took him into the jungle where they tortured him for hours and left him there. The villagers thought it was the soldiers seeking vengeance, but I believe it was the men my father had feared."

The shifting sands of power and politics in Zaire had left many unexamined murders, and her father, Kimoni Inyanga, was one of them. Unrest lasted until 1997 when the country changed its name to the Democratic Republic of Congo and became much more stable.

Sitting across from her and despite the resguardos bag and its influence, I could sense from Deka Inyanga Emery a strong awareness. Perhaps she had insights that helped her escape her country at the time she did. I believed she possessed a psychic ability, and I found it interesting that Jyanette did not — at least to the best of my knowledge.

An alarm clock beeped repeatedly, and a muttered curse came from the bedroom. I quickly poured Jyanette a mug of coffee and brought it in for her. After all the wine I'd seen her consume the previous night, she probably would need it.

I entered the lit room, and she was out of bed, without a stitch of clothing on, as she shut the blinds while murmuring curses about leaving it open under her breath. I smiled as she turned and faced me, her eyes half-closed as she teetered over to me and took the mug.

"How much did I drink?" she groaned.

"More than you usually do," I recounted. "You okay?"

"I'll let you know once I'm conscious. What day is it?"

"Saturday. I don't know why you set the alarm. I would've turned it off—"

Her head snapped up and her eyes opened fully. "Saturday? Omigod, omigod! My parents are here!"

"Yes, we saw them last night—"

"No, breakfast! They are taking me out to breakfast! Crap!" She glared at me with urgency. "You have to go."

"What?"

"Oh God, you've got no clothes on! Get dressed! Move it, move it! Be gone when they get here!"

"Gone?" I responded jovially, convinced she was joking. "Sweetie, I think they know we're sleeping together."

"No, they don't!"

"Christ, honey, we're both thirty—"

"Speak for yourself. I am about to turn twenty-nine…and you have to go!"

"Can I at least get a shower?"

"No!" she shouted as she reached down, gathered up my shirt and underwear from the floor, and threw them at me. "Get dressed. I need to shower—" Her hand went to her head. "Oh shit, my hair…"

I forced myself to put on a serious face and not burst out laughing. I also found it interesting that in the thirty years I have inhabited this male body, the sight of my girlfriend running about naked, her breasts bouncing in panic, could completely distract me from any other thought besides watching her.

"MOVE!" she bellowed, and I did. I hopped out to the living room, my hands filled with clothes, which kept me from using my cane. I stood next to her sofa and dressed as I heard the shower start. I had to use water from the kitchen sink to pat my hair into a more acceptable form and wash my face.

I walked to the bathroom and opened the door as a burst of steam puffed out. "I'm leaving."

"Good!"

"Call me?"

"Just go!" she hollered. "Oh, and don't have people phone me at the office."

I froze as a chill went up my spine. "What?"

"That guy who called my office. I am not your goddamn answering service. Now will you leave!"

The chill in my backbone felt more like frostbite. "What are you talking about?"

She yelled over the running water. "Some cop from MPD called my office and asked for your number. He said he was involved in your case and he had info you needed, but he had misplaced your cell number." Annoyance crept into her voice. "Really, I know that your cop friends are aware that we're an item, but you can't just have them call me at work!"

That's how he got my number...

She kept articulating her concerns, but I didn't really hear her. I felt like I was floating. Thin Guy had gotten my number from Jyanette. He had done his homework, and he knew we were together, so he called her office and said the right things. He knew eventually I would hear about it and that calling her carried with it an implied threat.

Sacrifices must be made...

"Len, are you still out there?" came Jyanette's voice as the water stopped. She grew louder as she approached the door. "Are you a voyeur now?"

She yanked the door open while drying herself with a towel, and I am sure she intended to throw me out until she met my eyes. Her demeanor immediately changed. "What's wrong?"

I shook myself. "Nothing."

"You look like you've seen a ghost, which I know you can do. What is it?"

"The guy who called. Did he give you a name?"

"He said he was officer something or other. I didn't know the name," she said, as a tone of calm focus came to her voice. "Is it important?"

I shook my head and lowered my eyes as I slipped my tie into my pocket.

"What are you not telling me?" Jyanette demanded.

"Just be careful, please," I insisted, and my hand went to her arm as I pulled her close and kissed her damp forehead.

"Dammit," she said and pulled back to meet my eyes. "This is the other thing I hate, like you getting all beat up. You don't tell me things! If it involves me, I need to know what's going on."

"I promise I will. After your parents—"

"My parents!" she squealed, and the panic returned. She all but pushed me down the hall. "Get out, get out, get out!"

I tried not to be fearful as I went to the coat rack at the front door to retrieve my overcoat. There, I stopped to glance in the nearby mirror, and the haunted look in my own eyes unnerved me. I pulled on my coat and stepped outside, just as Deka and George Emery strolled up the front walkway.

My mouth fell open, and I tried to get my mind to engage. "Mister and Missus Emery! What a surprise!"

They were both in winter jackets; Deka's was long and dark maroon. George had a shorter coat, which was navy blue and trimmed with faux fur. Deka reached out her gloved hand with a charming smile, and I shook it. George folded his arms and glared at me.

George spoke first. "I don't know why it should be. We made plans with Jyannie the other day to take her to breakfast. My question is what are you doing here?"

"Please, George." Deka smirked and looked at her husband. "You make it sound as if you and I were not once young."

"As I recall, we were young and married."

This made Deka laugh, much to her husband's consternation. "And yet there were nights in my dorm room before we were married," she beamed and gave George a wink. "I recall those nights fondly, even if you do not."

Her husband flushed a bit at this. I had not yet latched the door, so I opened it and gestured for them to go in. "Please come in. Jyanette is still getting ready." As they went through the door, I followed them.

As the door closed, I heard Jyanette's voice. "Len, I thought I told you to go before my parents—"

She walked into the room with a towel wrapped around her body and a second towel on her hair. She stopped at the archway between rooms, made a half-choked noise, and backed out quickly.

I looked at the guests. "Um...she's not quite ready yet. Can I offer you some coffee?"

"Deka doesn't drink coffee," George said as he sat. He still didn't seem happy about the situation, but with a glance from his wife, he didn't pursue it.

"My daughter has Bolingo Tea, I believe?" Deka asked.

I recalled seeing a small brown bag on the shelf in a cabinet where Jyanette kept her stock of coffee and tea. "Let me check." I headed into the kitchen.

"Huh," I heard George mutter. "Knows his way around here pretty well, doesn't he?"

As I went into the kitchen, I could hear Deka soothe her husband, though I couldn't hear the actual words. As I went to the cabinet and extracted the bag of African tea, I realized Jyanette had never offered it to me. I guessed she just kept it for her mother or special occasions.

I put the kettle on the gas range, lit a flame under it, and put together a mug for Deka. In the drawer with forks, knives, and spoons, Jyanette kept a strainer for loose tea. It was an interesting device, shaped like a large double-bowled spoon. Screens formed the two bowls, and a spring allowed them to open and close, creating a tight seal. I filled it with tea from the bag and placed it in the mug as the kettle heated.

By the time the water boiled and I'd poured it into the mug and returned to the living room, things seemed to have calmed down. George still watched me warily, but Deka took the mug of tea gratefully and had a sip. I limped to the only free chair in the room and sat down.

"This tea is an herbal tea," Deka informed me, breaking the silence. "It reminds me of a tea my father would make from plants he would grow and collect from the jungle."

"Your father was an herbalist as well?" I asked.

"Yes, as all Nganga have been. I believe I like this tea because I grew up near the plants it is made from. They have their own unique flavor that tastes like home to me."

All of us turned as Jyanette came into the room, still adjusting her hair. I wasn't sure if she used pins, clips, or wizardry to get it all into place, but she looked calm and completely put together. All three of us rose to our feet.

"Well, now." Jyanette forced a smile. "Good morning!"

She moved to Deka, who gave her a hug and looked at her father, who smiled and opened his arms. She moved to him to give him a hug as well.

Deka pivoted to me. "Leonard, will you join us for breakfast?"

I glanced at my girl and her dad. From the looks on both their faces, I decided it would be a bad idea.

"Thank you, Deka, but I have a case I am working on that requires my attention," I replied. I could see relief spread across Jyanette's face as her father visibly relaxed.

I headed to the door ahead of them and made polite noises as I went out and made the trek toward my van. The realization that Thin Guy had called Jyanette still shook me.

I took a quick gander at my phone, where there was a text from McGee from hours earlier:

Checked the address for Antoine Powell

He moved away months ago — no good.

I sighed and sent a reply to thank him for checking. I quickly hit the number for Darren Ward, who answered on the first ring.

"Ward."

"Wise. Did they get anything usable out of that scene yesterday?"

"Besides the locket? According to Kelly, they found about a million fingerprints all over the place. It will take days to collect them all, let alone identify them."

"The LKA for Antoine Powell was no good," I said, using the police abbreviation for 'Last Known Address'.

"Well, maybe you need to pull another one of those coincidences of yours."

"Synchronicity."

"What?"

"Jung said that focused will allows information to come to you through a process he called synchronicity," I pointed out.

"I don't care if you call it 'cheese and crackers'. If you can do it, I would recommend you do."

He ended the call without a further word. I put the phone away in my jacket pocket.

I was in the wrong mood to have anything come to me. Thin Guy's call to Jyanette for my phone number scared me. I was on edge because I was sure her father hated me. Add to that, the clock ticked away, and the hour approached when Thin Guy would sacrifice Erica Marconi.

The day was pleasant enough — late March with a chill in the air, which made me glad I wore my overcoat. But it was sunny, clear, and I knew the traffic would be less on a Saturday.

I needed more coffee and a shower, so I decided that heading home was the best choice. There I could get my head straight and try to figure out a better way to deal with the situation. Although my extra senses brought me information from unusual sources, I couldn't let it in until I was relaxed and open.

I unlocked the driver's side door with my electronic fob, and the seat automatically turned out to accommodate me and my leg. I sat in the chair as the mechanics hummed and rotated me to face the windshield. I took the resguardos bag that had remained in my pocket overnight and returned it to its plastic prison in the glove box. I then took one of the convenient wipes and wiped my hands to rid myself of any residual oils.

I pulled out of the visitor space to wend my way through the serpentine roads of the apartment complex.

As I drove toward home, my eyes kept being drawn to my rearview mirror, more than my usual occasional glance. At first, I thought I was just feeling paranoid from Thin Guy's phone call, then I noticed a car about two vehicles back that seemed familiar.

It was a black, sporty car — a four-door model. What was telling was the red stripe down the center of the hood. I had seen that same vehicle in the parking lot of the restaurant the previous night. Since this awareness was rather sudden, I decided I should probably pay attention.

To test my theory, I varied my route, not in any way sudden or surprising, but off the main road, which was well-traveled by many other vehicles. I took a right and went onto a back road, and sure enough, the car followed me, though the driver attempted to keep a discreet distance.

I didn't feel a need to change my route any further, as his actions confirmed my suspicions. This car was indeed following me. I wanted to get a peek at the driver. So far, he was keeping back far enough that I couldn't see who it was.

I hoped my knowledge of the back streets of Mountainview was better than his, and I had to make it look like I was still oblivious to him, or he might bolt. Of course, it was a guess that it was a he — I couldn't fight the feeling it might be Thin Guy. If so, could I get a look at him and possibly shut off an escape route? Maybe box him in?

My mind raced as I thought through streets in the imagined map in my head, and I had the glimmer of recollection about a nice little cul-de-sac close to my house that I might get him in, then block the egress with my van.

Bad enough I had to drive with controls on the steering wheel because of my bad leg, but now I wanted to do a car chase.

I often felt unprepared for my situation as a man of action, and if my life were a movie, I would insist the director recast my role.

I kept my speed low and telegraphed my turns with my indicators carefully — not too carefully, but with the attempt to drive nonchalantly. I drew near to the desired turn, and I gripped the wheel tighter. This was the moment of truth. If he knew these roads as well as I did, he wouldn't take the bait and he'd drive past the turn. If not, he couldn't see the turnabout more than a block away, and I might have him.

Vigilant to my prey, I made the turn as I maintained the twenty-five-mile-per-hour speed limit into the street. I knew another side street branched off up ahead, which was also a dead end. We went past it without him turning. I usually dislike the layout of New Jersey suburbia, but this time I was thankful for it.

I approached the hill I knew was ahead and waited until my van crested it. At which point I gunned the engine and flew down the hill, where I reached the turnabout going about fifty. I took the turn as gracefully as I could, and it pleased me that the curve of the dead end was clear, so I could whisk around it and head back the way I came.

I surprised the driver of the black sports car as he came gingerly over the hill, just as I had almost returned to it. Movement seemed to slow down as I looked over and saw a face look over at me at the same time. His mouth opened in surprise, and I instantly recognized him.

I went over the apex of the hill, planning to hit the brakes and throw the van into a stop that would effectively block the road. As I went over, a large horn blared at me, which shocked me to the bone. A huge moving van, probably far too large to be on such a small suburban street, was chugging its way over the hill. It was undoubtedly bringing new residents their belongings, but I was so stunned that I grabbed the brake control and swerved my vehicle all the way to the right side of the road. As I skidded past, I barely missed his extended mirror. I came to a complete stop, but I had been so flustered from the experience that I had barely blocked half the road.

There was the sound of a car engine, and I glanced back to see the black-and-red car easily go over the summit, to jet past the moving van and me, as easily as the hare runs beyond the famed tortoise.

Still in shock, I had neglected to note the license plate of the car, or anything useful beyond a general description of the vehicle itself.

Cursing to myself, I pulled my car to the side of the road to allow anyone else by and retrieved my phone to inform McGee of my close encounter with none other than Antoine Powell.

12. BYGONE BLESSINGS

The hot shower felt great on my skin, relaxing my sore muscles. I had been very active the last couple of days. Besides my workout with Ashwan, I had wandered around Staten Island in search of crime scenes, not to mention the vigorous bouts of lovemaking with Jyanette.

I found it humorous that Jyanette felt such a strong Puritan impulse to have me out of her apartment for her parents. In a way, it was a nice old-fashioned touch that she didn't want her father to know we slept together.

Our relationship presented complications on several levels.

I understood people are complex, and we all possess many conflicting impulses. I just hoped that her revelations would not cause problems as our relationship grew.

Jyanette was the best thing that had happened to me in years.

My phone call to Bill hadn't been very productive. I described the vehicle, but I had no idea of the model, make, or license plate. But he dutifully took the information and said he would work on it.

I turned off the water and stepped out of the shower, pulling a fluffy towel off a rack to dry myself. I wiped the mist from the mirror and set about shaving.

A few minutes later, groomed and in fresh clothes, I returned to my sitting room office where I retrieved my laptop from my bag and booted it up to look at my latest emails. After trashing the junk that offered me 'Hot Nubile Young Women' and 'Solutions for ED,' I found an email from my mentor, Doctor Fritz Kohl:

> **Dear Leonard,**
>
> **We have finally arranged funding to return to Scudder House and restart our investigation of the phenomenon. I would be delighted if you joined our team. Perhaps during your summer hiatus at GSU?**
>
> **Fritz**

I sat there for a moment and stared blankly at my screen. Return to Scudder House? Just the thought made me feel cold. And yet it was the location of my first major psychic achievement. I had 'channeled' energies or entities that resided in that house, which resulted in locating a treasure trove of money and precious metals hidden behind a false wall in the basement. The papers and television shows coast to coast trumpeted this find, as if we had stumbled on the tomb of Tutankhamen.

I knew there were still residual personalities that were trapped there. Because the house had a history of death and tragedy, I wondered if something else was imprisoned there. Perhaps it was best to keep it there, so it couldn't spread its dark fate out onto the rest of the world.

I quickly typed a reply:

> **Dear Fritz,**
>
> **I don't know if I can put in the time at Scudder House, but I will consider it. In the meantime, I am working on a case on Staten Island. I vaguely recall you have a student teaching there. Was he at Vanderbilt College?**
>
> **Let me know.**
>
> **Len**

I closed my laptop and looked out the window of my sitting room. The trees were still bare, but I could almost see the flicker of the green buds that would soon appear.

I closed my eyes and focused on my breath. Darren Ward had been right: if I had anything to help with this case, I needed to access it. But I couldn't do it by force. I needed to allow the next step to come to me. I needed to be open.

In... out, in... out.

There was nothing but my breath, no worries about my relationship, her visiting parents, hard-boiled detectives, time limits, or sacrifices. Just the sound of my breathing and the steady beat of my heart.

Mists seemed to appear in my mind's eye, breaking through the darkness. I sensed personal thoughts as they tried to pull my awareness — things thrown up by my ego to break my concentration. I relaxed through them and allowed myself to go deeper.

Colors burst through my brain, another attempt by the ego to distract. Fortunately, Doctor Kohl had trained me well, and I was familiar with the tricks my brain would play.

This also was my mind telling me I was going deeper into an altered state of consciousness.

I was going deep indeed, yet I felt it was what I needed to do. Suddenly, the image of that silly stuffed bear came to me, that well-loved toy that Constance had during her brief life. Mists seemed to swirl around it, and I worked on focusing only on it.

Hello…?

A small, feminine voice broke through in my head.

I'm here… I tried to share. I had experienced astral projection in the past, but the last time it didn't go well. I almost didn't make it back.

Who are you? came a response.

A friend,.. I replied silently. *Is that you, Constance… Connie?*

It's dark, I'm frightened…

I'm coming…

I was still going deeper and deeper. Everything around me fell into complete darkness. The last time I pursued a conversation with a disembodied spirit, it was in a haunted house. In that case, although released from my body, I was in a room with which I was familiar. This was different; there was nothing around me to keep me grounded.

I imagined earth beneath my feet, thought of myself standing on it and walking toward the source of the voice. "Connie," I called out, "do you know where you are?"

In the temple...

I stopped. "Yes, you were in a temple. That was where they took you."

They took me to the temple...

"That's right."

My clothes were gone, my pretty dress...

"I know," I said, as I felt a wave of sadness wash over me from her. She'd lost her life, yet the thing she mourned was her pretty dress.

The man has a knife...

A scream tore through the surrounding darkness, coming from everywhere and nowhere, and echoing inside my brain.

Followed by silence.

And then I heard him chuckle.

I knew that throaty laugh. There was only one being in all of existence whose voice could be so full of scorn.

A red light glowed brighter and brighter in the middle of the floor — or whatever made the base of my imagined location. I tried to back away, but it was like walking through mud.

The light grew brighter, and out of the middle rose a figure. It kept rising higher and higher as the darkness grew brighter. Soon it was a figure easily twelve feet high, with large horns on its head and blood-red skin.

It was the monster from the night I crashed the car — the thing that had unleashed my abilities and nearly cost me my life and my sanity.

"Nice of you to visit, though I guess you didn't come looking for me, boy!" the creature bellowed with its deafening voice.

I bent over double and slammed my imagined hands to my ears, but it was useless. The yelling was all inside my head.

"I could pull you down, boy, all the way, so you could never get out. But I'm not done with you. There are things I want from you," it boasted as it aimed a crimson finger with a long, pointed nail directly at me. "I advise you not to go so deep. You don't want to know what lives down here."

The floor began to churn and shift, and I could see things moving underneath it all around me. Hideous, monstrous shapes that one could only picture in tortured nightmares. They all moved and undulated sickeningly around me, all aware, all hungry to devour whatever they could find.

"Now," the demon demanded. "Leave me!"

I bolted upright in my chair, my head thrown back as if I had traveled at great speed and come to a sudden stop. I gasped, struggling to get air into my lungs. It was as if something had knocked the very breath out of me.

I grabbed the padded arms of my wheeled desk chair and bent over double as I gasped and wheezed. I wanted to vomit, but I'd only had coffee and had nothing to throw up.

I had gone too deep; I had accidentally descended into a place where I no longer possessed control, and it was a miracle that I had made it back. I was shivering from the experience, and I felt so cold.

It took me about twenty minutes before I calmed down enough to get my breathing slowed to a regular pace. My pulse was still high, but it slowed as I recovered.

I tried to think of anything I had seen or heard in that dark place that could help, desperate to make the horrifying experience worth it. Something niggled my mind, one simple word: temple.

The consciousness I had touched may have been Constance or the residual energy from her life, but it had given me an insight. Small though it was, this realization resonated in my mind. That was probably why that damn demon appeared. I was on the trail of something, and he needed to stop me.

But why should my attempt to help a kidnapped girl warrant his attention after all these years? Or was it that any time I went deep enough, he lay in wait to torment me?

Since there were no answers, I gave up the attempt and focused on the concept of the temple.

I pulled out my phone and hit the button to call Darren Ward. He answered on the first ring with: "Whaddya got?"

"Can you check abandoned churches in the area near where Thin Guy abducted the girls?"

"Abandoned churches?"

"Yes, especially if there have been any complaints of people breaking in or holding ceremonies."

"Churches?" he repeated dubiously.

I explained, "Or any kind of hall where people can perform ceremonies."

"The place they used for the rave was a pretty suitable space for that."

"No, this place needs to have religious or ceremonial history. Can you check?"

He considered it for a moment. "If we use the rave location as our point of origin, how far out?"

"I assumed they walked or were in a car, but not for long. So only a few miles from that location."

"I'll check with the 120th to see if there were any complaints of break-ins. They might know about any churches that are closed in the area."

"I'm looking for any religious order that would have an altar."

"An altar," he stated again. "I'm on it."

"I'm driving out there."

"Why?"

"Not sure, but if I'm going to pull a miracle out of my hat, at least I'll be close by."

"Call me when you're here."

I hung up and called Stan Frazier with the same request.

"Churches, huh?" Stan mused on his end of the phone.

"That's what I got. The private eye is checking on it."

"You called him first?"

This surprised me. "Yes, was that wrong?"

"Actually, it is, professor. I did a background check on your new pal, Darren Ward."

"Stan, he's not my friend. A... mutual acquaintance threw us together."

"Well, Ward got tossed out of the NYPD. Did he tell you that?"

"He said he'd been a cop, but I didn't ask for specifics."

"His father was involved with the Gambino crime family. Word on the street is that he was in the pocket of some crime boss."

"By any chance, Anthony Marconi?"

"Who?"

"I guess not."

"No, it was some made man named Romano. People I spoke to say Ward 'misplaced' some evidence to help him out of a rap. He resigned before they dismissed him. The authorities brought criminal charges against Ward, but a technicality caused them to dismiss the case."

I finally had the connection between Marconi and Ward.

Stan went on. "So, you'll excuse me if I insist that anything you find goes through me first, got it?"

"Sure, Stan, I'm sorry. I didn't know there was a problem."

"I just want to make sure no evidence gets lost on this case, understand, professor? Everything needs to be by the book."

"Honestly, Stan, I'm not trying to pull anything."

"Okay."

"I was about to drive to Staten Island and meet Ward to see if we could locate a church near the site of the rave."

"I'll check on that on my end. Keep me in the loop about anything you find."

"You got it, Stan. What has your team been doing?"

"We've been working with Kelly and the 120th. Today the team has a training exercise near the Clay Pit Ponds State Park."

"You still have to do those?" I wondered.

"I'm doing it for the team, mostly. It'll help us work together better. And remember, professor, I am a field agent. It doesn't hurt to train. But you can interrupt if you discover anything important. We can move pretty quickly."

"Good to know. Thanks, Stan." I got off the phone.

I had now committed myself. The problem for me was that I had no logical idea why I should drive all the way out there, except that I had a feeling.

Then again, following my 'feelings' had worked out in the past.

I quickly checked my email before I got on the road and found a reply from Fritz Kohl:

> **Leonard;**
>
> **You are quite right. You worked with him your first year. His name is Doctor Walter Addison. He is a Doctor of Divinity and teaches Religious Studies and chemistry at Vanderbilt College on Staten Island.**

He ended the message with a phone number that I quickly added to my phone.

I remembered Addison; we had called him 'Walt,' and sometimes 'Uncle Walt.' He had no resemblance to Walt Disney, who was a famous 'Uncle Walt,' but he possessed a full beard, and though young, he wore the quiet demeanor of an older man. He possessed a good sense of humor, and several women in our class remarked that he was like 'a favorite uncle,' so the name stuck.

I considered calling Jyanette to tell her that her ex-husband had followed me from her apartment, but I couldn't see that it would do anything productive. If her ex was following me and involved in a cult that killed people, shouldn't I warn her?

The memory of the vision of her hanging upside down in the car and saying 'sacrifices must be made' flashed through my mind yet again. And that Thin Guy knew that phrase — and also was aware that I referred to him as Thin Guy — was disconcerting.

Where was he getting this information? I knew how he got my cell number. He'd called Jyanette, pretended to be a cop, and she gave him my number. No mystery there.

Bill, Darren, and Stan all heard me use the term 'Thin Guy', but who else could have known it?

Finally, that phrase, 'sacrifices must be made.' I'd told that to no one.

Yet, he said it.

And when I attempted to go deep and reach Constance, the demon that caused the car accident had been there, lying in wait.

What was the connection between Thin Guy, the demon, and Antoine Powell?

And what was Thin Guy playing at?

13. DUTIFUL SEARCH

I would love to say that since it was Saturday, there was no traffic, and I had a fast and easy ride to Staten Island, but that would not have any connection with reality.

Driving through New York City or any of its boroughs, there was always traffic, except late at night or in inclement weather.

The only fun part was finally getting where you wanted to go.

I got in my van, stopped to fill up the tank, and headed down the NJ Turnpike and across the Goethals and onto the island.

I kept watching my rearview mirror to see if the black car with the red stripe appeared behind me, but I saw no sign of it.

The Staten Island Expressway still went at a crawl, and it was afternoon when I pulled off on Clove Road to make my way to the courthouse lot where I had parked the previous day.

My route took me again past the turnoff for Vanderbilt College, and the sign caught my eye.

Vanderbilt…

There was that buzz again. It was time I did something about it, so using vocal commands, I had my phone call Walt Addison from the number I downloaded from Doctor Kohl's email.

He picked up on the second ring.

"This is Doctor Addison," he greeted in a businesslike manner.

"This is Doctor Leonard Wise."

I could hear him chuckle. "Len Wise, as I live and breathe. How are things in California?"

"Actually, I'm teaching at Garden State University in New Jersey."

"Really? Wow! What courses? Religious studies? Comparative religion? Metaphysics?"

"Parapsychology."

I could hear him snap his fingers. "That's right, I heard GSU had a parapsychology program this year. I didn't know it was you. I shouldn't be surprised after Scudder House."

"To be honest, Walt, I also work with the police."

"Really? That must make Fritz happy! He always saw parapsychologists as forensic investigators. How did you get them to use you?"

"As a matter of fact, they came to me. But I'm working on a case here in Staten Island."

"Really?" he pondered with excitement. "What's it about?"

"I can't give you too much detail, for obvious reasons. You teach comparative religion at Vanderbilt, is that right?"

"Yes, and chemistry, which has always been a love of mine."

"I'm wondering if you know of any abandoned churches near the Staten Island Ferry terminal."

He considered this. "There are quite a few all over the island. The Arch Diocese closed twenty-one parishes starting in 2007."

"I see."

"But if you want the lowdown, I know a guy."

"A guy?" I asked.

"Yeah, he collects artifacts from closed religious institutions here on the island. In fact, he does it all over the city."

"He does?"

"Yes, and he's got a warehouse on the north end of the island, near the ferry terminal. It's filled with statues, chalices, even altars. He sells them to needy churches throughout the country."

"He might help," I told him, elated at the prospect.

"His name is Shaun Henessey. He's been a great resource for me for the Catholic course of study in my comparative religion class. He's collected relics from old parishes and knows the history behind each item. If you want someone who could tell you about closed churches, he's your man."

"Walt, could you text me his number?"

"I'll do even better. I'll text you the address of his warehouse as well."

"Thank you so much, Walt."

"Yeah, well, one of my students, Claude Vandersteen, is interested in the same subject. He's the one who put me in touch with Shaun."

"I appreciate it. How can I repay you?"

"I might ask you to do a lecture for one of my classes on Fritz's concepts of residual energy. You always had a better grasp of the concepts than I did."

"No problem. Mondays are good."

"Thanks, Len. Stay in touch."

As soon as I hung up, I made the turn into the same parking lot I used the previous day, just as a name, address, and phone number text appeared on my smartphone. As I exited the car, I also sent Darren a text to let him know I'd arrived. He asked to meet at the same bench in front of the courthouse where we'd met the previous day.

I pulled my coat around me. The weather was taking a cold turn, and I could see my breath as I walked down the block and past the courthouse.

There on the series of interconnected benches waited Ward. He wore a heavier coat than I'd seen him in the previous day and rose as I drew near.

"Any luck?" I asked.

He rubbed the back of his head. "Not much. I called Sergeant Kelly, who has friends born and raised on Shaolin—"

"Wait, Shaolin?" I questioned.

Ward smirked. "That's the name locals call the island. The problem is, there are a lot of closed churches in the area."

"That's what I just found out. I spoke to a teacher I know at Vanderbilt College."

"How does a teacher know about churches?"

"He's the comparative religion professor," I explained.

Ward's forehead furrowed. "I guess that makes sense."

"He also gave me the name and address of a guy who collects artifacts from abandoned places of worship," I offered.

"Do you think we'll get anywhere talking to him?"

"Yes, I do," I suggested and showed him the text on my phone. "This is the address."

Ward looked over my shoulder at the small screen. "This isn't far. We could walk it."

He stood and walked in the direction I'd come.

I limped over to catch up with him. "I have to let Stan Frazier know. In fact, he asked me to let him know first."

He glanced over his shoulder. "So, text him and walk at the same time."

I indicated my cane. "I can't really do that."

He exhaled heavily, and his breath frosted up around his head as he turned to face me. "I feel he talked to you about me. Maybe even warned you."

I met his eyes. "Yes, in fact."

His mouth was a hard line. "Text him and let's go."

I quickly input the information into my phone that I would be in touch if I found out anything.

"Okay," I said as I pocketed my device and caught up to Ward. "It's all set."

"Good, let's walk."

We started down the street, and I pulled my coat closer. "Man, it got cold."

"They say we're due for snow."

"I was hoping we were past that. I've been in California for seven years, and this winter has been rough."

"Gotta toughen you up, Wise." He smirked. "So, what did Frazier say about me?"

I hesitated for a moment, considering whether I should tell him. It was probably things he'd already heard. "He said you were a corrupt cop. That's why you left the force."

He shook his head. "I'd been told he was looking into me."

"So how much of it is true?"

His jaw clenched. "I really don't have to explain myself to you."

I shrugged. "He said you lost evidence against a gangster, and here you are working on a case for a man that I know is a crime boss."

"So why did you agree to help?" he sneered.

I exhaled heavily. "I'm not sure. I don't approve of Marconi. Hell, I don't even like him. But his niece is an innocent."

"He's an unusual guy," Ward muttered as he stared at the ground. "Truth is I didn't misplace that evidence. Someone else did and set it up so I took the fall. I resigned, got brought up on charges. Marconi hired a fancy lawyer who got me off."

I frowned. "Why?"

He smiled sadly as we turned a corner and walked through a residential area. "Craziest thing. He met me here, right at the courthouse where you and I met. He told me he knew I didn't lose the evidence and that he'd hired me a lawyer." The smile grew broader. "He said he owed it to my dad that I shouldn't go to jail for what someone else did. Since then, he's thrown work my way."

"And now with his niece…"

"He told me I was his first call." Ward gritted his teeth. "Look, growing up, I knew my dad was with the mob. Marconi was a young guy back then. One day my dad didn't come home. Someone murdered him. That's when I decided I wanted to be a cop, to do things differently from my old man." He sighed wearily. "Didn't work out the way I expected. Now most of the time, I'm taking photos of cheating husbands and tracking down deadbeats. But at least I know that what I'm doing is legal. Kelly knows it, too. That's why he's willing to keep me in the loop."

I walked next to him, my cane moving on the sidewalk. "I just wanted you to know what I've been told."

He considered this. "Look, I get it. Marconi threw us together. You don't know me, and I don't know you. But I got to say, you seem to have a knack for finding things out. Maybe you really can read minds."

"The problem is, it comes as it comes," I explained. "That's pretty inconvenient when we're on a tight schedule."

"Agreed," Ward said, and we turned onto another side street as he indicated a building down the block. "We're almost there."

By now the cold was getting to me. "We should've taken the van."

He snickered at me. "Take it like a man, Wise."

We drew near the building. It was an interesting contrast, as most of the street was residential, and there in the middle of the block was a two-story brick structure with large metal garage doors.

Unlike the building that was the home for the rave where the girls vanished, this building was in excellent condition. The brick was bright and maybe even recently sandblasted. There were several round windows, almost like portholes in the facade. I considered this a clever way to avoid break-ins, as they appeared too small to allow a grown man to get through them, yet they allowed light to spill into the space.

We walked to the door, and there was a small box with a button that Darren pushed.

"Maybe I should do the talking?" I suggested.

"If anyone is even here," Ward grumbled.

"I guess we should've called first."

Yet after only a minute, a white-haired gentleman opened the door. He was rail-thin and only about five-foot-four. He gazed up at the pair of us.

He cleared his throat. "I am sorry, gentlemen, but I don't sell to laypeople."

"We're sorry to bother you, Mister Henessey, but Professor Walt Addison gave your name and address to me. He said you might help me in some research I'm doing."

His face brightened. "Oh yes, Walt. Because of him, the New York Times ended up doing a wonderful article about me. That was a big help to my business." He waved at us. "Come in, come in, don't stay out in the cold."

We came through the door into a vestibule, with another door a few feet away. It was a small space for the three of us. Henessey shut the outer door with a shiver and pulled the cardigan he wore closer to his body.

"I'm Doctor Leonard Wise," I continued as I offered him my hand. "This is Darren Ward. We're looking into closed churches in the area."

"Oh? Are you a professor as well?" he asked me.

"Yes, at Garden State University."

He chuckled. "Priests and ministers have visited me from all over the country. Now I have college professors and students coming by." He moved to the second door. It was heavy metal, but he'd left it ajar and easily opened it. "Well, let me give you the tour, and I'll see if I can rustle up a list of the places I know about."

He stepped into the large warehouse with the pair of us right behind him. He hit a switch on the wall, and fluorescent lights blinked on overhead.

The vast open space unfolded before us like a hidden trove, densely packed with an array of religious artifacts. Rows of statues representing saints peered out cautiously from layers of bubble wrap, as if waiting patiently to be restored to their sacred places.

I could easily picture each one nestled within the alcove of a quiet church, where the faithful might pause to light a candle, seeking blessings and grace.

He moved forward with us trailing closely behind. Narrow pathways wound through the dense collections, guiding our steps past a pallet of metal and wooden organ pipes precariously stacked like industrial plumbing, cold and impersonal yet essential to the music of worship.

"My office is at the far end," he mentioned, pulling his cardigan tighter against the chill. "I can look things up on my computer in there. Plus, the heat's on — I was still hoping spring had truly arrived."

"We were all fooled," I replied, as we passed a cluster of votive stands and a grouping of ornate chandeliers glittering quietly to our right.

Ward's gaze drifted left, where a dismantled set of marble railings sat just beyond a collection of massive church bells, each weighing a quarter-ton and resting silently on individual wooden pallets, suspended slightly above the floor.

At last, we reached the back of the warehouse and a modest door, I assumed, led to his office.

On the wall beside it hung a dozen crucifixes of varying sizes, each carefully sheathed in protective bubble wrap. Some were small, only a foot or two tall, while one stood life-sized—a solemn figure of Christ poised in quiet suffering.

Nearby, someone carefully stacked a neat collection of decorative frames and portraits of various saints. The frames varied in size and wear, many richly gilded with gold leaf that caught the light, casting a warm gleam over the pile—a testament to the reverence and history cradled within these walls.

He opened the door, and a blast of warm air washed over us as we stepped in.

"You're lucky you caught me," Henessey began. "I'm usually not here on a Saturday, but I have a church in Cincinnati that needs the stations of the cross and vigil light stands. I was taking photos and emailing it to the sacristan."

"The what—?" I asked.

"The sacristan," Henessey repeated casually, as if this was an everyday term. "He's the person in charge of a sacristy and its contents."

"I see." I exchanged a glance with Ward, who shrugged.

Henessey moved to his cluttered desk and sat in a battered chair that faced his computer monitor. "Now, let's see, closed churches. You're looking for one in this area?"

"Yes, somewhere here on Staten Island," I suggested.

He gazed at his screen and input a few keystrokes, and moved the mouse. "That covers a broad range. I've emptied about five churches, just this year. What is this about?"

"We're looking for a place that might be misused," I suggested.

Henessey turned back to me and lowered his glasses to peer up and into my eyes. "What does that have to do with religious studies?"

Ward shifted forward and pulled out his wallet to extract one of his cards. "Actually, we are searching for a pair of abducted girls. We have reason to believe they're being held in an abandoned church."

"Oh my," Henessey blurted and looked at the proffered card. "You're a private investigator? Are the police aware of what you're doing?"

"Yes," I disclosed. "So are the FBI. We're looking into avenues they may have not considered."

"I see," Henessey commented and turned back to his computer. "Well, let's have a look-see, shall we?"

I decided to give him more information. "We're seeking an abandoned religious site with a stone altar."

"That certainly limits the choices," Henessey conceded, and his face scrunched up as he peered at his computer.

Ward watched the pair of us as I leaned forward, my weight on my cane, as Mister Henessey plunked away at his keyboard one letter at a time.

He typed slowly, and several documents appeared on the monitor. He gazed at them and muttered under his breath, before pulling up the next one and then the next.

I stood upright as Ward and I exchanged another glance. I could see he wasn't happy about the time this was taking.

Finally, after what felt like an eternity, Henessey turned back to us. "I'm afraid, gentlemen, that I have nothing nearby, if that's what you meant."

"Did you find anything at all?" I asked, disappointed.

"Well, there's an old chapel in the southern part of the island that might fit, in the Coopertown section. It isn't completely deserted. There just aren't services there on a regular basis."

"What can you tell us about it?"

He thought for a moment, observing the ceiling before looking at me. "Well, I'm just going by memory, as I was there about a year ago. It wasn't to clean it out; they wanted replacement parts for a chandelier. But they had an altar made of stone."

"Would this altar be large enough for a person to lie on?" Ward asked, cutting to the chase.

Henessey frowned. "No, I don't believe so. In fact, it was more like a stone table elevated off the ground with legs. But it was all marble. A delightful piece, I must say." He then shifted from Ward to me and back again like a referee at a tennis match. "You think these missing women are lying on an altar of some kind?"

Ward opened his mouth, but I raised my hand to stop him and spoke instead. "We have reliable information that there was a woman, and she was lying on some kind of stone altar. They had drugged her, and she might have been recalling things incorrectly."

"A stone large enough to lie down on? And someplace abandoned…" His voice faded away as he leaned back in his chair and considered the ceiling again. He then abruptly sat upright and stared at me. "I am aware of a place that's isolated, and no one lives in it. Would that be more to your criteria?"

"It might," Ward interjected. "You got an idea?"

"Well, it doesn't serve as a church, but it stands quite isolated. I was thinking of the Vanderbilt tomb in the Moravian Cemetery."

Vanderbilt…

I felt the buzz pass through my mind. Was this why I got a buzz every time I saw that name?

Henessey went on. "It's famous here on Staten Island but sealed off from the public with heavy metal doors. I had a chance to go inside about two years ago. There was a little storm damage to one of the stained glass windows on the roof."

"You do stained glass as well?" I asked.

Henessey smiled. "That's how I got into this line of work. My father was a glazier, and his hobby was stained glass. It got me interested as a kid."

"How unusual," I commented.

"Yes, I did repairs on churches for years. Then when they closed down, I decided collecting the artifacts would be a service. I wanted to ensure they were treated devoutly and found a new home in other churches. That's when I got this warehouse."

"What about the tomb?" Ward insisted.

"Hm? Oh, well, you see that was the thing. Cornelius Vanderbilt has his coffin right in the middle of the room. I guess you would call it a sarcophagus."

"Like the Egyptians?" I questioned in amazement.

"Yes, yes," Henessey spoke reverently, a light in his eyes. "But that was the thing, it was smooth and made from black limestone. I remember, when I did the repair, I had to climb a ladder, and I looked down on that dark casket." He shook his head. "All I kept thinking was that it looked like some kind of altar for human sacrifice."

14. CONSECRATED GRIND

"Vanderbilt's tomb," I repeated into my phone. "That's what I said."

"I dunno, professor," Stan Frazier replied through the speaker of my phone as Ward and I headed back to the garage and my van. "Based on my knowledge, the tomb has remained locked for years! A chain-link fence and gates cordon off that entire area. Besides that, the cemetery has security…"

"Trust me on this one, Stan. I have a strong feeling this could be where the girl is being kept," I insisted as we walked.

Stan sighed loudly. "Okay, I'll call the NYPD and see if they can get anyone from the cemetery office. This would have been a lot easier on any other day than a Saturday."

Surprised by his reticence, I said, "Stan, if this is where they killed the other girl—"

"All right, I'm on it. Give me a half-hour. Can you meet me at the cemetery?"

"I'm on my way, as soon as I get to my van."

"Do me a favor and stay in the van until I get there. For once, okay?" he chided as he ended the call.

I returned the phone to my pocket.

"What did he mean by that?" Ward asked as we approached the garage and stepped toward the elevator.

"I've been... um... involved with a couple of incidents with Stan..."

"Do tell?" He smirked.

I exhaled in frustration. "Both times I got out of the van when he told me to stay in it."

The smirk grew larger as we got into the elevator.

"It was important both times," I argued, wondering why I felt such a need to defend myself. "Should I use the van's GPS?"

"No, I know where it is."

We walked to the van, which I opened with the electronic key fob. Ward watched as my driver's seat turned out and I got in. Then, as the mechanism shifted me to face forward, he jumped in the passenger's side.

"That's pretty neat," he remarked.

"Yes, it is," I stated as I secured my cane and started the car up. Warm air filled the cabin.

"That's better," he sighed. I had to agree. Who knew the end of March would be so cold?

I pulled out of the space as Ward guided me.

"You want to head to Victory Boulevard and go south until it becomes St. Paul's Avenue."

Something odd struck me. "How long will it take to get there?"

"On a Saturday?" Darren considered. "I guess about twenty minutes."

I frowned, as Ward looked at me carefully. "Something wrong?"

I fought to articulate what I was feeling. "Yes…I mean…no…I mean…it just seems to me that Thin Guy took the girls to someplace closer to the rave location."

"You're the one who jumped all over the idea of this tomb."

"It's because the word Vanderbilt keeps popping into my head. I don't know why," I explained. "At first, I thought it was because I knew someone at Vanderbilt College. And he gave me the connection to Henessey."

"I hope you can appreciate me not having a clue what you're talking about."

"I'm not sure I do, either."

"Great," he murmured cynically. "I'd hate to be the only one."

As we headed further south, St. Paul Street gradually transformed into Van Duzer Street. After another five minutes of steady driving, we made a turn onto Richmond Road.

The scenery was a blend of everyday life—shops and businesses lined the street, ranging from bustling tire stores to quaint, aromatic bagel shops.

Not long after, a large white church came into view, perched majestically atop a gentle hill. Surrounding the church were expansive lawns, still tinged with the pale brown hues of early spring, slowly awakening from their winter slumber.

Encircling the property was a sturdy stone wall about three feet high, topped with an elegant metal fence.

"That's the Moravian church," Ward said and pointed.

We continued to drive past the property.

"They have a lot of land," I remarked, as tombstones began to appear up the hill from us.

"You got that right," Ward declared. "The church owns over a hundred acres."

I was sure my eyebrows all but shot up. "Really? All that land, right here on Staten Island?"

"Part of it was the Vanderbilt estate. They were very involved in the Moravian church," Ward reported. "If we get in, you won't believe the place."

At his direction, I made a turn onto Locust Avenue, made a left, and then came down Otis Avenue to face the closed and locked gate of the main entrance.

I parallel parked into a space and shifted the gears into park, and we waited, the heat running in the car to keep us warm.

"Wish I'd gotten some coffee," I complained.

"We got time," Ward suggested.

But apparently we didn't, as the sound of sirens approached from two different directions at the same time. With lights flashing and sirens blaring, two NYPD cars pulled off the street and onto the cemetery access road, where they stopped at the secured gates.

"Whoa!" Ward exclaimed. "I guess they are taking this seriously."

"I have to admit, the FBI can make things happen," I observed. "Should we walk over there?"

"No, it's cold. Let's wait for the Feds."

We stared at the police cars that had now shut off their sirens and lights and sat unmoving. We all remained in our vehicles for another five minutes, until a large black step-van pulled off the road behind the police vehicles.

"That's Stan," I noted, and opened my door. Ward and I left the van and crossed the busy street to the dark FBI conveyance.

The metal rear door rolled up as we drew near. Stan stood there, dressed in black, wearing a tactical vest emblazoned with 'FBI' and a sidearm. In the van were four other agents — two women and two men — wearing SWAT garb as well: full body armor, helmets, and machine guns hanging from a strap on each of their shoulders.

"Hey, professor!" Stan bellowed as the door rose. He nodded to Darren, which was returned half-heartedly.

"You guys got ready fast!" I exclaimed as Stan offered a hand and pulled me up and into the back of the vehicle.

"No, you just got lucky," Stan explained. "Like I told you, we were doing a field training exercise near the Clay Pit Ponds State Park. We had just finished when you called. We grabbed our transport and got right over here."

"So that's why you're in combat gear?" I nodded. "It seems like overkill for going into a tomb."

"Well, if the bad guys are there, we are certainly prepared," Stan observed. "I gotta talk to the NYPD, find out when the caretaker is going to get here."

He stepped out the open door, and I pulled my coat closer to me as I moved in. The two women moved a bit and made space for Ward and me on the bench attached to the right side of the van. I nodded to both of them as we sat.

We didn't have long to wait, as Stan stepped back up into the van followed by a uniformed NYPD officer. They lowered the door behind them, and a light on the ceiling created shadows in the van.

"This is Officer Milton," Stan announced to the group. "We are working in cooperation with the 122nd precinct on this matter."

Milton was a tall African-American man, a bit chubby, but he possessed muscled arms that looked like he could crush you with a hug. He took off his hat, revealing a shaved head, and he looked around at the group. "The caretaker is on his way. Won't be more than a few minutes. Please introduce yourselves. I want to know who I'm working with."

He pointed at the man at the end of the bench who spoke his name and followed it with "FBI Field Agent."

He went down the bench and pointed at Ward, who admitted he was a private investigator.

Then he came to me.

"Doctor Leonard Wise. Civilian consultant."

He gazed at me with suspicion. "What does that mean?"

"I work with the police in Mountainview, New Jersey. I'm a university professor."

He frowned. "Are you a profiler?"

"More or less."

Stan chimed in. "I've worked with Doctor Wise before. He can be a great help."

"I hope so," Milton said and crossed his arms. "Agent Frazier tells me you're the reason we're here."

I shrugged. "Actually, we're here because a witness claimed he saw a stone sepulcher inside the Vanderbilt tomb that fits the description of a sacrificial altar we've been trying to locate."

He stared at me for a moment, then turned to Stan. "What is he talking about?"

Stan held up his hands in a calming manner. "We have reason to believe that a young woman is being held someplace similar to a church."

"And how did you get that intel?" Milton demanded.

"I am not at liberty to share that," Stan maintained, which got a lifted eyebrow from the cop. "Come on, Milton, we're just going to take a look. If there is nothing to see, we'll take off."

"We pulled a lot of assets to get here in a hurry," Milton objected, "and you're not at liberty to explain?"

"It's an underage girl that was abducted," Stan explained, trying to ease the officer's annoyance.

"We thought this was an imminent situation. Now you're telling me you just want a 'look'?" The big man shook his head in exasperation.

There was a knock at the roll-up metal door, and Stan, in one swift movement, pulled it up to find a uniformed officer standing outside.

He was an average-height white guy with a brown mustache, and he looked right to Milton. "Sir, the caretaker is here."

Milton nodded. "I'll get him to open the gate and we can drive in. Are you familiar with the Vanderbilt tomb?"

Stan looked to me and I shook my head.

Ward piped up. "I've been there. We can drive all the way up to it."

Milton nodded. "That's right. But we may have to walk a bit." He glanced at my cane and extended right leg. "Can you handle that?"

"Yes, sir," I replied.

Stan cleared his throat. "After he opens the front gate, ask him to join us here."

Milton turned to Stan. "Good idea. Let's get ready to move out."

Milton went out, and Stan rolled the door back down. He then went to the front and opened a small window between the back and the cab and spoke to the driver.

He watched what was going on through the front windshield and signaled to one of the agents, who got up and opened the rear door once again. The agent then helped an older man into the van. He was a short fellow with white hair and a mustache. He was wearing one of those winter coats that looked like a series of interconnected inner tubes and added some much-needed bulk to his thin frame.

As he stepped into the back of the van, he looked around at the group of us and muttered, "Oh my."

Stan turned to him. "Please, come in, Mister—?"

"Jacobson," he offered and smiled. "Sorry if I seemed surprised. It's just that we don't usually have armed men..." He glanced to the two female agents. "Um... people... here in the cemetery."

Stan moved over and sat on the bench opposite us and gestured for Jacobson to sit next to him. The timing was perfect, for just as the old man sat, the vehicle shuddered and began to move.

Stan went on. "Have you seen any activity around the Vanderbilt tomb?"

"Hmm?" Jacobson considered. "Oh, there are always thrill-seekers and young people trying to get to it, probably because it's thought to be haunted. A woman tried to get through one of the iron doors back in the sixties, and it fell on her and killed her. We had to put a fence up around that section of the cemetery, to keep out the curious."

I cleared my throat and spoke. "I understand there's a stone coffin inside the tomb."

Jacobson looked over at me. "Oh yes, quite spectacular. But how do you know about it? That tomb has been locked up for decades." He sat back as the van jostled us. "Of course, we occasionally get people interested in the architecture. It was built in the Romanesque revival style, and the landscape was done by Frederick Law Olmsted with—"

Stan interrupted, "That's all well and good, Mister Jacobson, but we are more interested in whether anyone could have gotten into the tomb without you knowing it."

"What?" Jacobson responded, perplexed. "I don't see how. The metal gate is locked, and that area is completely surrounded by the chain-link fence. We also have private security at night and weekends, and we have staff here during the week, and I'm always on call."

I inserted myself. "Could someone have found a way in? Have you been aware of any odd happenings or events?"

Jacobson sighed heavily. "Unfortunately, we've been listed on the internet in a lot of sites that feature 'haunted' locales. But our security team is very professional. They've found and turned away many a drunken 'ghost-chaser' on a Saturday night, I'll tell you that." He sat up straighter in the seat just as it bounced over another bump in the road. "The metal doors on the tomb are checked once a month by me, and I would notice if there had been any tampering."

I smiled. "That's good to know. When did you last check them?"

"Oh, about three weeks ago, I imagine."

The truck came to a stop, and Stan got to his feet and went to the small sliding panel. He opened it and looked out through the windshield of the vehicle. "Mister Jacobson, we've reached the gate."

Jacobson extracted a large ring of keys from one of his pockets as the back door rolled up. He was helped down by Stan and two other FBI agents, and they walked out of sight.

I peered out the large open space. I grabbed a metal handle that protruded outside the back of the vehicle, and using it, I swung out to see the road ahead of us.

We had ventured deep into the cemetery, surrounded by rows of weathered gravestones and timeworn tombs, their surfaces etched with names and dates long past.

Ahead, Jacobson was approaching a monumental stone archway alongside Stan. The arch soared nearly thirty feet into the air, its elegant curve framing a massive opening beneath. Securing the entrance was a wrought-iron fence, at least eight feet tall, spanning wide enough to accommodate two lanes of traffic.

Towering earthen walls flanked the arch on both sides, and the builders constructed them from enormous, rugged boulders that they must have carved and stacked with great effort.

Rising above these formidable stone walls was a chain-link fence, about ten feet high, reinforcing the barrier around the perimeter. Jacobson produced a key and inserted it into a large silver lock mounted on the gate. With a satisfying twist, the lock clicked open.

The two FBI agents pulled the heavy gates apart, clearing the path ahead as our vehicle bounced steadily up the hill, the gravel crunching beneath the tires.

In just about two minutes, we came to a halt, and through the open back door, I saw the grassy expanse of a courtyard before us.

The team swiftly and silently dropped to the ground, weapons raised as they halted and meticulously scanned the terrain.

Ward graciously helped me lower myself to the ground, and I took in our surroundings more fully. It truly resembled a courtyard of an old castle, bordered by a low semicircular wall constructed from neatly cut stone.

Beyond that wall stretched a dense wooded area, the trees still barren and skeletal from the grip of winter.

The FBI agents eased their machine guns down so they pointed toward the ground, the weapons hanging from the slings looped over their shoulders. Yet, each agent kept one hand firmly on the pistol grip, a silent testament to their readiness.

I realized they could swiftly bring their weapons into action at a moment's notice if the situation demanded it—a quiet but constant vigilance etched into their movements.

Stan turned to Darren and me. "You two stay behind the truck until we've cleared the tomb. You got that?"

Both of us nodded in agreement.

The tomb loomed ahead of us, a formidable gray sentinel rising at least two stories high. Constructed from massive, rectangular blocks of stone—granite, I presumed—it ascended in a stepped, pyramid-like fashion. From the center of its flat roof, two rounded domed towers soared upward, their stained-glass windows glittering vividly in the bright sunlight.

I stared at that shimmering glass; it must have been the very panes Henessey had repaired during his recent visit to the tomb.

Around us, the only sounds were the measured crunches of footsteps breaking the silence as they pressed across the frozen earth. This was a group of seasoned professionals, well-trained to approach a crime scene with restraint and quiet precision.

Yet something was unsettlingly off. I saw no squirrels or birds, and despite the cold weather, they had been appearing in New Jersey, but in this stretch of land, I didn't see even one. The woods around us were as dead as the cemetery itself.

As we neared the front of the building, I paused to admire the intricate stone carvings, a testament to the remarkable skill the builders achieved using only simple nineteenth-century tools.

The craftsmanship was nothing short of stunning.

Builders meticulously etched massive, solid stone blocks to form elegant pillars that rose proudly from the foundation. Several gracefully rounded arches framed three sturdy gray-painted metal doors, each secured with multiple heavy-duty locks, suggesting a fortress-like strength beneath the beauty.

Above, they adorned the second level with slender, ornate pillars and narrow openings, too thin even to slip a hand through. Yet these delicate features had been carefully hewn and shaped, transforming the façade into a standing work of art that blended strength with refined detail.

Mister Jacobson pulled his large ring of keys again and began to go through them as the FBI agents and the NYPD officers waited. Ward and I stood by the truck in silence, awed by the edifice that stood before us.

Ward whispered to me, "You did say you were looking for something like a church."

I nodded and murmured in reply, "This certainly has the feel of one. And it is a place where no one would be around to disturb you."

"I dunno," he clucked. "I doubt you could bring people here without it being noticed."

Jacobson finally pinpointed the correct key from his large ring and stepped forward to insert it in the top lock of the middle metal door. It turned grudgingly but came open. He then bent down and attempted the lower lock.

Ward spoke in a hushed tone. "Seems like a lot of trouble to keep a few vagrants away."

"But if our guy was using it, it makes it difficult for anyone to interrupt him," I pointed out.

Jacobson finally got the key to turn and removed it, then pulled at the door, which creaked on long-unused hinges.

Twin flashlights appeared in the hands of two of the agents, who got on their knees on either side of the open door and cast the beams into the vault. The other pair, a man and a woman, raised their weapons, which also appeared to have flashlights, and carefully entered the dark room, going low and high as they went.

Ward and I stood less than two dozen feet away, and I could see some colored lights inside the darkened tomb, which I assumed was sunlight coming through the stained-glass windows at the top of the building.

A voice yelled "Clear!" from inside.

Stan nodded and signaled for me to approach. As Ward stepped forward, Stan held up his arm to stop him.

"Not you," he growled. "You stay out here."

I saw anger flash on Ward's face, but it quickly faded. He made a curt nod and stepped back.

As I drew near, Stan pulled out two pairs of nitrile gloves and offered one pair to me. I put on the gloves as we approached the burial chamber, and Stan pulled a flashlight off his belt and showed the light around the room.

The air was thick, stale. Clearly, no one had opened the tomb in a very long time.

As Henessey had promised, dominating the center of the room stood a magnificent sepulcher crafted from gleaming black marble —so grand and imposing it could have rivaled those built for a pharaoh. The polished surface shimmered with intricate white veining, tracing delicate, natural patterns that enhanced the stone's striking beauty. Mesmerized, I reached out my hand to feel the cool, smooth texture beneath my fingertips.

Stan stopped me. "Hold on, professor, let me check it." He went over the surface with his light.

By now, Mister Jacobson had come into the room and was speaking. "Beautiful, isn't it? The outside of the tomb is carved from Quincy granite, but the coffin, the centerpiece, is Nero Marquina marble that had to be imported from Spain."

Stan was looking closely at the surface of the coffin, and he glanced up at me. "I don't see anything." He showed the light around the room, where there was a layer of dust that had only been disturbed by the pair of agents and ourselves. "Look at the footprints we're leaving. No one but us has been here in a long time."

"Let me try something," I suggested.

"Your special way?" Stan inquired quietly.

"Exactly."

Stan turned to the older man. "Mister Jacobson, could you leave us alone here for a minute?"

The little man blinked in surprise and headed for the door.

Stan then called out to the pair of agents, "Kent, Thompson, clear the room, please."

The two agents, who had long since lowered their weapons, exited behind Jacobson.

"Is it okay if I watch?" Stan proposed.

"It's fine. McGee usually listens to me babble when I get impressions."

"Okay."

I closed my eyes and focused on my breath as I moved into an alpha state. As I did, I pulled the glove off my right hand and touched the side of the large casket.

I caught fleeting glimpses: first, a massive stone being laboriously heaved from the earth; then an elderly stonecutter, his weathered hands and keen eyes studying the raw block before him with quiet reverence, cautiously beginning to chisel away at its rough surface.

Later, I saw the same man tenderly hand-polishing the now finely crafted stone box, his touch gentle as if honoring something sacred.

In the next vision, the scene shifted to this very room, filled with a somber gathering of men and women dressed in dark, formal attire. Faces etched with grief and solemn respect as they lowered the heavy lid slowly, sealing away the lifeless corpse of Cornelius Vanderbilt beneath it.

I tried to go deeper, to see if there was more, but all I received were the same images as they repeated themselves.

Finally, I dropped my hand and took a deep breath.

"Anything?"

"Nothing." I shook my head grimly. "I was wrong. This isn't the place."

15. HALLOWED RENEWAL

"There you go, off in your own world again."

Jyanette's smile across the small kitchen table at my house brought me back to awareness with a start. The twin candle centerpiece reflected brightly in her eyes as she leaned back in her chair and watched me.

"Sorry," I admitted sheepishly. "I guess I'm still going over the case."

She reached across the table and took my hand. "Well, tomorrow is my birthday, and I fully expect all of your attention tonight."

"I can't help feeling that maybe I was overconfident."

"I think you're being too hard on yourself," she reassured me.

I sighed. "You aren't the one who led everybody on a wild goose chase to an empty tomb."

"And I don't see that I ever would. But you and I have different jobs and distinct skill sets."

"I can't understand why I'm doing so badly on this one."

Jyanette sighed. "You chased a lead that didn't pan out. I'm sure you know this happens to the police all the time. Ask McGee if you don't believe me."

"I believe you," I said and squeezed her hand lightly in response. "I'm just a little frustrated."

"I can see that." She sat back, grabbed her glass of wine, took a sip, and gave me a knowing look. "I believe I can help ease some of your frustrations."

I smiled and picked up my mug to have a sip of tea. We had the kitchen to ourselves as Mrs. Higgins had gone out for the evening with a friend.

"Sounds nice," I agreed. "I have to say, your call informing me of your availability was a surprise. I thought you'd be with your parents."

"I insisted Dad take Mom out for a romantic dinner," she explained. "Was calling you last minute too much trouble?"

"No, it gave me a reason to leave the scene, even though it was with egg on my face. You gave me an excuse to run home and cook."

"And you made a fine dinner, too," she confirmed, indicating the empty plates in front of us. "The pasta with a cream sauce, and those little peas. You know it's one of my favorites."

"Sorry I couldn't swing dessert."

"After cake last night, I don't need it. Besides, I wanted to tell you you're officially invited to join us for brunch tomorrow."

"Your father's all right with that?"

It was her turn to sigh. "Len, I really want him to like you."

"That's what I want as well."

"Then try to win him over, please? I know how charming you can be. Consider it my birthday present."

"Actually, I have your birthday present."

"Do tell?" she said as an evil grin grew on her face. "Are you planning to ravish me here on the kitchen table?"

"That wasn't it. However, I might be persuaded."

She chuckled and took another sip of wine. "You know, I would do it, except we don't know when Margery is due home. I wouldn't want her to catch us doing that on her table."

I couldn't fight the smile myself. "Might be awkward. But wait here and I'll get you the humble gifts I have." I rose and headed for the swinging kitchen door.

"You really can't afford to buy me things," she called after me.

"I know. That's why it's just some small things, but I thought you'd like them."

"It's a them?"

"Indeed." I pushed through the door and reached over to the small table where Mrs. Higgins and I throw our keys in a candy dish. Down on the lower shelf near its feet, I grabbed a plastic bag I'd placed there earlier.

I heard her voice through the kitchen door. "I hope the people you're working with weren't too upset that you missed."

I pushed my way in with the bag and limped over to the table, carrying my cane. "Stan was good about it. The PI, Darren Ward, was pretty annoyed." I placed the bag in front of her. "He didn't speak to me the entire drive back to his office."

She gazed at the plastic bag and one eyebrow went up. "Is this the wrapping?"

"No, the presents are inside and wrapped," I told her as I sat. "I'm an underpaid professor, not a dunce."

She pulled out the first package, cylindrical and tied with red ribbon. She giggled like a naughty child. "It's not a sex toy, is it?"

I pretended to be shocked. "I thought I was your sex toy."

"You'll do," she chortled and ripped the paper.

"How often does a man get a compliment like that?" I wondered aloud.

She pulled the cloth from the cylinder, still unsure what it was. "Don't worry, I don't feel a need to replace you."

She unrolled the T-shirt, looked at the message on it, and broke into loud guffaws. "This is perfect." She turned it to face me and held it up to her chest. It read: "Hands Off My Hair." The word 'Off' was in a bold black font, and the rest of the sentence was in swirly pink letters.

"You've told me stories about people touching your hair, which I completely understand as it fascinates me," I said. "I thought this might help."

"It's a black woman thing, honestly," she replied, a big smile still on her face. "Some people just reach out and touch my hair without asking, and it is very disconcerting."

"So, that's the comedic gift."

"Well, it's perfect for when I go to the gym, and it's a big step, you buying clothes for me."

"A T-shirt is pretty easy. I'm glad you like it."

She reached out and took my hand. "I like it because it shows you listen to me, even something as small as complaining about people touching my hair. That makes it a great gift."

"There's more."

She reached into the bag and pulled out the second present, which was a box wrapped in the same bright paper.

"We should save this for tomorrow. That way, my parents can see me open it." Her voice grew conspiratorial. "Unless it's something I can't open in front of them."

It was my turn to laugh. "No, it's fine. You can open it in public with no repercussions."

"Good, then save it until then." She stood, came over to my side of the table, and got down on one knee. "I guess I should thank you."

She brought her lips to mine, and we fell into a passionate kiss. Her hand slid down my leg and touched me as I groaned. "I got the desired effect."

"Oh yes," I said breathlessly as she continued to rub me intimately. "Can you stay?"

"Long enough to take care of this," she murmured and kissed me again. She rose, pulled me upright.

"I adore you, birthday girl," I sighed.

She took my left hand and led me toward the hall and my end of the house. "I believe it's time I put on my birthday suit."

"I would love to help."

"Oh, I have several tasks for you."

We soon were in my room where I lit several candles on top of my bureau, kicked off my shoes, and got into bed.

Jyanette undressed slowly, pulling off each piece of her outfit gradually in an impromptu, tantalizing dance. She undressed at a frustratingly leisurely pace, as I yanked off my clothes while watching her.

Finally, in nothing but her magnificent naked body, she approached the bed.

She slid next to me like silk. I lost myself to desire from one inhale of her musky scent. Her right hand dropped to my thigh, as my hands moved to her breasts, touching, caressing, arousing.

My fingers cavorted over her flesh, making goosebumps appear as I fondled her in an intimate frenzy. The heat was powerful, but we took a quick moment for my lady to place a condom on me.

We then moved together to join our bodies in an intoxicated choreography of limbs, never moving the same way twice as both of us moaned in ecstasy, caught in the ancient dance of love.

We lay in the warm afterglow, both of us breathing heavily from our exertions and coming down from the intense flush of passion.

The candles burned on top of the bureau; the flickering light showing each contour of her dark body as I held her.

She sighed as she rolled to the edge of the bed. "That was a great birthday present, but I have to get dressed and go home."

I placed my hand on top of hers to stop her.

She smiled. "I know you want me to stay, but I—"

I sat up. "There are some things I have to tell you. For your own safety." I took her hands.

"What's wrong?" She questioned as she turned and slipped back under the sheets.

I leaned against the headboard with a serious expression. "That phone call you got asking for my number? It wasn't a cop. I think it was the man I call Thin Guy."

She frowned. "Is he the perp?"

"Yes."

She rolled her eyes, annoyed. "I would've preferred to know about that sooner."

Gesturing helplessly, I said, "I've only known since you told me about that phone call this morning."

"You knew this morning?" she scolded. "You should have told me then and there."

I couldn't suppress a smile. "If you recall, you were busy showering and insisting I leave."

"Okay, I'll give you that," she conceded, and her expression darkened. "Is there anything else you're keeping from me?"

I thought of the glimpse I had seen of her ex-husband when he followed me in the black and red car.

"Why are you hesitating?" she demanded, her eyes narrowing in suspicion.

"It's just..."

"Damn! I knew it!" She turned her back to me, her temper flaring, her arms crossed over her chest. "You always keep things from me."

"It's not that."

She slid out from the sheets, stood, and glared down at me. "Okay, so what exactly is it?"

"I don't want to upset you on your birthday... with your parents here."

She went around the bed and grabbed her bra, placing it over her breasts as she spoke. "You do only two things that upset me: you show up looking like roadkill and you keep things from me!"

She shouted the last few words.

"I wanted you to have a nice—"

"Talk!" she insisted as she pulled on her panties.

I exhaled heavily. "I think your ex-husband has been stalking me."

This surprised her. She stopped dressing and stared blankly at me. "Antoine? Stalking you? How?"

I reached out and grabbed my cane, getting up from bed in the nude. "When I drove home from your place, a car followed me. I trapped it in a cul-de-sac and saw it was your ex. And I should tell you, I think I saw the same car at the restaurant where we all ate."

She considered this seriously as she grabbed her dress and stepped into it, saying nothing.

I went on. "I didn't want to tell you because I didn't want to scare you. I thought with your parents here, you would be safe."

"He followed you," she repeated. "And at the restaurant…"

She turned, and I pulled the zipper on the back of her dress up as I told her, "He's somehow involved in all of this."

She spun to stare at me, different emotions passing over her face.

I felt the need to push my point. "Can you understand why I'm concerned?" I again took her hands in mine. "I want to make sure you're on your guard."

"Len, you know that as an ADA, I have a firearm for personal protection and a concealed-carry permit."

"I know, but you might think your ex-husband is harmless."

She gazed at our combined hands. "No, I don't think he's harmless at all. That's why I divorced him."

"So, it was more than the drugs?" I asked.

"Yeah," she whispered and pulled her hands away, grabbing the small, short jacket that was part of her outfit and slowly putting it on. "It was the day I finished law school. Man, I worked so hard, I had only been home to sleep during my finals. Besides, at that point, it wasn't a marriage anymore. I didn't enjoy his company, and he never spoke my name with softness. He had a rage he couldn't suppress, and I was his only target, so I avoided him. But I graduated and, to my surprise, Antoine came to the ceremony."

"That was nice."

"Sure, but it was all part of his game. He was high at the ceremony. I mean, he wasn't yelling or calling attention to himself, but I could see it. I recognized the indicators." She shook her head. "I guess anyone married to an addict recognizes them."

"What did you do?"

"I got my diploma and found my parents. Antoine came up to us and congratulated me. He told me he was proud of me."

"I see."

"Daddy told me not to go home with him. I explained we had separate cars and that I wouldn't drive with him."

"Good choice."

"Well, my folks and I went out to dinner, and then I went back to the house. Antoine was there, and he'd taken something after the ceremony." She couldn't meet my eyes. "He began yelling that I thought I was too good for him. He told me I was his wife and he was going to prove it."

"My God, Jyanette."

Her lips were a tight line. "He slapped me. I never saw it coming. It was the first time he'd ever struck me." Her eyes were far away, lost in memory. "The force of it surprised me. I hadn't expected him to be so strong. It was like being hit with a piece of meat." She turned away from me and summoned the courage to continue. "He—he forced himself on me, ripped my clothes. I should've fought, should have yelled, screamed, something."

"You were in shock," I suggested.

"He yelled words at me, all of the anger spilling out of this man who once spoke of love. We had... sex... It certainly wasn't making love. I just wanted him to get it over with. He grabbed me by my throat and choked me as he... you know."

I took her hand and kissed it, regretting I had brought this up and wishing I could take her pain away but knowing I could not.

"He finally let me go and rolled off me. Then he went off to take another toke of whatever he was smoking." She looked at me, her eyes wet. "He used me, like I was nothing. No love, no compassion. I was just a warm place he could stick it. I lay in the bed, my clothes askew, until I heard him lie down on the sofa. I waited until he fell asleep before I went to the bathroom and cleaned myself up. Then, I packed what I could and left that night. Fortunately, Daddy helped me find a new apartment the next day."

"I don't know what to say," I murmured helplessly.

"There's nothing to say, nothing anyone could say. I filed for divorce, and that took almost a year. But I got free, and I got myself together. I saw therapists and fought to not let him define my life. That incident was over two years ago, and you're the first man I've been with since him."

I opened my arms. She stepped into them, and we just held each other.

After about a minute, she spoke softly. "You've shown me that sex can be good again, Len. That it can be beautiful, wonderful, and fun."

I couldn't think of anything to alleviate her pain. I moved my mouth to hers and kissed her gently, almost chastely.

She pulled back with a weak smile. "It's almost eleven and I have to get home. Did you know it's supposed to snow?"

"Snow?" I repeated dumbly. "How early do I have to be at your place?"

"I guess about nine. I have to get up earlier than that and put my hair in shape, and you know how long that takes."

"Yes, I do. And I know not to interrupt you once the process has begun." I needed to add something to let her know it was all right. "I love you, Jyanette Emery, and I'm grateful that you are in my life."

Her eyes sparkled in the candlelight. "And I love you, Leonard Wise. Now let me get home."

She rose and headed for my sitting room, going out the side door that led directly outside.

I looked over at the candles flickering on the bureau and thought that I should probably blow them out before I fell asleep. On the other hand, they were in protective holders, so there was no danger of causing a fire. I had mixed feelings — pleased that my darling trusted me enough to tell me of this experience and angry at the man who had once been her husband.

My phone rang with its odd musical tone.

I groaned and looked around for it. Had I plugged it in to recharge it? Or in my lust, did I just leave it in the pocket of whatever I had been wearing?

I glanced over to the candles and there it sat, vibrating madly, jiggling and slowly creeping along the surface of the dark wooden dresser.

I limped naked to my phone, which listed 'Unknown Caller' on the screen.

The same thing as when Thin Guy called me.

I glanced around the room to make sure the drapes were closed. I suddenly felt very exposed.

I hit the button and spoke. "H-hello?"

"Is this Leonard Wise?" came an unfamiliar voice.

I exhaled, surprised that I had been holding my breath. Whoever it was, at least it wasn't Thin Guy.

"This is Leonard Wise. Who is this?"

"This is Antoine Powell, Mister Wise. And… you've got to help me."

16. APPLIED ACCOMPLICE

I stood, unmoving, trying to get my mind around what I was hearing. "Antoine Powell?"

"Yes, can you meet me? I need your help."

"Considering the girls you abducted the other night, I don't know how safe that would be."

"You know about that?" he fretted. "That's why I need your help. Claude's gone crazy."

"Claude? Is that Thin Guy's name?"

"Yes, it's the drug, the damn drug he made."

"You mean like the one he gave the girls?" I demanded. "Purple on one end, green on the other?"

"How did you—? No, that's the one that lets him control people. It's the special one only he takes," Antoine went on, his voice tinny as it came through my phone. "I thought it was just to get high, but now he's killing people. He stabbed that girl, and he's going to kill the other one. You gotta stop him."

"Go to the police. You can tell them what you know."

"No, if he senses a raid, he'll kill her."

"I don't see how I can help—"

"Can you meet me?" he pleaded.

"What? No!"

"He's going to kill that girl tonight at midnight."

I looked over at my digital clock, which read 10:30. At midnight, it would be Sunday — the day of the full moon and the Equinox.

McGee had been off by a day.

I exhaled in frustration. "I'll meet you. Tell me where."

There was a short hesitation. "I just pulled into your driveway."

"What?"

"I saw Jyanette leave your place and I thought—"

"You're spying on me?" I exclaimed, shocked by this revelation, and even more upset that my extra senses didn't pick up on it.

"I had to. He's crazy! I waited until Jyanette drove off before I pulled in the driveway."

Danger...

Now, I received a buzz, like it was any kind of warning at this point. I didn't need ESP to know that I was being invited into a trap. But, if I didn't go with him, Erica would die.

"Are you still there?" he asked. "We have to move if we're going to save that girl."

"I'm not dressed," I rationalized. "Give me five minutes."

"Okay," he blurted and ended the call.

I decided that for once, I was not walking into jeopardy without backup. I quickly hit a familiar number on my phone.

"Frazier," growled the voice over the line.

"Stan, it's Len," I said, as I picked up my underwear from the floor and pulled them on.

"What the hell are you doing calling me at this time of night —"

"Stan, I don't have time to talk. Antoine Powell is in my driveway. He says his partner is crazy and he's going to kill Erica Marconi at midnight."

"Jesus!" Stan bellowed. "Have you got a location?"

"He's insisting I go with him to stop Thin Guy, whose name is Claude."

"Professor, you're not seriously considering going with him?"

"Listen to me! Is there anything I can do to my phone so you can track me?" I threw on my shirt and began to button it.

"Len, I cannot support—"

"Stan, we only have a little more than an hour, and it will take half that long to get to Staten Island. Stan, please tell me what to do! There's no time to send anyone here."

"All right," he griped. "This is against my better judgment."

"Mine as well."

"Turn off your passcode, and make sure your location services are engaged…"

As I dressed, Stan walked me through everything I needed to do, including giving him my cloud account and password, so he could follow me in real time. I got dressed as quickly as I could and was sent an authorization code. I spoke the six-digit code to Stan, which allowed him total access.

It took a total of eight minutes, but I was dressed and headed for the front door to grab my heavy coat. I ended the call with Stan, turned the ringer off my phone, and stashed it in an inner pocket. At least if I was searched, the device would be a little harder to find.

I stepped out into the cold night, my breath misting around my head as I pulled gloves on. Antoine flashed the headlights of the familiar black and red car, and I limped over, cane supporting my leg.

I was glad to bring my cane, which meant that at least I had a weapon, albeit not much help if I was caught in a gunfight. But if Claude — who I still thought of as Thin Guy — came at me with that kris knife, maybe I could defend myself.

I walked to the car, pulling the passenger door open. The light inside went on, and I could clearly see Antoine, his expression anxious.

"Thanks for coming out," he murmured.

"You left me little choice," I fumed as I manipulated myself into the front seat. At least it had room for my leg. Some sports cars have so little legroom that I can't get into them at all.

"I'm sorry about that," he lamented. "In fact, I'm sorry about all of it."

He shifted the car into gear and pulled through the circular driveway to take us to the street.

"Did you know Claude was going to kill Constance?" I demanded, as we moved quietly down the darkened streets on our way to the highway.

"Was that the blonde's name?" He exhaled sadly and looked pained as he manipulated the gearshift.

"Yes, and the other girl is Erica. Why is he doing this?"

"At first, I thought he was kidnapping them for money or something," Antoine whined as he drove. "I didn't question him."

"Why do you do what he says? Is it so he'll give you the drugs?"

"No, it's more than that, and more than one drug. He's a chemist. He invented these pills. One makes you stop thinking, the other…man, it's like you're one with the universe." He shook his head.

"The one he gave to Constance, is that the one that makes you stop thinking?"

"It gets you high, but more than that, you become very open to suggestion, to doing what you're told," Antoine explained. "That's how I got involved in the Following."

"The Following?" I repeated. "What's that?"

"It's the group that serves us. Well, serves him." Antoine pulled the car onto Interstate 78 and we headed toward the turnpike. "According to Claude, it was all to serve the will of Astarte."

"Astarte?" I frowned, the name vaguely familiar. "What is that?"

Antoine was frustrated as he tried to clarify. "I'm doing the best I can. I'm straight right now, but I'm going through withdrawal."

"What are you coming down from? Benzodiazepine? Cocaine? Heroine?"

"None of that. I told you, it's stuff he invented. Makes you feel good and obedient, depending on the dose. But coming off it, you get really paranoid."

I sat back in my seat. "Are you okay to drive?"

"Yeah, in fact, my head's clearer than it's been in a while. But I'm hurting." Antoine's mouth became a tight line. "It wasn't my fault, you know, the drugs."

"Yeah, they just jump down your throat," I spat.

"I got injured in a car accident years ago. Got addicted to OxyContin, then Xanax. Most of the time, I could keep it under control, but now and then, I lost it."

I struggled to control the anger that suddenly flashed through me. "Yeah, I heard what you did to Jyanette the day she graduated law school."

He hung his head. "She told you about that?"

"Damn straight," I fumed. "If it weren't for the fact that I want to save Erica Marconi, you and I would go at it right now, you bastard."

The car was silent as he continued to drive.

"You're right," he muttered. "I was a bastard. A stupid bastard who lost the finest woman I ever knew. Drugs became more important than her, and I abused her that night because I was just so angry. I regret that every day."

"Really? You say that now while you have the blood of that innocent girl on your hands?"

"I didn't know he was going to kill her!" he stormed.

"What did you think he wanted with that special knife you got for him? Look, Potts has given you up. You made the devices that allowed him to steal the knife. What did you think Claude wanted it for?"

"I didn't know!" Antoine shouted, his voice loud in the little car. He focused on the road. "Man, that's all we need."

"What?"

"Look for yourself," he said with a shake of his head toward the windshield.

I looked straight ahead to see white flakes falling onto the roadway in the beams of the headlights.

Snow.

It wasn't coming down heavily, but he slowed the speed of the vehicle.

"Just like he said it would," Antoine marveled.

I watched the flakes as they fell onto the road. We'd reached the NJ Turnpike and were heading south toward the Goethals Bridge.

"Big deal," I pointed out. "So he heard a weather forecast."

"You don't get it. It's the other drug he created. The one he takes. It lets him see the future."

"That's utter crap," I spat.

"No, it's not. You see, he found a plant. He called it Jimsonweed."

I glanced over. I was familiar with Jimsonweed. It had a history of being used by Native Americans in sacred rituals. It was part of the nightshade family and known for producing hallucinations and intense visions. Controlling the dosage tightly would be crucial, as it could otherwise be deadly.

"What about it?" I inquired. "It's a common enough weed."

He nodded. "You know better. He said you would know better."

"What about it?" I repeated.

"He combined it with Henbane, then examined the molecule. He studied it and synthesized an artificial version."

"What?"

"I only tried it once, but it was amazing."

I stared ahead of us. The snow was coming down more heavily. "What do you mean?"

"It opened my mind," he spoke excitedly. "I could see…things. I knew things, I could feel people's thoughts." He weighed his next words. "It was like being a god."

"You said you only took it once. If it was like being a god, how come?"

"The comedown was terrible." He shook his head sadly and slowed the speed of the car. "I saw monsters, demons, things that scared the hell out of me."

"How does Claude avoid the crash?"

"He never comes down."

"You mean he keeps taking it?"

"Exactly."

I considered this carefully. Jimsonweed was a powerful alkaloid and a famed hallucinogen. Combining it with henbane, which also had a history of psychogenic effects, would alter one's brain chemistry.

Both could be fatal in their natural states. But if Antoine was correct, had Claude created a synthetic version with the toxicity removed? If so, could it have the effect of opening the latent abilities of the human mind?

Even if it wasn't toxic any longer, constant drug use could lead to dangerous side effects in the body. It sounded to me that Claude had become an addict of his own creation, and I was sure it had to be affecting his mind.

"You mentioned the Following? How many are in this group?"

He exhaled heavily, his eyes focused on the road as we crossed over into Staten Island. "Uh, eight…no, ten."

Ten people I might have to face, along with Antoine and Claude. I had faced a cult of true believers the previous November and barely gotten out of that situation alive. The odds looked terrible for me. I needed to keep Antoine off-balance. "Who are these people, and why would they assist Claude in killing Constance?"

"They're students, like Claude."

I turned to face him. "Students? Claude's a student?"

"Yeah, at Vanderbilt College. He said you knew that."

I was now aware why I kept getting the name 'Vanderbilt' over and over, and the reason the sign for the college caught my eye, as well as my mind. It wasn't so that I would call an old acquaintance, which is what I ended up doing. The buzz was to get me to investigate the college.

But I had gotten Antoine to open up, and he went on. "It started so innocently. I was there to do an upgrade on computers at the college when I met Claude. He seemed to know everything about me, like he could read my mind. Turns out he could."

"Because of the drug — what did he call it?"

"He just referred to it as 'Miracle'."

"Were you using at the time?"

"Not steadily. I'd been trying to straighten out. But the first time I took that purple and green pill—"

"That was the one that makes you high?"

"That's right. When you're on it, you really will agree to anything. That's the one he gave to the kids in the Following."

"What else did he do?" I proposed. "Did he suppress negative thoughts against the group and re-label people's feelings towards their family? That's what cults do."

"It wasn't like that."

We were traveling on the Staten Island Expressway, and the snow was coming down in large, heavy flakes. He'd slowed down to about twenty-five miles per hour as he took the Clove Street exit.

"You mentioned Astarte. What is that?"

He watched the road. "The goddess."

"Goddess?"

He nodded solemnly. "The goddess made flesh."

I felt a chill up my spine. "What does that mean?"

"According to Claude, she speaks to him. In his head."

"So it's a she?"

"An ancient goddess. I talked to her once as well."

"The time you took his 'Miracle'?"

He nodded. "When I spoke with her, it seemed like it all made sense. But now, it's just crazy."

"It's a pity a girl had to die before you realized that," I seethed.

We crossed over the highway, and in a few hundred feet, we turned onto the side road that led to the college.

I considered what he had said. The name finally clicked in my head. There was a Hittite fertility goddess whom the Greeks called Astarte. The Babylonians had also worshipped her as Eaoster. Judaism and Christianity had almost erased her because her rites required her followers to sacrifice their children.

As I considered this, Antoine spoke. "We still have time to stop him. He told me you were the only one who could stop him."

If I had been unsure that I was walking into a trap, it was now obvious. I hoped Stan was still on my trail.

As we neared the front of the college, Antoine steered the car onto a quiet side street. Towering beside us was a sleek, modern sports center constructed of gleaming brick, its multi-story facade stretching upward against the grey sky.

We passed it smoothly before Antoine turned into a spacious parking lot. He reached out and swiped a magnetic card, prompting a small gate to lift silently, granting us entry.

The ground was now blanketed with over two inches of pristine, freshly fallen snow, which continued to drift gently down, shimmering softly in the bright beams of the overhead lights that cast a cold glow across the lot.

Neatly lined rows of cars nestled beside a cluster of dormitory buildings. From the layout, I guessed this was the students' preferred parking area—conveniently close to their dorms.

"He did this here?" I wondered aloud. "I was sure it was a church." I turned to Antoine. "Is he using a chapel on campus?"

This made him smile. "So you don't know as much as Claude thought."

He turned so we faced away from the buildings and moved the car to an empty space that faced a forest across the road we'd just come up.

Antoine indicated the dark wooded area. "It's there."

"He's doing these things in the woods?" I gasped, completely dumbfounded. I recalled the visions I'd had with the stone altar and the room with all the candles. Had that been outdoors?

"It will be clear when we get there." He shut off the car and pushed his door open. I followed suit, opened my door, and used my cane and the door to help me get to my feet in the blanket of white that covered the ground.

I looked past the falling snow at the ominous woods. "So we're going in there to stop Claude?"

"To meet him," Antoine said and reached into his coat to extract a small handgun.

"Shit," I muttered as flakes fell around us.

He gestured with the gun. "I know you have your cell phone. Give it to me."

I reached into my hidden pocket and pulled it out. "I still owe some payments on that," I mentioned as I handed it to him.

He took a step back from me. "Funny," he muttered. He drew back and threw my cell high into the air and into the woods.

As he watched the phone fly, I swung my cane up, and with one forward thrust, brought the heavy cobra end up and against his left temple with surprising force.

He grunted as I made contact. The pistol fell from his hand, and he went down, falling onto the snow-covered pavement and sliding several inches. More concerned with my survival than his, I moved to the gun, grabbed it, and turned to face him with the weapon extended.

Antoine lay unmoving as the snow continued to descend. It was deathly quiet, except for the sound of the wind.

I was about five feet from him, but I watched him in case he was still conscious. I quickly pulled the magazine from the grip and looked into it, illuminated by the light from the street lamps.

It was empty. No bullets.

I hit the slide release and examined the chamber, but it was empty as well. The gun was unloaded. Apparently, he only wanted to use it as a threat, but his only option would be to hit me with it.

I slipped the gun into my pocket and approached Antoine, who lay unmoving as the snow collected on him. I pulled a glove off to touch his neck and feel for a pulse.

It was there and strong.

I couldn't leave him out there in the elements, though a part of me wanted to do so. But with a glance at my watch and the awareness that it was 11:40, I needed to take action and locate Claude and Erica.

I pulled the car keys from his pocket, popped his trunk, and unlocked the doors. In the trunk was a roll of duct tape, a blanket, and a flashlight.

All of them would come in handy.

I dragged the unconscious man to his car, which left a serpentine trail in the sea of white. I got him to the car and opened the rear doors. With effort, I lifted him up and pushed him onto his back seat, face down.

Pulling his hands behind his back, I taped the wrists together, just past his gloves. I then taped his legs over his pants at the ankles. I knew he could freeze in the car as well, so I took the blanket from the trunk and covered his body, leaving his head exposed. Hopefully, the situation would resolve before the temperature dropped any lower.

I closed and locked the car, then pocketed the keys. With the flashlight to light my way, I trudged through the snow, out of the lot, and across the street. I didn't know what was in those woods, but if Claude was there, then Erica would die unless I ventured forward.

17. COVETED CULT

As I shone the light up and down the shoulder of the road, I noticed a gap in the wooded curtain about the width of a driveway.

A chain blocked the path, attached to two bright-yellow posts. Snow had already layered the tops of the posts and chain, forming a ghostly white web across the path.

I cautiously unhooked the chain and dropped it. I then made an arrow heading inward with my gloved hand in the snow. This was probably a useless task as the arrow would soon fill in with fresh snow and the wind would erase it, but I wanted to leave something for Stan to follow if he found the way.

I walked down the snowy lane, leaving footprints as I went. My feet were already growing cold, and I wished I'd thought to wear more sensible footwear before I had undertaken this journey.

But that was before the snow, and my loafers were rapidly becoming wet.

I looked to the sides of the road and kept the beam of my flashlight pointed toward the ground so no one could see my approach from a distance. I observed the denuded trees that were just beginning to bud as their branches grew heavy under the wintery onslaught.

Up ahead were a pair of rounded, thick pillars constructed from cut stone and mortar, slowly disappearing under the blanket of white. One had fallen halfway over and leaned at an eccentric angle, looking like a crouching predator in the darkness. There was an open space beyond the pair of monoliths.

I observed a sign resting diagonally, since one support that held it had rotted away. It read:

St Albertus Magnus
School for Boys

This made sense: a Catholic school for boys. Here was the abandoned church I had been seeking.

I moved between the pillars and carefully lifted the light. In the open space before me, about twenty feet away, stood a forbidding building. It was at least five stories high and made from brick with stone apertures around windows long gone. The lower floors were probably classrooms, and the upper ones at one time had been living space.

The empty sills seemed to silently watch me.

Found the way, did you…?

I turned at the sound and flashed my light, my cane at the ready as a weapon. I saw no one as the heavy flakes continued to fall.

"Where are you?" I muttered.

A place you cannot harm me...

The voice was inside my head. I closed my eyes and concentrated.

Claude...

Ah, that's more what I expected from the 'Super Psychic of Scudder House'...

You must stop this...

When I am so close? Nonsense...

There is no reason to kill this girl...

A blood sacrifice is necessary. I was told that you must be a witness...

The ground seemed to glow, and a pathway of yellow light appeared.

Come and see what I can do now...

I cursed and focused my mind on white, nothing but white. The last thing I wanted was this maniac getting into my head and taking up residence. I used every technique I could to block my mind, and I grudgingly walked on the illuminated path. I knew that the light was merely a mental projection to guide me, and I also knew I was walking into a dangerous situation.

I could only hope that Stan was tracking my phone, and that the toss into the woods hadn't rendered it non-functioning.

I could really use the cavalry about this time.

Trudging through the intricate patterns of snow crystals as they floated down on me, each one swirled and danced and made the world seem pure. However, I was heading toward the impure, with a life in the balance.

I shivered from cold and fear, and pulled my coat tighter around me. There before me stood the silhouette of a bell tower yards away.

Just beyond the old school building, a stone chapel loomed large, dwarfing its surroundings with an air of solemn grandeur. The chapel stood about two stories high, its sharply pitched roof slicing into the sky like a dark arrow.

At its forefront, a towering bell tower soared above everything on the former school grounds. Rising to at least six stories, it culminated in a slender, pointed spire that pierced the winter night. Arched openings adorned the belfry on all four sides, allowing faint echoes of silent bells to imaginatively whisper through the cold air.

Halfway up the tower, intricately carved gargoyles clung to the stone, their grotesque forms twisted in eternal grimaces.

Under the shroud of the snowy twilight, these statues seemed alive—casting menacing shadows and evoking a chilling sense of ancient, lurking evils. They stood, silent sentinels of stone guarding forgotten secrets.

It wasn't necessary to dispatch Antoine...

The words appeared in my mind, with the sneering voice of Thin Guy. He got in despite my protections. This was not good.

He threatened me with a gun...

I focused on walling my mind away, not letting him in.

The mental chatter went silent again as I continued toward the chapel. As I drew closer, I could see an unsteady glow through stained-glass windows. The glow ebbed and flared, and I was sure it was candles elevated on the stanchions I'd seen in my vision.

I was still using the flashlight to watch my step as I passed through the snow, leaving footprints as I went. I noted that mine were the only ones in the fresh snow, so Claude might not be getting reinforcements. Or was his Following already there performing the desired rituals?

I directed the beam of my flashlight onto the uneven stone steps beneath me, their rough surfaces worn smooth by countless footsteps over the years. Slowly and cautiously, I climbed higher. As I reached the top and glanced upward, my eyes locked onto a face emerging from the shadows.

Startled, I uttered a sharp "Oh!" and nearly lost my balance. But as my vision adjusted, I realized it was only a statue— a solemn figure carved from stone. A skullcap adorned the man's head, a small rounded yarmulke like those my family wore for holidays.

His unblinking eyes, carved with meticulous detail, gazed down at me with an expression of pious pity. Draped in gracefully flowing robes that seemed to ripple in an eternal breeze, he stood as a silent sentinel. Clasped firmly in both hands was a stone book, while a quill pen rested flat against his arm, poised to inscribe wisdom. In his steadfast presence, he seemed to watch over the place with solemn reverence.

From the look of him, I decided it must be Saint Albertus. He stood gazing down the steps from his perch on the side of the entrance into the narthex.

Large wooden doors stood in front of me. I saw faded graffiti letters painted on the fine old wood, but the doors appeared undamaged.

I grabbed the handle and gave it a pull, and the door creaked slowly open. Once the opening was large enough for me to squeeze through, I went inside and pulled it closed behind me.

I was surprised that it was warmer inside the place of worship. Not a comfortable temperature, like at home, but better than the cold on the other side of the door.

Before me was a stoup, a waist-high, freestanding basin carved from stone. During the church's active period, people filled the central bowl with holy water. The container was currently empty.

I noticed a faint glow further inside the church, shining through a door that stood slightly ajar. Moving cautiously, I wished I had my phone, some bullets for the gun I'd taken, or anything to tip the odds in my favor.

My mind was shielded tightly—I'd locked down all my mental defenses—so I wasn't even open to the subtle warnings my heightened senses might have detected.

Stepping through the narthex, I approached the second door and edged a careful peek inside.

On the chancel stood a group of robed and hooded figures, perfectly still as if frozen in time. Large candles flickered atop five-foot-tall metal braziers beside them; their golden light cut through the gloom enough to relieve the darkness but not enough to bring the entire scene into sharp focus. The candles' flames cast towering, eerie shadows that stretched and twisted across the walls, transforming the figures into looming giants that seemed to hum with silent menace.

The floor was littered with debris where the pews had been long removed, giving the room a neglected, abandoned feel. Near the center, two small propane tanks sat side by side, each topped with a pair of heaters. Their glowing elements stared back at me like a pair of angry, unblinking eyes, adding another layer of unsettling presence to the dimly lit sanctuary.

There was a low chanting, Gregorian in style, that echoed throughout the space.

"You may as well come in, doctor," Claude called out over the sound of the intonation.

I pocketed the flashlight and slipped into the nave, my cane at the ready, the button that would release the sword near my finger.

My footsteps creaked on the wooden floor as I drew nearer. I could see the peeling paint on the walls, and the withered mortar which held together the stone arches that supported the roof. On the walls were the heavily cracked stained-glass windows, and the reflected candlelight danced and moved on them like waves, making them appear almost liquid. Thick cobwebs hung on every surface as I approached the transept and the stone steps that elevated the chancel and led to the raised altar.

The altar was stone; I guessed marble and elevated about four feet off the ground. Someone unceremoniously and clumsily chiseled away the cross originally carved into the stone on the side that faced the congregation.

On top of the altar lay a large blanket with a shape in it. As I drew nearer, I realized that there was a head sticking out the top of the cloth.

From the hair and the features, I knew who it was — Erica Marconi.

She appeared to be sleeping, but given Claude's fondness for pharmaceuticals, he had likely drugged her. On top of the blanket, near her feet, lay the silver Kris knife with the golden handle that had dispatched Constance. Removed from its sheath, both the metal of the knife and the jade on the sheath glimmered in the light of the nearby candles as their wicks blackened and the wax ran down the sides of each of the large white cylinders.

One of the robed figures turned to me. He was thin with a patchy beard, rotten teeth, and those bulging eyes — my Thin Guy, Claude.

He moved away from the ring of robed figures who continued to face the altar with their heads down. The chanting continued as he stepped down the stairs and approached me. The robe's sleeves hid his hands, and he raised one arm to expose a small handgun, which he happily aimed at me.

His voice was feverish. "I don't wish to shoot you, doctor, but I am aware of your habit of performing heroics. And let me assure you, I loaded this gun."

I stepped toward him, but Claude drew back to remain out of the range of my cane, the pistol fixed on my abdomen. Cautiously, I merely raised my hands in a pose of surrender.

"Did you kill her?" I demanded, with a glance over at Erica, who seemed terribly pale in the candlelight.

"Not yet. I had to wait until you were here to witness the act. I'm afraid Astarte insisted on it."

I made a sound of disgust. "Is that your demon girlfriend?"

Claude grinned his evil smile. "More likely your demon girlfriend."

I stared at him, my brow furrowed. "What does that mean?"

The smile grew. "You have to be careful what you conjure, boy."

The look on my face must have been shocking because Claude raised the gun, as if afraid that I might charge him.

"My, my," he laughed. "That really does hit you where you live. She said it would."

I tried to calm myself. That one phrase conjured all the loss and suffering gaining my abilities had caused. I needed to keep control of myself and keep him talking because if he was bragging to me, then he wasn't killing Erica. "You hear Astarte in your head. How? That drug you invented?"

"You have no idea. Then again, perhaps you do. Being able to hear thoughts, see visions. She said you could do that."

"Look, Claude, Antoine told me about the drug you made, based on Henbane and Jimsonweed—"

"Of course he did. I instructed him to do so."

I paused. Everything Antoine had revealed to me was merely to keep me involved and willing to go along. "You know those are two powerful hallucinogens. He said you were a chemist. You must know how dangerous those alkaloids are…"

"Yes, but I learned so much about them from Astarte. Did you know those two combined were what the oracle at Delphi used? The Pythia took the combination in tiny doses. Even so, it eventually drove each one mad. I synthesized a version that has all the benefits and none of the side effects."

"That's not possible."

"Isn't it? My drug opens the mind. My first attempt allowed me to contact Astarte, and she told me how to improve it. You know she can; you've heard me in your own head."

"Even if it has given you these abilities, the drug is affecting you. You can't go around killing people."

"You don't see what I see. These actions empower Astarte."

"You don't know that!"

"I do. She comes to me, speaks to me. I was told she will speak to you as well, this very night. It appears she has plans for you. Yes, such plans. And I am merely sacrificing two stupid girls to her. In ancient times, her shrines received hundreds of offerings at once."

"Humanity has moved beyond ritual killing!" I exclaimed.

"Have we?" His voice grew louder. "We sacrifice thousands of animals every day just to fill our bellies. This energy is what Astarte requires to feast upon."

"To what end?" I demanded, which made the smirk on Claude's face slide away. "There is no way out of this, Claude, where you don't end up in a cage. You have blood on your hands."

The smile returned. "You don't understand. I love her. I am more than willing to die for her."

I indicated the still figures who continued to chant around the altar. "Are the others in your Following willing to die for her as well?"

"You will know, you will see." He gestured with his gun. There was a lone chair, an old wooden one with a pair of armrests and four stout legs, close to the steps. "Get in that chair and drop the cane on the floor. Don't bother with the sword inside it."

He also possessed that information, which surprised me. Was he reading my mind, even with my barriers in place? Or was he pulling knowledge out of the very ether? And how did he know the one line from the night the demon appeared to me?

These questions ran through my mind as I limped over and got in front of the chair.

He spoke, his weapon still pointed at me. "Before you sit, I'll take Antoine's gun. Even though it has no bullets, I might need it."

I reached into my pocket and extracted the pistol.

"Easy," he warned.

I shifted the weapon to my left hand and held my arm out straight, the handle facing him. I looked down at the floor and watched him with my peripheral vision.

As he reached out, I shifted my weight and shot my other arm up to strike him with my cane.

With surprising agility, he moved close to me, blocked my right arm as it swung, and clocked me in my forehead with his gun. I staggered from the blow, and he grabbed Antoine's pistol from my hand and shoved me into the chair.

I collapsed into it, the room spinning, and it creaked under my weight. He pulled my cane from my hand before I could recover and threw it several feet away.

He pulled out a roll of duct tape and stepped behind me. "You can't win. I see your every thought, every action…"

He wrapped the tape about my upper body and forced me against the chair back with surprising strength. He rolled the tape around my body again and again, tight enough to hold me, but not so tight as to close off my breathing. Then, watching me carefully, he moved to my right side and wrapped tape around my right forearm, securing it to the chair.

"Tape seemed appropriate. I knew you would use it on Antoine. Nice of you to cover him with a blanket. I wasn't sure if you would do that or not."

He moved to my left side and taped that arm as well.

The stars that filled my vision faded, and my eyesight cleared. I noted that there was a small, battered table next to me, on top of which sat an ancient mantel clock about a foot tall. It had a battered outer case and cracked glass on the clock face, but I could hear it ticking away noisily, as if damaged mechanics took great effort to express the time. The hour hand was almost on the twelve, and the minute hand showed that midnight was a mere three minutes away.

I spoke up. "Why are you doing this? Why not one of your drugged minions?"

"They must not break the circle or cease the chanting," Claude responded as he finished securing my arm. He stood and surveyed his handiwork. "Now that you are here to witness, all is prepared for the sacrifice, at which point you will get to know Astarte. Intimately, in fact."

I wanted to open my mind and see if help was nearby, but if I dropped my guard for even a moment, he might read my thoughts, and there would go any surprise that might stop him. I fought to keep my barriers in place.

He stepped up, and taking his forefinger, he snapped it against the bruise on my temple. The fresh round of pain made me grimace. I spoke through clenched teeth, "You don't have to do this, Claude."

He glanced at the clock, and my eyes followed. Two minutes to midnight.

He straddled his legs over my right one that was stuck out, unbending, at an angle to the floor. He leaned directly in front of me and met my eyes. I immediately realized I should turn away, but it was too late. I could feel him reach into my brain.

In a flash, an image appeared. An image of her.

I don't know if I was inside Claude's head or he was inside mine, but all I could see was a woman, so beautiful she took my breath away.

She stood in front of me, darkness all around her, as if she lay on a blanket of black velvet. She wore a robe that barely covered her hips and stunning chest. Her skin was an amber shade, and her hair was in the style of an ancient Egyptian. That, combined with the thick eyeliner she wore, made it appear that she'd just stepped out of a hieroglyph.

She smiled at me and projected thoughts into my head. *Glad you could be here...*

What do you want with me...? I demanded in return.

I have need of you...

I will not serve you...

You shall be my new home...

What...?

I grow weary of the body I am inhabiting...

This surprised me. She was inhabiting a body?

Her voice interrupted my conjecture. *I have need of your gifts...*

With every bit of strength I possessed, I turned my head away and closed my eyes. This broke the connection, and the mirage faded.

I kept my eyes closed but heard Claude chuckle. "You have won her favor. She likes you."

"How nice," I grumbled sardonically.

The small clock chimed.

We both looked at the clock as it tolled the moments to midnight. I looked at Claude, still crouched over me.

He leaned close and whispered in my ear, "Once the sacrifice is complete, the mistress will have the power to take you."

"I will fight her with everything I am. I will never accept her willingly."

He smiled. "Never say never. Not when she has the power to use anyone you care about. Like that black bitch you're dating?"

"Don't you dare!" I spat.

He looked over his shoulder at the unmoving form of Erica Marconi. "Guess I need to take care of business."

There was a crash behind me and a man's voice yelled, "FBI!"

18. REVERENT RAID

Everything happened so fast, yet time seemed to slow down.

Claude's head snapped up to witness the noise, but he remained crouched over my body that was taped to the chair. He lowered himself a bit, perhaps to use me as a shield.

Pulling out his gun, oblivious to me, he raised the weapon. He'd also forgotten the fact that he had not secured my legs with the duct tape. In one swift move, I kicked up with my good left leg. Claude straddled my stiff right leg, leaving his legs open. I then kicked his unprotected crotch.

He grunted at the impact.

He doubled over and fell to the floor in one move. The gun dropped as his hands went protectively to his groin.

My back was to the door as several agents ran in yelling: "Hands in the air! No fast moves!"

I turned my head to see two uniformed agents in full SWAT gear with the letters 'FBI' on their black vests. An agent grabbed the small pistol Claude had released, while the other threw my adversary to the floor, flipped him onto his chest, and applied handcuffs to his wrists behind his back.

Stan Frazier came into my view. "You okay, professor?"

I nodded as I tried to catch my breath. I could still hear the chanting and was facing the robed figures. None of them had moved since the arrival of the FBI team. I saw two helmeted agents dart up the steps of the chancel and approach the stationary figures.

Stan, in the meantime, had retrieved a black knife from his boot and neatly sliced the duct tape holding my right arm.

"Sir?" one agent said as he looked at the robed participants.

Stan yelled back, "Yeah, what is it?"

"These ain't nothing but dummies!" the agent explained. He pulled a hood back from one figure to reveal a white mannequin like they use at clothing stores. It was a male doll designed with well-defined pectoral muscles. It appeared old and there were cracks in several places.

"This one, too!" yelled another agent, who pulled a robe off a white-plastic naked female figure that smiled blankly with unseeing eyes and slim hips that jutted to her left side. She was missing her hands, and each arm ended at the wrist.

"Can you turn off that damn chanting, for Christ's sake?" Stan bellowed as he sliced the tape from my left arm.   H e   g o t behind me and cut away the tape that secured me to the chair, as he bent low to my ear. "Talk to me. Are you okay, professor?"

"Yeah, I'm fine," I replied, discovering I felt winded. My body was experiencing the adrenaline rush of the 'flight or fight' instinct, which activated my sympathetic nervous system, made my heart beat faster, and shot blood to all of my muscles.

The chanting ceased abruptly, and an agent held aloft an MP3 player and a battery-powered speaker unit. "I got it!" he shouted.

Up on the chancel, a shorter agent, one lady I had met the other day, approached the supine Erica.

Stan handed me my cane. "Can you stand?"

I nodded and made my way to the stairs, Stan following me like a mother hen. I glanced back to see the other male agent pull Claude to his feet. He still seemed in pain, and I was glad to see it.

I ambled up the stairs to the female agent who was checking Erica's pulse and asked, "How is she?"

"Pulse is there, but not strong," she replied and looked up at me, curious that Stan had brought me over.

Stan spoke up, "He studied to be a medical doctor. Let him look at her."

I moved close to Erica on the altar as Stan instructed the agent, "Lydia, go to the truck and call for an ambulance. I can't get a signal for my phone in here."

She nodded and headed out.

I felt for the pulse in her carotid artery with my left hand. With my other hand, I lifted an eyelid to look at her pupil, which was a tiny pinprick. I moved my hand under the blanket and then yanked it away.

"What happened?" Stan asked at my ear.

"I didn't know she was naked," I explained, and reached under the blanket again to put my hand on the middle of her chest to feel the rise and fall of her lungs. I also leaned close to her mouth to feel her breath against my face.

"How is she?" Stan worried.

"I believe she's overdosing on a narcotic: clammy skin, pale features, shortness of breath, small pupils, shallow pulse rate," I rattled on as I carefully turned her on her side.

"What are you doing?"

"The major cause of death in an overdose is aspiration of one's own vomit into the lungs. Turning the patient on their side can prevent this."

"Can you give her something?"

I turned to Stan. "If we had some naloxone — hell, maybe even activated charcoal. I don't really carry things like that on me." I stared over at Claude, who was finally able to stand up straight and gazed up at me with his cocky grin.

I raced down the steps with my bad leg and grabbed the handcuffed chemist by the lapels. "What did you give her? What dosage?"

"Enough to accomplish what was necessary," he volunteered, and his smug smile returned. "After all, sacrifices must be made."

There it was again. A reference to the demon that changed my life and still haunted my nightmares. It was as if he knew of the dream in which Jyanette Emery said those very words, upside down and dying in a crashed car.

Blinded with fury, as the smug bastard just stared arrogantly at me, I leaned back and smashed my head into his nose with surprising force, making a satisfying cracking sound.

Claude fell to the ground and landed heavily on his right arm.

The agent pulled him back to his feet.

"My arm! You broke my arm!" Claude whined as blood poured down his face. "Police brutality!"

"This isn't helping, professor!" Stan roared and pulled me back as the agent turned to Claude and spun him away from us. I had to agree as my head throbbed. Stan looked at Claude's nose and pulled out a handkerchief.

"I can't hold the cloth," Claude complained and looked at me. "He broke my arm."

"All right, all right! Cuff him in front, so he can hold the cloth," Stan ordered.

The agent shook his head, unlocked the cuffs, and brought Claude's hands to the front of his body. Claude took the handkerchief with his left hand and held it to his nose, as the right arm hung limply from the cuff. The agent helped him up the steps to the altar.

The other agent had been pulling the robes off the remaining mannequins, which revealed their white-plastic bodies. He threw the robes into a pile and muttered, "Nobody here but this one guy."

Stan gestured at Claude as we climbed the steps back to the altar. "What's Thin Guy's name?"

"Claude," I said, my head pounding as I collected my wits. Striking him had felt good, but it hadn't helped Erica's situation. I gently removed her hand from under the blanket and felt her pulse again. Still weak.

"Okay, Claude," Stan began as the agent brought Claude to stand beside us at the altar. "Tell us what you gave this girl and fast. If she dies, that's murder one."

Holding the handkerchief to his face with his cuffed hand, Claude mumbled thickly, "It's already murder one. You'll find the other girl in the basement, worse for wear. I'm afraid she's been down there for a few days."

"Bastard," Stan muttered and turned his back to Claude to face me. "Can you do anything with him, professor? I mean, with what you can do?"

"No, Stan. He's been taking a drug that gives him abilities similar to mine, maybe even stronger. If I open up to him, he could pull things out of me."

Just then, the door at the far end of the hall opened, and Lydia came back in. "The ambulance is on the way!" she yelled.

Once again, everything seemed to slow down. Stan and the other pair of agents had all turned to face the woman at the door, their attention focused on her. At the same moment, I saw Claude reach to the bottom of the table, and in one blazing fast move, he lifted the Kris knife with his cuffed hands. His right arm was undamaged, and I realized he'd been faking the injury.

I dove across the table to protect Erica, knowing full well that I might end up stabbed instead of her. I did it without hesitation, in an instinctive reflex to protect this innocent girl from death.

But I guessed wrong. In a move that took only a fraction of a second, Claude, his eyes bright, turned with the knife. With surprising speed and strength, he plunged the knife into Stan Frazier's shoulder, taking advantage of the neck opening in his body armor.

Time sped up again, as the agent near him pulled his weapon and fired at close range into Claude. Claude doubled over, releasing his grip on the knife as he fell to the ground.

Stan crumpled, the shiny gold handle sticking grotesquely out of his body. The third agent helped him as I rolled off the table and fell to the floor, where I grabbed Claude.

I pulled Claude up from the ground as blood poured from his mouth. He struggled to speak, "I told you; there must be a sacrifice."

"Not the one you wanted," I answered.

The chuckle he gave sounded like it came from a tomb. "You...don't get it. Exactly the one we wanted. Now my precious one is waiting...to give me...my reward..."

His head lolled back, and his eyes stared up at the ceiling and at nothing.

He was gone.

I gently closed his eyes and lowered him to the floor, then turned to the agent who held Stan.

The man looked at me. "Should we pull out the blade?"

"No, that will make the bleeding worse," I said, and I moved over and carefully supported Stan's head. I looked down at the man I had worked with over the last few months, who had rescued me when we'd first met. "Stan, can you hear me?"

His eyes flicked open. "This fucker hurts," he grumbled.

"Stay with me, Stan. An ambulance is on the way," I reassured him.

"Don't know if I can, professor," he said, and his eyes met mine. "Claude?"

"He's dead."

"Won't hurt... any more girls..." he said, and a pained smile came to his lips.

"No, he won't," I assured him. "Or anyone else."

The door at the narthex banged open yet again as a pair of men in heavy coats and dark uniforms burst through the door, pulling a wheeled gurney. They moved rapidly toward us.

I called out, "This one's first!"

"No," Stan croaked. "The girl goes first."

The men drew near, and I stared stupidly at their steel-toed boots as I tried to fight the feeling of detachment from all the death occurring around me.

One of them had pulled a phone and was yelling into it. "We need another ambulance... I know it's snowing, but Christ, it's a goddamn war zone."

One man went to the girl to check vitals as the other man, a big blond fellow, knelt behind Stan's head and said, "Let me look."

His hands moved to open the Velcro on Stan's body armor.

Danger...

The buzz made me raise my hand in a stopping gesture. "Don't open it."

His head snapped up and he glared at me. "I need to look at the wound."

I nodded. "I know. But the body armor is holding everything in place, and if you release it, he could bleed out."

"But internal bleeding—"

"I agree, but that won't stop if you release the armor."

He frowned. "You a doctor or something?"

"I was supposed to be."

Stan grumbled. "I'm still here, guys. And it still fucking hurts."

The other EMT came over. "Doug, help me with the girl. We gotta move."

The blond, Doug, nodded and joined his partner.

"Geez, she's got no clothes on," Doug blurted as he put his hands under her.

"Just keep the blanket on her. We gotta move. It looks like an OD."

Sirens were howling nearby, flashing lights blinking garishly through the stained-glass windows.

I turned back to Stan. "You gotta hold on, Stan."

His eyes were half-closed, and he muttered something incoherent.

I glanced up from Stan, and before me stood Claude, looking down at me from above his body. The spirit was all in sepia tones, and he smiled at me with that arrogant smirk. Next to him was the beautiful woman who had been in my vision, the temptress, the creature that had led him down this dark path.

He gazed at her adoringly.

"And now for your reward," she said, and took a step back as her body mutated, changed, and grew. In the blink of an eye, the gorgeous woman changed into the giant demon I had seen the night of the car accident when Cathy had died.

Claude watched the transformation, but he did it with the joy of a genuine believer.

The monster opened its mouth; in one fast move, it bent forward and sunk teeth into Claude's neck. As the monster fed upon the soul of its most devoted follower, Claude's eyes widened in shock and disbelief. His sepia ghost-form dwindled, faded, and the monster absorbed it.

In mere moments, it had consumed the shadow-shape of Claude. The demon looked down at me, energized by his hideous meal.

"See you soon, boy," he said to me.

The door of the narthex burst open again, pulling my attention away.

I glanced back at the demon, but it was gone.

Sergeant Kelly from the 120th precinct strode in with a pair of other officers. He stopped, looked over as the girl was being taken out on the stretcher, then at me, Stan, the naked white mannequins, and the body of Claude.

He shook his head. "This is one hell of a mess."

19. EARNEST EXCUSES

The detective cleared his throat. "Tell me again, doctor."

I sat across from the tall African-American detective and Sergeant Kelly, who sat directly across from me in the interrogation room at the 120th precinct. I rubbed my forehead in exhaustion, as it was past one-thirty in the morning.

After informing the police of Antoine Powell still locked in his car, and waiting until the ambulance took Stan away with the Kris knife still sticking in him, Kelly had demanded I come to the precinct and explain myself. The black detective, whose name was Kwame, though I was unsure if it was his first name or last.

I had taken them through the story once, and the pair of them exchanged glances repeatedly, with the suggestion that I was telling tall tales.

I sighed. "Must we go over it again?"

The detective looked stern. "I have to tell you, doctor, you've confessed to repeated assaults. I also am trying to understand why you were involved in this situation at all."

Kelly exhaled angrily. "I say we throw him in a holding cell and ask him in the morning."

"I'll go over it again, if you will update me on Erica Marconi and Stan Frazier."

"You are not in a position to bargain," Kwame insisted.

Kelly rose and went to the door in response to a quick knock. He murmured to a uniformed officer on the other side as Kwame paced in annoyance.

"Okay," Kelly said and shut the door. "Wise, it seems like your lawyer is here."

"I have a lawyer?" I questioned. There certainly was no end to the surprises this night.

There was another knock at the door, and Kelly pulled it open. A thin man with unkempt hair entered like a shot. He looked as if someone had yanked him out of a sound sleep and poured him into a wrinkled suit.

He spoke before anyone else could. "Gentleman, I am Jared Franks, but you both know that."

"Good evening, counselor," Kwame replied, obviously familiar with Franks and not pleased by the attorney's presence.

"No, detective, it is not a good evening when I get pulled out of bed because you're holding a client and not allowing him to return home."

"He was a witness to a police shooting—" Kelly attempted.

Franks went on like a steamroller. "Yes, and I will be happy to arrange a time for this witness to be interviewed about what he saw. But not without me being there." He turned to me and inclined his head toward the door. "Doctor Wise? We are out of here. Your ride is waiting."

I rose, still a bit overwhelmed by another surprising turn of events, and limped after the lawyer.

"You had a cane when you came in, right?" he asked as we slowly made our way out.

"Yes, and my wallet, keys, and winter coat."

"I'll get those for you," he said and moved away from me.

We were near the processing desk, and there stood Darren Ward.

I frowned. "What are you doing here?"

He smiled. "I'm your ride. I also have this for you."

He held out my phone. The case had scratches, but Powell had thrown it a couple of dozen yards, so I considered that a win. I pushed the button and the unbroken screen lit up.

"The FBI team left it for you. Good way to have them track you."

I sighed. "What's the word on Erica and Stan Frazier?"

"Stan is still in surgery. Erica responded to the drug they gave her."

I nodded. "Probably naloxone. I'm glad. Where are they?"

"They're over at Staten Island University Hospital."

"I'll want to visit them tomorrow."

The lawyer returned with my cane, which I gratefully took and leaned against. Then he handed me a large manila envelope that had my other personal effects.

"I'm in court Monday," Franks stated simply, and he held out a card, which I took gratefully. "Call me, and I'll set up a formal interview. Until then, say nothing to nobody."

I nodded, resisting the urge to correct his double negative.

Darren and I trudged out of the precinct, onto the street, and down a small hill to Richmond Avenue, which we crossed. The snow had stopped, and the temperature was a little warmer. The road was pretty much clear, although there was a layer of snow on the sidewalks and in the middle of the four-lane road.

Darren spoke as we crossed the empty streets. "They say it's all going to melt by morning, and Tuesday the weather might be as high as seventy. Just a strange meteorological occurrence."

"There was a lot of strange last night," I murmured.

Darren's car sat parked on the street, a little ways down from the precinct. It was a mid-sized car, one of those super-safe, boxy foreign jobs.

"I have to have brunch in about seven hours," I noted with a glance at my watch.

"With that black eye?"

"No, with my girlfriend's parents," I said in an attempt to be funny. "And with this black eye."

He unlocked my door, and I got in, bone-weary. Darren activated his GPS, and I gave him my address, and soon we were moving.

"You okay driving all the way out there?"

Darren kept his eyes on the road. "You've been driving out all week. I figured I owed you one."

"How'd you know where I was?"

"Marconi called me," he said with a shrug.

"I should've figured that out. I guess that's where the high-powered lawyer came from."

"Also correct."

"It figures. I don't have the clout to get a lawyer out of bed in the middle of the night. Do you mind if I doze?"

"Go right ahead."

I leaned my head back and closed my eyes.

Darren spoke. "I'm going to visit that abandoned church tomorrow. Thin Guy was using it as a headquarters."

I stayed unmoving, my eyes closed. "Whatever for?"

"I want to see if there was anything the police might have missed."

I replied wearily. Wearily, I replied, "Everyone might have missed things because of all the excitement."

"Psychic flash?"

"Just a feeling," I commented sagely.

"I'll look at where they were keeping the girl. If I find anything of interest, I'll call you."

"It's my girlfriend's birthday, so I might not be available."

"Fair enough."

As we crossed the Goethals Bridge and headed up the NJ Turnpike, I opened my eyes occasionally to note that the roads were clear of snow, the remnants only on the shoulders. I couldn't help the strange concern that Astarte might have caused the bad weather.

I was still trying to understand the transformation from the beautiful temptress to the demonic creature from my nightmares. The whole thing still made little sense to my exhausted brain.

We pulled into my driveway at about two-thirty in the morning, the snow still covering the sidewalk on the side entrance to my living quarters. I thanked Darren, carefully walked to the door so I didn't slip, and went in.

I set an alarm for eight a.m., pulled off my clothes, which I threw in a pile in the middle of the floor, and fell into bed in my underwear.

The morning came far too quickly, and the alarm was beeping madly when I turned it off and fought the urge to throw it across the room.

The spectacular amount I ached in every part of my body should not have surprised me. Nor should the bruise on my forehead and the amazing black eye I wore from my confrontation with Claude.

Thinking back, I came out of it much better than my last confrontation with a cult, where I spent a night in the hospital. However, was Claude really a cult? From what I could fathom, it was only himself and Antoine who were the actual members. It seemed quite apparent that the story about other members put forth by Antoine was all a lie.

I showered, shaved, and made myself look presentable, and used mousse to move my hairstyle so as to cover the forehead bruise a bit.

About eight-thirty, fully dressed, I walked to the kitchen, where Mrs. Higgins was pouring a cup of coffee into my favorite mug.

She turned to offer it to me. A momentary look of shock crossed her face, which she immediately quashed. "Good mahrning, doctor."

"Thank you, Mrs. Higgins," I murmured as I took a sip. "You — um — might wonder about my eye."

"Not half as mooch as Jyanette will, no doubt. Here, sit ye down and let me look."

I dutifully sat on a straight-backed kitchen chair, and she looked carefully at my face. "It's bruised, aye, but not too swollen. I may have joost the thing."

She took off my jacket and hung it on the back of a chair, then disappeared out the swinging kitchen door. Returning in mere moments with a black bag, she pulled out a small cosmetic jar, unscrewed the top, and applied a flesh-colored paste to my face.

"Ow," I complained.

"Hoosh now! If ye were man enough to get this, ye're man enough to have an old lady touch you with a finger."

"Yes, ma'am," I grimaced.

"Oh, ye're such a baby," she chided. She then took out a powder puff and placed powder on the spot. "There, that should do!"

She handed me a small mirror, and I looked at my face. I had to admit, she'd done a great job of concealing my ill-gotten bruise and black eye. Would it be enough to fool Jyanette?

"Won't fool yer girl," Mrs. Higgins remarked as if reading my thoughts. Which she might have been doing. I wouldn't put it past her. "Now go, doctor."

I smiled at her and grabbed my coat, pulled out my keys, and headed outside. Today felt warmer, and the snow was now only visible in a few small patches.

I got in my van and headed out.

After the twenty-minute drive, I parked in front of Jyanette's apartment, only a few moments after nine. I strode up the walkway to knock on the door.

It opened to a beautiful sight. My tall, dark lady stood before me, delight in her eyes. She wore her hair in another amazing, relaxed style falling to her shoulders, but I knew she'd spent a lot of time arranging it. Her teeth were sparkling white in contrast to her ebony skin. "Right on time!"

I could see George and Deka standing in the living room behind her.

Jyanette frowned for a moment. "You changed your hair," she stated, and with a free hand moved my hair. I brought my hand up to stop her, but she had seen the large bruise the hair had covered.

There was a sharp intake of breath as her eyes moved over my face, assessing the damage. I saw a momentary flash of anger, then she pushed my hair into the position that hid the bruise and forced a smile. "Actually, maybe it's better in this new style."

She moved aside, and I stepped into the room to greet her parents again, while she eyed me with suspicion.

Brunch was actually quite nice. We went to a little place in the center of Mountainview that went by the name 'Toast', specializing in breakfast fare. We sat at a simple wooden table with a sheet of white butcher paper covering it to act as a tablecloth.

Jyanette had ridden over with her parents, while I brought the van and parked it in a nearby handicap space. Since I possessed the correct plates and the blue tag to hang from my rearview mirror, it seemed an appropriate choice.

I made it a point to attempt conversation with George and could finally get him to open up about historic buildings, which was his passion. Restoration and construction actually were interests of mine, so I could ask the right questions.

He regaled me with stories of building successes and disasters and a very humorous account of Jyanette's attempt to move an ungainly load of bricks in a hod.

By the end of the tale, all of us were laughing, even Deka, who I was sure had heard the anecdote many times, and Jyanette, who was the brunt of the tale.

As we ate, Jyanette opened her present from me. She unwrapped the little box and opened it to a simple necklace. At the end of a silver chain was a silver disc laser-cut with her astrological symbol: Aries. When she turned it over, the other side had a diagram of the star constellation associated with the star sign.

It was a lovely, if inexpensive, gift. She gave me a peck on the cheek in response, and I put it around her neck as she held up her hair.

George sipped his coffee, the empty plates before us. "If it's okay, Jyannie, we thought we'd just leave from here."

She nodded. "I understand, daddy. I'm just glad you both could come up for the weekend."

Deka turned to me. "And I am so glad to have met you, Leonard."

"Likewise, Deka," I responded.

"Though I am concerned..." she said.

"Oh?" I said with a frown.

She looked my face over carefully. "I fear you may have an enormous challenge ahead of you." She then turned to her daughter, very serious. "Both of you."

George leaned forward. "Sorry, Len, but Deka gets this way sometimes."

"I know," Jyanette croaked.

I interjected. "Can you tell me what challenges? Maybe you have some insights?"

Deka shook her head. "I cannot tell you more. Except there is a very bad Bakisi which seeks you. I pray you have the strength to defeat it."

"Sweetie," George attempted. "It's your daughter's birthday…"

"I am sorry," Deka said, and stopped staring at me, and tried to smile. She then turned her attention to Jyanette. "Ebele, I wish you many, many years of happiness. But please take care."

"I do, momma," Jyanette answered. "Don't worry."

"A mother always worries."

After that, George paid the bill, and we all rose to leave. Outside on the street, her parents hugged Jyanette, and I shook hands with George and received a hug from Deka.

As she drew close, she whispered in my ear. "Swear to me you will protect my daughter."

"What?" I whispered back.

"Swear!" she hissed.

"I swear I would give my life for her."

"Let us hope it does not come to that." She sighed, and we parted. Then, all smiles, they headed away toward their car, as I stood surprised by her mother's plea.

20. SOLICITOUS SURVIVORS

Jyanette and I rode back to her place in my van, and she was oddly quiet. I wasn't sure if I should speak or not, still pondering the request her mother had made.

Once we arrived at her house, we stepped inside, and she turned to me and demanded, "What happened?"

"I didn't have time to tell you," I attempted. "We rescued Erica Marconi."

"At a personal cost, of course," she added.

"Jyanette, I just—"

"No, you wait right here." She stormed off into the bathroom and quickly came back with a cloth in her hand.

I closed my eyes, and Jyanette slid the damp rag around my eye and removed the makeup put there by Mrs. Higgins. When she finished, I opened my eyes to see a fire burning in hers.

I put up my hands defensively. "Hey, the bad guy ended up dead. I only got a black eye."

"Anyone else hurt?" she snapped.

"Thin Guy stabbed the team leader, Stan Frazier, with that knife we were looking for."

"Is he dead?"

"From what I know, he pulled through."

"So it could've been you that got stabbed."

"It seems Claude — that's Thin Guy — wanted me to be a witness."

She folded her arms. "I think it's time for you to leave."

"Jyanette, I didn't have a choice," I whined.

"You always say that!" she bellowed, and turned to toss the soiled wipe into the trash. "And then you show up looking like this." She stood facing away from me and exhaled heavily. "Or worse. I can't take it, Len. I just can't take it."

"It was your ex-husband who abducted me, told me he wanted to help!" I shot back.

She turned to face me. "Antoine? He really was involved in this?" she inquired skeptically.

"Yes. He told me he was concerned that Claude had gone crazy. He drove me to Staten Island and threatened me with a gun."

Her mouth fell open. "Antoine did that?"

I nodded. "Turns out the gun had no bullets, and I knocked him out. He's under arrest now."

Her jaw clenched. "A part of me always thought he would end up in jail."

I stepped closer and took her hands. "He told me there was a group called the Following. Turns out that was a lie. I got there and it was only Thin Guy and some mannequins."

She eyed me. "And you saved the girls?"

"One of them. Claude had drugged her, almost gave her an overdose, but we saved her."

She pulled free from me and turned her back to me. "And you show up for brunch with my parents with a black eye — on my birthday!"

I moved close to hug her from behind, but she pushed me away. "Jyanette, I—"

"Look, you should go. I'll call you when I want to see you."

I looked at her sadly. "I love you."

Her expression hardened. "And I love you, dammit. But I want a life, marriage, kids, the whole thing. And you showing up like this every time you're on a case convinces me you are not the man to build a life with."

I stared at her in shock. "That's really not fair…"

"Len, I made a mistake with Antoine. I married him in a rush and on a whim. I should've examined him much more carefully than I did. Not only as a worthy spouse, but in his ability to take on the responsibilities of a partner and a family."

"That's the direction I see this relationship heading," I tried to console her.

Her forehead creased. "Really? Then why do you insist on taking on such dangerous cases?"

This stumped me for a moment. "I—I want to help."

"That's noble. But I'm more interested in a man who will put me and our children above everything else."

"I can do that!"

"You couldn't even do it on my damn birthday," she scolded, and her hand went to her neck to rub the silver disk I had given her. "You need to go."

Fear clutched my heart and unimaginable grief.

"Are you…breaking up with me?" I gasped.

"No, I'm not, though I am tempted," she chided. "I need to cool off and see how I feel. Don't call me for a few days."

I hung my head, seeing no point in arguing. "All right."

I walked to the door and gave her one last look before I left. She stood at her full height, adamant in her decision, but I could see it had not been easy for her.

I went out the door and closed it, using my cane to guide me as I walked to the van and got in.

She meant it, and I could tell. The fear that tore at me when she told me to go had been devastating. I had wanted to be with a woman who was her own person, that I could share goals and commitments with. She had just clarified that my showing up as the battered hero was no longer an acceptable part of our relationship.

Since my day had not gone the way I planned, I looked up Staten Island University Hospital on my smartphone and drove out there.

I was tired, but I wanted to meet Erica and make sure Stan had pulled through. Something to make everything I had gone through seem worth it.

As I drove, I noticed that the day was warming up nicely, and I saw very few reminders of the previous night's snowfall.

I argued with myself the entire trip, both taking Jyanette's side and repudiating it. If I were honest with myself, I had to admit she was right. She had expressed her fear for what I did, and I knew that it was a sticking point if our relationship was to move forward.

But of anyone I'd ever met, she had to know that being involved with someone in law enforcement was risky, and that's what I'd spent four years training with Doctor Kohl to accomplish.

I also realized that these were the same arguments repeated over and over, as with most couples. Plus, with the story she'd told me of how Antoine forced himself on her, I could understand why she insisted on being much more careful with any partner.

But I shared her goal: a long-term relationship with one person and all the trappings of such a commitment. This meant balancing career with the requirements of family obligations, as well as the possibility of children.

Our relationship was still only six months old, and we both were digging in our heels to make our demands clear. I could completely understand, from Jyanette's past with Antoine, that she wanted our relationship to be different.

I also understood that it would have to be on her terms.

I wondered if I was being sexist. The days when the man dictated the relationship were over, and it made sense that Jyanette should demand and expect the things she wanted.

And I honestly didn't enjoy getting my ass handed to me with every case.

Coming out of my thoughts, I turned off the Staten Island Expressway, which was much less busy this one Sunday. I drove into the large hospital facility and parked.

In a few short minutes, I was at the main desk, showing my driver's license to the bald security man at the desk.

"Who are you visiting?" he asked as he checked his computer.

"Erica Marconi and Stan Frazier."

He nodded. "She's on the third floor, but Frazier is in the Heart, Lung, and Surgery Center, which is a different building. Do you know where that is?"

Since I had driven past it on my way in, I nodded.

A small printer spat out a visitor's badge, which the guard put a plastic clip through, then handed to me.

I clipped it to my jacket, and the guard gave me directions.

I went into the large nearby elevator and hit the button for the third floor. The elevator had about eight people in it, but could have easily fit twenty. Some of the other patrons carried flowers and gifts, and I was shy about showing up empty-handed.

The door opened on three, and I limped out and headed down the hall toward the nurse's station. As I passed a private room, I saw the name 'Erica Marconi' on a card inserted into a plastic holder on the wall and stopped.

There were several people, including a man and woman that I assumed were Erica's parents, along with other assorted family members. They had been quietly talking with Erica, who sat up in bed, looking gaunt but uninjured.

They all turned to face me, and I recognized Anthony Marconi.

He immediately opened his arms and moved toward me. "Doctor Wise, hey, here is the hero of the day."

Before I could protest, he took my arm and pulled me into the room. "Erica, this is the guy who rescued you, Doctor Leonard Wise. He led the police right to you."

One man who had been sitting got up and pulled me into a bear hug. From the resemblance, I decided he must be Marconi's brother and Erica's father.

"Thank you," he sobbed in my ear. "Thank you for saving my little girl."

Marconi put his hands on his brother's back. "Hey, Dominic, let the guy breathe, okay?"

He immediately released me. "Oh, sorry."

"Quite all right," I asserted. "I helped a little, but the actual heroes are the FBI and the police."

Dominic went on. "We appreciate what you did. Tony tells us some guy took you there with a gun, but you had the FBI track your phone or something."

I raised an eyebrow as I looked at Mister Marconi. "Interesting that 'Tony' knows so much."

Anthony Marconi just shrugged.

Dominic turned to his daughter, who still seemed a bit out of it. "Erica, what do you have to say to Doctor Wise?"

She looked at me with wide eyes and spoke quietly. "Thanks for getting me out of the place." Tears appeared in her eyes. "They killed Connie."

"I know," I lamented. "Did you see anyone else besides the thin white guy or the tall black man?"

"I'm not sure. I spaced out for most of my time in that cellar."

"You were in a basement?" I asked, remembering how Claude had said that Constance was downstairs.

She nodded. "I think they put drugs in my food." She wrinkled up her nose. "The toilet was this portable chemical thing."

"I'm glad you made it out of there," I told her.

"Hey, you all keep visiting," Anthony Marconi declared to the group. "Doc Wise and I gotta talk."

Everyone in the room mumbled words of thanks and praise, and Dominic took my hand to shake it one last time before I stepped into the hall with Marconi.

"I thought you were gonna call," Marconi pointed out, skipping the usual niceties. "You still got that phone I gave you, right?"

"I do. It's in my glove compartment. But I thought it would be better to visit in person."

"Yeah, well, Erica is going to be fine. The doctors say she'll make a full recovery."

"I wanted to thank you for the lawyer and the ride home."

Marconi shrugged. "I thought a limo might be too ostentatious. And since you did Ward's job for him, I figure at least he could be your driver."

"He was a big help. I couldn't have succeeded without his input."

He chuckled and shook his head. "I like that about you, Doc, you're always givin' everyone else the credit."

"It was a team effort. Have you heard anything about the FBI agent?"

"I heard it was touch and go for him, gettin' stabbed and all."

"I'm planning to visit him as well."

"Doc, I owe you one. And I always pay my debts. What can I do for you for saving my little niece?"

I considered this for a moment. "By now I am sure you know the man behind her abduction is dead."

"Yeah," he snarled. "Let me tell you, if the police hadn't shot him, he'd be dead now anyway."

"Since you asked what I want, it's this: his partner, Antoine Powell? I want you to assure me you will not have him killed."

The crime boss considered this for a moment. "What's it to you?"

"He's my girlfriend's ex-husband. But he was under Claude's control because of a drug Claude invented. He'll go to prison. Let that be enough."

He considered this thoughtfully for a minute. "Geez, I could give you anything you want, and this is what you ask for?"

"It's the only thing I want, Mister Marconi."

He shook his head and went on affably. "You're a pistol, Wise."

I glanced back at the room down the hall. "I'm glad I could help save your niece."

He took his index finger and tapped my chest. "I won't forget this, Doc, you hear me? You still got that phone. If you ever need me, you call me, you got that?"

"Yes, sir," I demurred.

He nodded to me and headed back to the hospital room and his family.

I considered this as I headed back to the elevator. Maybe I would need his help someday, but I couldn't imagine asking a criminal for assistance.

I soon walked out the front door and pulled my coat around me as I headed for the Heart, Lung, and Surgery Center.

After a short walk, I went into the Center and up to another desk where a different security officer checked my badge.

He looked at his computer. "Stan Frazier is still in intensive care, so you can only see him if he is conscious and for only ten minutes," the older man behind the desk informed me.

He sent me up to the correct floor, with the admonition to check at the nurse's station to make sure he was conscious and that it was convenient.

I took another elevator and walked past many people in white lab coats, all with different plastic-encased badges. I finally reached the nurse's station, and a thin African-American woman looked up at me from behind her glasses.

"I'd like to see Stan Frazier," I explained.

She picked up a clipboard and glanced at it. "You and everyone else. We've had police, FBI, everything but the damn Canadian Mounties comin' through here."

I grinned. "I'm just a friend."

She glanced up at me and her look softened. "I guess he could use one about now." Her mouth became firm again. "Only ten minutes, you got that?"

She pointed at Stan's room, and I walked down the wide hall and turned in.

Stan lay in the bed, still pale, and there were numerous machines hooked up to him, beeping away and tracking his vitals. An IV went into his arm.

As I tapped into the room, he opened his eyes and glanced over.

"Had to be you, professor," he muttered. "Only guy I know who has a cane and that footstep."

"You have the ears of a bat," I conceded. "How are you?"

"I ain't dead," he recounted. "It was touch and go. They said I almost didn't make it. But the doctors also said, if I hadn't kept the body armor on like you told them, I would've bled out."

"We did what we could. What's the prognosis for recovery?"

"Both lungs are working now. I'm gonna have problems with my right arm 'cause he cut some of the muscle, and the specialist they brought in is worried that my heart isn't in the shape it should be." He looked closely at my face. "You look like crap."

My hand went to my bruised eye. "As my girlfriend pointed out." I sighed. "She did not appreciate me showing up like this on her birthday."

"I imagine that didn't go well?"

"Not well at all. She asked me to leave and said she'll call."

"Ouch."

"I don't know what to do, Stan. I mean, on one hand she's right, I keep getting injured and it scares her."

Stan smirked. "That eye is nothing. I've had perps shoot me, stab me, punch me, and every damn thing. It takes a special woman to love a law enforcement officer."

"Are you married, Stan?"

"Thirty years," he boasted.

"How do you — I mean her — I mean, how do you handle it?"

"My wife is one tough lady," he disclosed. "But it isn't easy. She knew it would be difficult, and she's seen me in hospitals, and coming home late bruised from head to toe. When the kids were little, she'd sometimes be up half the night waiting for me."

"How… did she do it?"

"She fell in love with a cop. Take away all the federal bullshit, and that is what I am: a cop. She knew what I did when she married me but wanted to build a life with me anyway. Believe me, I had relationships where I got injured once, and they headed for the hills, but not my Julie. And now the kids are grown and on their own. It makes things a little easier."

"When do you think you'll be back on the task force?"

He looked over at the IV in his arm and exhaled loudly. "I don't think I will be, professor."

"What?" I was stunned.

"Look, professor, I'm fifty-five now," he speculated. "Ten years ago, this wouldn't have happened. I would've kept my eye on the perp and moved a hell of a lot faster."

"You can't blame yourself—" I attempted.

"I don't, professor. But I gotta be realistic. I ain't coming back a hundred percent from this. McGee is right: work local. I've been lying here thinkin' I want to spend a few more years with the missus, maybe enjoy life a little."

"I see."

"Yeah, my wife's on her way right now. She had to pick up our daughter. She's expecting."

"Your first grandchild?"

"Yup."

"I'm glad you have people who love you," I confided.

"It's what it's really about," he insisted. "But you gotta find a good one."

"I'm sorry we're losing you."

"Eh, it's time for me to hang it up. You'll have to work with somebody else in the future."

We spoke until my ten minutes were up, and the very efficient nurse told me to go. I walked out of the building sadder. Stan had been one of the good ones, but he was getting out.

Law enforcement was a tough job, and I was only on the outskirts of it, involved on the fringes. Even so, I sustained my share of injuries.

I got into my car and pulled out the money to pay the parking lot attendant before I started the car. My phone rang before I could even turn the ignition.

"Wise," I stated glumly.

"Doc? It's Darren Ward. Can you come out to Staten Island, to that place you fought that guy last night?"

"I'm on the island right now. Why, what's up?"

"There's something here you really need to see."

EPILOGUE

In about fifteen minutes, I arrived at the turn for Vanderbilt College. I pulled off the main road and headed up past the wooded area to the college grounds.

It was much less foreboding in the daylight, and very different from the previous night. In fact, the campus was lovely. I pulled onto the side road and parked in an open space on the street.

I walked to the driveway with the yellow metal posts. The chain was still lying on the ground, and I could easily see the cracked, ancient roadway without the layer of snow. Police vehicles and officers were on the grounds as I walked up.

An officer saw me and approached. "Sir, this is a crime scene."

I quickly pulled out my Mountainview Police Department ID. He just gave it a cursory glance and let me pass.

"You should wear your ID while you're here," he added.

I nodded, clipped the ID to my jacket pocket, and walked on, still melancholy about my fight with Jyanette and with the idea that I would no longer see Stan. He was right about finding a relationship that worked.

The chapel rose and was not as frightening in the bright sunlight. The gargoyles on the building were less menacing; the structure less disquieting.

As I reached the door, another officer looked at me and stared at the ID clipped to my jacket.

"Mountainview, New Jersey?" he pondered. "Isn't this a bit out of your jurisdiction?"

"Darren Ward requested I come."

"The PI? Geez, he thinks he runs this case." The cop grimaced. "Yeah, head on in. Forensics is done, so there ain't much you can muck up."

I walked through the door and into the narthex. Ward was up near the altar, standing amongst the exposed white mannequins that stared unblinking into nothing. He turned at the sound of my cane as it echoed through the room while I tapped my way over.

He came down the steps and met me halfway, where the heaters stood. The police shut them down, and they no longer offered heat to the cold room.

"Any problems?" he wondered.

"No, my Mountainview ID got me in," I explained. "Does Kelly still want to arrest me?"

"He'd like to, but I talked him out of it."

"Thanks. Did they find Constance?" I added grimly.

"Yeah. There are really old monk's cells in the basement. Apparently, it was a monastery before it was a school. That's where both girls were being held, and where they found Constance. It wasn't pretty."

I shook my head. "I'm sure it wasn't. What do we know about our perp?"

At this, Darren pulled a small notebook out of his pocket and riffled through a few pages. "Claude Vandersteen. A master's student here at Vanderbilt. I interviewed one of his teachers, Walter Addison?"

I frowned. "I know him. We studied together in California."

"Well, he was shocked and went on and on about how brilliant Claude was, and what a loss it was because his 'genius was gone.' Seemed like he was more upset about Claude getting shot than the fact that his student abducted and killed young women."

"I'm still trying to understand any of this myself. The things he could do, to suggest that a drug was capable of doing that…"

"I heard they found a bunch of his writings in his dorm room."

"That might prove enlightening. So why did you ask me here?"

"We found something down in the monk's cell, and it freaked everyone out. I thought maybe you could clue me in about its origins. You studied things like demons and all that, right?"

"We covered religious lore for many faiths in my years with Doctor Kohl."

He nodded. "Then let me show you. It's in the monk's cell downstairs."

We walked to the left transept, and in the corner where the opening met the chancel, there was a small door that opened to a stone staircase that spiraled into the dark.

Darren pulled out a flashlight, and I used the light on my phone. The stone staircase descended in a tight spiral, the inner part of each step very narrow. It curled downward with no handrail and only our flashlights to provide illumination. The stones were cold, and there was a chill in the air as I followed Darren down.

There was a smell, a sort of sweet, putrid redolence that hung just inside my nose like a stagnant pool of water.

I flashed my light on the stone walls, which seemed much older than the church above us. The mortar was weeping out from between the stones and lay in heaps along the walls.

Darren led me to a room with a small doorway. We slid into a cold stone room only eight by ten feet. He illuminated the wall with his lamp, where there was a figure painted in exquisite detail on the wall.

"Is that a fresco?" I asked, looking at the artwork.

"Yup, plaster and paint combined to push it out from the wall, making it more dimensional."

It was a woman about three feet tall, totally naked with surprising detail. She was beautiful, and whoever had done the fresco had made the flesh as smooth as a real woman. In one hand she held an ankh and another a Kris knife. Her feet became claws like a bird of prey at the bottom of the portrait. The words 'The Following of Astarte' appeared on the wall above, with 'The Goddess is made flesh' written below it.

"Who did this?" I asked.

"I guess Claude, while he was drugged out," Darren commented with a shrug. "But that's not the one that bothers me."

He turned his light and shone it on the wall opposite the woman's portrait, and I gasped.

"That's something isn't it, Doc?" he gloated.

But I could not reply.

It was an artfully created fresco of the red body and face I had known so well. Even though it was only about three feet tall, I recognized the large horns on the head, the crimson skin, the yellow eyes, and the muscled body of the demon I had seen outside the car the night Cathy died.

Under this figure were the words, 'And walks among us.'

This was startling enough, but then under that, written with what appeared to be nothing more than a marker, were words that haunted my dreams and filled me with dread.

Sacrifices must be made.

ASYLUM IN THE MIND

DOCTOR WISE BOOK 6

ARJAY LEWIS

MIND
BENDER
PRESS

ASYLUM IN THE MIND

She surfaced slowly from the fog of unconsciousness, her eyelids fluttering as if reluctant to reveal the world again.

How long had she been out? Minutes, hours, days? The disorientation clung to her mind like a choking veil, thick and suffocating.

She fought to gather her scattered thoughts, clutching to the fragile fragments of her identity.

I'm Mary Gillian. I'm a nurse.

The words felt distant and unreal, like echoes from a life that belonged to someone else.

A hazy memory flickered: her cramped, cluttered apartment bathed in the cold morning light, the worn bathroom mirror. It reflected an image of an attractive dark-haired woman with fair skin, a roundness of cheek and chin, perhaps carrying a bit too much weight.

Then came the painful sting of recollection: the bitter argument with Todd, the boyfriend she had broken up with days —or was it weeks?—ago. It was a stupid fight, another stupid fight on top of all the other ones, but they decided it would be best to end it. She wished he was here with her in this horrible place, where she would beg his forgiveness.

How perfect her life had been before all this darkness swallowed her whole.

She glanced around the room, struggling to determine whether it was night or day. But the chamber was perpetually shrouded in darkness, broken only by a faint sliver of cold light sneaking beneath the door.

A frigid shiver ran down her spine—not from the chill, but from dread. If night had come, then the torment would begin again.

He would return. He always did. What fresh horrors awaited her this time? She flexed her bound hands and legs, feeling the raw bite of the strips of torn bed sheets wrapped tightly around her. The knots were cruelly precise; the more she struggled, the tighter they constricted, threatening to steal the feeling from her fingers as they had before.

He had made that painfully clear—his twisted parting gift on the first night, leaving her bound so long that numbness had blotted out sensation for two agonizing days.

Better not to resist, she told herself.

He seemed to savor her defiance, inventing new ways to break her spirit, pushing her to the edge where resistance felt like a desperate gamble. He feigned escape routes—mocking traps designed only to crush hope and twist her agony anew.

This wasn't how her life was supposed to be. A week ago… maybe less… her days had been filled with mundane joys: the doctor's office where she worked, the comforting chatter of coworkers, the occasional laughter of friends. Now, nothing remained but the horror of his face and the perpetual nightmare of his hands on her body.

She shifted her injured ankle slightly. Pain shot sharply up her leg—broken, surely—but over time the torment had dulled to a merciless throb.

Her face—her beautiful face—was a ruin. He had carved into her with a scalpel, cruelly fast, making deep slices that burned and stung, branding her with violence. Was the damage permanent? She dared not hope.

Suffering had become her sole companion, a shadow that clung to her with merciless persistence.

A faint glow spilled beneath the door, casting eerie shadows on grimy walls slick with dirt and neglect. She spotted the chair she was tied to, centered in a disturbing pattern scrawled on the floor—no mere circle, but a pentagram, dark and ominous beneath her.

She had awoken here after the attack. That terrible, senseless moment in the parking lot outside the office—a man had approached out of nowhere, striking her down with a heavy blow.

She remembered nothing beyond the pain and darkness swallowing her.

He fed her scraps, brought water, but mostly left her tied to that chair. Once a day, if he was merciful, he'd escort her to the filthy bathroom—if not, she was forced to soil herself.

The humiliation was endless.

"Oh God... Fluffy? Who's feeding Fluffy?" she whispered hoarsely.

An image—her black and white long-haired cat—flashed into her mind. He had always curled around her feet at night, a silent guardian. The thought of him suffering alone, hungry and scared, broke something inside her.

Tears welled unbidden, salty and hot, and she cloaked her sobs in a fragile whisper, afraid he might hear.

Or perhaps he wasn't here at all. But she couldn't stop crying. The tears came in helpless waves just as they had that first night—until his harsh slap silenced her, searing pain exploding across her face.

Now, a faint sound stirred from the other room. She swallowed hard, her breath catching in her throat. Panic clenched her heart.

It was going to start again.

The door creaked open, and he appeared: tall, menacing, his white lab coat stained dark with blood—her blood. Her gaze locked on the gloved hand that held a gleaming instrument, sharp and cruel.

"Please... no," she whimpered, her voice raw and trembling.

"Shh. It'll be all right," he said, an unsettling smile curving his lips—a smile she knew too well. The smile that promised pain.

"No, no, let me go. I swear, I won't tell anyone—"

"No, you won't," he replied coldly. "You've been an excellent plaything, perhaps the best yet. But it's time I moved on. Fairness demands I share myself with others."

Her eyes darted to the glinting scalpel. Panic roared in her throat, choking the words out.

"No, please!" she said, just a whisper.

He stepped closer, his gloved fingers trailing lightly over her cheek like a venomous touch.

"One last night together, sweetheart," he said, his voice low and terrifying. "And know this: of all the women I've ever had, you are — the most recent."

In one fluid, horrifying motion, the scalpel flashed.

The screaming began.

AUTHOR'S NOTE

Hail to you, aficionados of the odd!

I think that **Devotion In the Mind** pulls in all the elements of a good Doctor Wise tale. The weird, hand in hand, with the real-life situations we all go through.

It surprised me when Anthony Marconi showed up, as I thought he was a one-off in Portland, Maine. He appears in the series several more times, but I'll let you find that out as you read the books.

I'm glad I got the chance to bring in Jyanette's parents and all of those 'meeting the parents' situations guys go through, and showing her own family dynamics. I also explored Jyanette's past and her relationship with her ex-husband, all of which added depth to her character.

I came up with the special psychic drug, *Miracle*, for an original concept for the Leonard Wise character. I wrote an outline for a story that took place in the future, where cops worked with psychic investigators who used the drug. As it had terrible side effects, officers who used it had a limitation of two years. Len was a police officer's new partner, who didn't need the drug, but relied on his inherent psychic powers. I decided not to go the Sci-Fi route and kept Len in present time.

Things are about to become very dark as the story arc of the demon that Len saw on the fateful night of Cathy's death rises to its zenith in the next book, *Asylum In The Mind.*

—Arjay Lewis

ABOUT THE AUTHOR

Known as the "Wizard Of Odd", Arjay Lewis is an actor, magician, and multi-award-winning author.

I write tales of the strange and the horrifying.

I have spent my life as an entertainer, amusing people as a street-performer in the 1970s; a Broadway and casino artist in the 1980s; a party performer in the 1990s and 2000s; a cruise ship performer in the 2010s.

Stories have always been in my mind, and I have been writing since the 1990s. My reason to write is simple: to entertain. I write the type of books that I like to read: murder mysteries, strange tales of unnatural gifts, odd happenings and horror.

Please visit my web site and sign up for my mailing list to be "in the know" for upcoming books. Visit me on Facebook, Twitter, or my Amazon Author page.

And thank you for reading. You are the reason I write.

www.arjaylewis.com

www.facebook.com/arjaylewis

www.twitter.com/arjaylewiswrite

www.amazon.com/Arjay-Lewis

BOOKS BY ARJAY LEWIS

Doctor Wise Series
Fire In The Mind
Seduction In The Mind
Reunion In The Mind
Haunted In The Mind
Devotion In The Mind
Asylum In The Mind
Specter In The Mind
Vengeance In The Mind
Echoes In The Mind
Infection In The Mind
Justice In The Mind
Ritual In The Mind
Vanished In The Mind

Horror
The Muse
Kept In The Dark
The Vanishing
Digger
Ghost Writer

Romantic Suspense
(with Debra Snow)
A Study In Murder

NYPD Wizard Detective
The Wizards Of Central Park West
The Vampires Of Greenwich Village
The Werewolves Of Washington Square